The Rifting Crow

By Matt Egner
Copyright © 2015, Matt Egner

(Originally titled "Johnny Crow")

Table of Contents

Contents

Prologue 11

ONE - The Drive.. 15

TWO - The Homestead 57

FOUR - The Visit.. 107

FIVE - The Winter.. 137

SIX - The Tribe 167

SEVEN - The Engineer.. 189

EIGHT - The Girl.. 227

NINE - The Spies... 259

TEN - The Departure.. 277

Epilogue... 287

Dedication

The author would like to thank Shinobu, Sumika and Koujiro for helping inspire the content of this story and for reviewing the novel. A special thanks goes to Lisa for constant encouragement and excellent editing.

Preface

The true journey of man is to a place of wonder, excitement, fear and adventure. If these feelings are never explored, a man's life is wasted, clinging only to ignorance and complacency. Humans evolved into beings of modern, intelligent proportions by examining the unknown for no other reason than knowledge. The capacity for awareness is governed only by our own self contrived limitations; limitations most of us are never aware of. Every now and then a unique person is born with both the capacity for understanding and a broad, open outlook. With each new generation, there comes along a few individuals with talents and insights, ready to explore a world that permits change. Only people with both talent and determination ever succeed. These are the leaders.

Prologue

I'm out there. I'm way out there. If you shot a gun at me, you wouldn't hit me. If you shot a laser at me, you wouldn't get close. If you shot a rocket at me, I'd be safe, because I'm way out there. Where am I? Well, that's a long story. I'll try to recount it as best I can. I suppose it all starts at birth. Don't all stories start at birth? I'm Johnny Biskit. I was born smart. Perhaps I was an evolutionary jump that had come to mankind, or maybe I was an anomaly, ahead of the evolutionary curve. Either way, I was like Michelangelo, Beethoven, or Einstein. Even as a four year old, I could solve spatial problems with intuition. I finished high school at 12, thanks to my parents who let me read anything I wanted and the school I attended that saw my advanced abilities. I finished a bachelor's degree in physics at 14. I went straight into a PhD and finished by 17. I loved math and physics and how they could be applied together. I was interested in two things: energy and motion. I also loved to explore. As a child I occasionally wandered off into a field or forest to search for bugs, snakes, salamanders, rocks or whatever looked interesting. Discoveries were a thrill. After completing my PhD, I was given a Post Doctorate and assigned an associate teaching position at UBC. I had a nice little office that I never used because I also had a lab that consumed all of my time. At the age of 20, I had 17 patents. A medical company had reviewed one of my patents and offered to buy it from me, but I was so wrapped up in my own work I just dismissed them. They said they would be back. I was working in the lab one night on a new way to harness electricity in a compact device when I made a miscalculation which resulted in an explosion. I was safely out of the room, but the shock wave was so strong it blew out the wall and burnt much of the lab. Security came running. The fire department was called, police were contacted, and needless to say the dean of science was irate. Although I had published many papers and secured many patents, I was seen as an academic snob for not turning these ideas into money for the school and my research. As a result, I was asked to leave. This was a bitter pill to swallow. My research had come so far. Most of my accomplishments had not been published. I wanted to create something substantial rather than publish bits and pieces. I wanted to complete a puzzle, rather than waste time describing every little piece of the puzzle. Now I had no lab, no funding, and no work. I was still living at home where I was comfortable. I had no motivation to enhance my personal life, only to further my work. Just prior to my twenty first birthday, I sat in my bedroom pondering how I could regain what I had lost. I needed money and a place to work. I devised a plan to setup a lab of my own. This was really the first streak of independence I had ever had. I remembered the medical company interested in my patent and contacted them. This was my opportunity to get the funding I needed. Everything hinged on this cash. I called them and we met. After a day of negotiating, I secured $650,000 in return for their exclusive rights to the patent for two years with the option to renew.

They would not own it, just lease it. Frankly I didn't care if they owned it or not. The patent was useful in production methods for a chemical process. I retained the right to use it, but told them I simply had no desire to mass produce anything. So there I was, lots of money in my bank account. I scoured the internet for two days to find a suitable lab. I wanted a place I could live and work away from any prying eyes or thieves, and somewhere I could blow up a lab and not be scrutinized, not that I expected to do that again. I looked in B.C., Alberta, Yukon, and the N.W.T. I came across a home on the Liard River in the southwest corner of the Northwest Territories. That was where I would go. This marked the path to my destiny. This was when my life changed.

ONE - The Drive

As always, plans are just starting points. From there, fate takes over. I was quite excited, and nervous about starting a journey. I realized I would need a good vehicle. Thank goodness my parents pushed me to get a driver's license when I was sixteen. I went downstairs to the kitchen where my mother was making lunch and my father was sitting at the table reading the newspaper and I announced my plan.

"What do you think? Is it a good idea?" I asked.

I'm not sure what I expected them to say. On the surface it sounded ludicrous. But they knew I was not an average fellow, destined for a desk job at some bureaucratic company. I think my father's mouth remained open for two minutes and he never blinked at the news of my more than half million dollar windfall from the sale of a patent.

"Well, have you thought about what it's going to be like living all alone out there in the wilderness?" my mother inquired, nervously. "That's far away. It's almost winter, and winter up there is horrible. You might have school all figured out, but you don't really have any experience with, you know, life stuff. Why don't you find a place near home?"

"I'm not going away just to get away from here, I'm going somewhere I can be left alone and do my work without interference. Anyway, everything here is expensive and small. Up there I can get lots of land and buildings for a good price. I have to make this money last a little while," I said.

My father finally chimed in. "I think it's a good idea, but your destination is a bit questionable. It's very rugged up there, and cold."

"I know dad, but everywhere is cold compared to Vancouver. I'm not building a cabin, I'm buying a home," I explained.

"I understand," he said.

If anything, my father was understanding. He was always reasonable. I could tell he knew what I was aiming for, even though he knew I had no idea what I was getting myself into. That's right, I had no idea what I was getting myself into. I had a pipe dream. I had it all figured out in my head like a simple equation, though ignoring some pretty important variables.

My father continued, "You will need some good wheels. May I suggest you buy a pickup truck? I can help you out with that."

"Thanks dad. I will indeed," I agreed.

My father was, predictably, more of a Toyota Corolla man, or any other midsize, reliable car. But my father was also a bit of a mystery. He was a quiet man. He had worked most of his life as an accountant for the city of Burnaby. He was also older than you would expect for a man with a twenty year old son. He had retired two years ago which placed him at sixty two years old now.

My mother, a lifelong homemaker and early tutor for me, was also older, nearing sixty one now. That's not to say they are old, quite the contrary. They both seemed young and active. My father played tennis and golf, mostly with my mother, and curled in the winter with his friends. He continued to work part time for small companies who needed occasional help with their books.

My mother was active in charities and tutored other kids after school. There was a lot I didn't know about my parents. They were somewhat private and talked little about life before I was born. I had learned from an early age that other people did not grasp concepts as easily as I did, nor were they as aware of things as I was and I dealt with that. So I seldom inquired about their knowledge, instead I assumed they were just average people living mundane lives. So there could have been more to my father and mother than I knew. As such, I always gave them the benefit of the doubt when it came to life experience.

"When do you plan on starting this journey?" my father asked.

"Right away," I replied, rather sharply.

"I see. Well whenever you want to go look for a truck, let's go," he answered.

I was a little taken aback by his commitment to my rather hasty plan. I could see in my mother's eyes great hesitation and worry. "OK. Anytime is fine with me," I said.

I think there was also a newfound appreciation for money and what it could do for me. I never spent much before. I owned one thing, a television. It was the only thing I ever bought worth more than $100. Of course I never really had much money before. Now I could go on a shopping spree.

My father and I drove to a few car dealers. He gave me advice along the way. "Buy a used truck, gently used, with low kilometres. Always negotiate. Start around $2000 less than the asking price. Don't tell them you have cash until you get close on price, then spring that on them. Listen to the engine. Get 4 wheel drive. Be prepared to walk away." It all sounded like a game, and I think he enjoyed it. We saw a few F150's and they were nice. We saw a GMC and a couple Chevies.

Then we landed at a dealer who had three Rams. One was a blue Ram 1500, two door, off road tires, only 20,000 KMs, two years old, loaded with features, leather seats, navigation, and stereo. This thing would have been $55,000 or more new. The asking price was $24,000. I sat in it and felt like the captain of a luxury yacht. So this is what it's like to have money. I could buy anything I wanted, and I liked that feeling.

I sat in the truck after a test drive and discussed it with my father. I liked it a lot. So we negotiated. My father was tough. We sat there for two hours until finally we got it for $22,650. My father looked so proud of that accomplishment. He brimmed from ear to ear. I told him to drive it home and I would take his car. He did not argue. I was happy to share this moment with him. We really hadn't done much together growing up. I was not into scouts or sports or any leisure activities. I think we missed out on those moments.

Back at home my mother was busy cleaning the house. No doubt this was a reaction to the news that I planned to leave. Keeping busy kept my mother from thinking. Nothing though kept my mother from worrying. I could only imagine what was going through her mind. I had always been a fixture in the house. There had never been any indication I would socially grow up or move out. My parents were not eager to see me leave. They had no desire for privacy and freedom. We had a nice little peaceful family and all was good. This sudden change would be a major adjustment for them to overcome.

"Mom!" I yelled as I entered the house. She came to the front door to ask what was going on. "Come see what I got." I turned, opened the door again and stepped outside followed closely by my mother. There in the driveway of our average suburban house was a monster pickup truck, sparkling under the sunlight.

"Oh my goodness!" she exclaimed. "I think you could drive that over Spruce Mountain."

"Go ahead, sit in it," I said, excitedly.

She stepped up on the running board and pulled herself into the cab as my father and I watched on with big smiles. "Good gravy, this thing is huge!"

"Not exactly a town car, is it?" I said. "I wouldn't care to park it in some downtown underground parking lot. But for up north it will be rugged and safe, and keep me warm and comfortable at the same time." My mother seemed unimpressed, maybe even intimidated by the truck. I didn't blame her. She had probably never even been in a truck that big before. She squirmed in the chair, trying to find a comfortable position. Just wasn't happening. She finally twisted her legs around and stepped back down on the running board. I reached up to help her down and she grunted as she stepped off the board onto the ground.

"OK, maybe it'll be safe on those roads up north," she said. "But you're not planning to leave for a while, are you?"

"Why not?" I asked. "I see no reason to wait around. The longer I wait, the further behind I'll be in my research."

"You know, John, there is more to life than your research. Maybe you should try taking a break, having some fun, try a hobby." My mother does not give up easily. The fact that I studied since I was very young without any desire for social activities is perhaps a commentary on my ambitions. This did not feel like a good time to change my habits.

"I'll think about that on my ride up north, OK Mom?" I grinned. Mom did not respond. "How about helping me pack some gear, Mom? I could use your advice on what to take. We can all sit at the table tonight and work out a route to get up there." The inclusion of my mother in this scheme seemed to perk her up a little. At least it would keep her busy.

We stepped back into the house and I went to my room to start pulling out clothes to pack. It became clear I was not terribly prepared for a northern, outdoors environment. I had a handful of clothes, mostly slacks and pullover shirts. I had very little that would keep me warm. That was OK, I would find what I needed along the way. I would take it easy and stop at towns to find proper gear. The question was, what is the right gear? I was hardly qualified to make that call. Warm clothing was definitely at the top of the list. Some tough boots and rubber boots were essential.

But there would be so much more, like axes, saws, ropes, hammers, tools, blankets, furniture, etc.

This was indeed a learning experience like none I had ever gone through before. I packed as much of my clothes as I could into a suitcase and then put more into a garbage bag. My mother came into the room. She had a bag filled with towels, soap, and an assortment of things that I would never have thought to pack, and probably would never need. But I had a monster truck with a ton of room. I'd have taken the kitchen sink if they'd given it to me. We piled all the bags at the front door. Most of my lab work was in the garage in boxes, so that all had to go.

Next, we sat at the table with the laptop and looked at Google maps to sketch out a good route up to Fort Simpson. "OK, Dad, what do you think? You've travelled around a bit, eh? How do I get up north?" I asked. Dad entered Vancouver to Fort Simpson into Google maps to see a route. It was a long way, so far that you couldn't see the roads all the way on one screen shot. It was 2300 km or thirty hours of driving. That seemed like the other side of the world.

"Looks like there are two routes you can take," Dad started. "There's the shorter route, but that's over into Alberta and then north. So you'd have to cross the Rockies. Not sure that's the best thing this time of the year. The second route is straight up to Prince George. From there you can go east into Alberta or keep heading north to the Territories. That's the way I would go. So that would be Highway 1 up to Cache creek, then the 97 through Prince George to Dawson Creek. From here you have to be careful because 97 goes east and north. Make sure to turn north toward Fort St. John and Fort Nelson. Just past Fort Nelson, turn north on 77 and stay on that all the way into the North West Territories where it becomes 7. Further up it branches to Highway 1 and head north to Fort Simpson. I better print this all out for you."

"That's a good idea. I have the GPS in the truck too, so maybe I can set it up as a route," I said.

"Oh yes, I forgot you had that fancy GPS. Thank God for that. This is a mess of highways to remember. Looks like you can make it to Williams Lake the first night. That would be seven hours. But don't push it. You have never driven that far before. If you're tired, just stop anywhere at a motel. After that you could make it to Dawson Creek. That's about 8 hours. Then stop at Fort Nelson. That's only five hours. There's not much past that for a long way. Your next stop is Fort Liard. I don't know if there's anything there. It's tiny. But it's still ten hours from Fort Simpson, so you have to stop, even if you have to stop and sleep in the truck. You can't drive fifteen hours, especially up there on those rough roads. Remember, you can go all day and not see anyone else on the road. So be very careful. Lots of Moose, Caribou and Bear up there." As my father spoke these last words I could see my mother tense up, almost gasp. I was feeling a little anxious myself. I had never really considered the true isolation and hazards.

"OK," I answered. Dad plugged the printer into the laptop and it started to make grinding noises as the papers came sliding out, one after another. As they came out, my dad highlighted the route in yellow and then circled the towns to stay in with a red pen. Once assembled and edited, he stapled them all together for me. It was really happening. Was I going through with it? What if I got scared or didn't like the home? Would this be a failed adventure and waste of time? A lot of doubts started building in me. Maybe I'd be lonely. As I was feeling this sudden unease, my mother said, "You know if you aren't happy or things don't go as planned, you should come back home."

"Thanks, Mom," I replied. Maybe she sensed my hesitation, or just had impeccable timing. Either way, I was glad I had the escape route. Mom had already made dinner and was serving it up while dad put the computer away.

"Have you ever been up north, Dad?" I asked.

"Yes. Before I met your mother, I was in the army, stationed in Whitehorse. I was there for three years. I got to drive around lots of highways and back roads, not that there were that many back then. It was wilder than it is today, believe it or not. Sure saw enough wildlife too. Caught some massive trout in the lakes. It was a great place to be as a young guy. But I remember the winters. Oh boy were they bad," he recounted.

"Maybe an adventure will do me good. Maybe I'll get some of that 'life stuff' mom was talking about, ha ha ha." We all had a good laugh at that. As much as I had no use for developing life experiences, I felt there may be something in life I was missing, and this could force me to get those experiences I would otherwise avoid.

Mom was pretty quiet at dinner. I think she was feeling quite emotional. After dinner, we all settled in the living room to watch television. My dad got up, went to the kitchen and returned with a couple of beers. This was the first time I ever shared a beer with him.

****

I'd like to say I got a good night sleep, but I didn't, and I'm sure no one else did either. I awoke at 7:00 AM and made breakfast for everyone. To my surprise they were all up by 7:30 AM, perhaps worried that I might just leave before they even got up. I dished up scrambled eggs, sausages, toast and juice for us all. They both seemed rather groggy.

"Well what's your plan, John?" my father asked.

"I'll pack the truck after breakfast and then get going. I have a full tank and the routes you gave me, so I can hit the road right away. I think you said 7 hours to the first stop, and I plan to take it easy, so I'll get in around five-ish if I leave at 9:00 AM."

"John," started my mother, "would you please call me a couple times a day? I want to make sure everything's OK."

"Alright. I'll call you when I take a break and when I get into town. How's that?"

"That would be fine. Thank you John." My mother forced a smile. Really, I would have called anyway.

Who else would I talk to in the day? For some reason the breakfast that morning tasted extra good. I had butterflies in my stomach from anxiety, but not in so much a bad way, more of an excited nervous way. "How's the weather forecast, Dad?" My dad was always up on the weather. He spent an inordinate amount of time watching the Weather Network.

"Good!" he exclaimed fervently. "It's a perfect October day. High in Vancouver of +16 and sunny. I also checked all the way up the line. Williams Lake +13, Fort Nelson +11 and Fort Simpson +3 and it'll be clear for the next three or four days. Shouldn't have any weather trouble unless you're up in the mountains, but you'll skirt those on this route."

"Great. Nothing like a road trip, eh?" I said.

My dad nodded. My mother did not.

After breakfast, we all loaded bags and boxes into the truck and then flipped the tonneau cover overtop, sealing in all the goods for the long haul. I actually wished we were all going, like a family trip we might have taken when I was young.

Once, we went to Calgary and then Banff for a whole week. Another time we rented a cottage on some turquoise coloured lake in Manitoba. I loved the sound of the screen door as it opened and closed. I remember the hot summer days and the smell of the meadow outside the cabin, and the row boat we used to glide around in on the calm water. But this time I was on my own. This was my adventure.

Once the loading was complete, there was only the GPS to program and then no reason to stall any longer. I started the big V8 engine and it rumbled. I kissed my mom and hugged her.

"Be careful." she whispered.

"I will," I replied.

I hugged my dad and he wished me luck. I hopped up into that big cab, opened the window and revved the engine with a smile. One last wave and I was off. I was really off, rolling down the driveway, out into the street, and down the road. As I looked back, I saw my mother turn and hug my dad, and cry.

I settled my emotions to focus on the task at hand; getting out of town. I shouldn't be looking in the rear-view mirror. It was time to look ahead. The highways would be easy compared to navigating these city roads, especially in this big truck. The GPS kept nagging me to get into the left lane, turn left in 200 metres, get into the right lane, merge right, etc. I swear it was more stressful following these directions than just watching the signs.

At last I found the Trans Canada and merged with the flow of traffic. Thankfully, everyone else was going into town and not out of town. Traffic on my side was light compared to the other side.

I was headed for Hope, literally and figuratively. I had been there before. It was a nice town with beautiful mountains and green farms and occasional rock slides. It didn't take long to get there. I was tempted to pull over and call home, just to make a crack about Hope, but saner heads prevailed and I stuck to the highway.

The truck drove like a dream. It was smooth and quiet inside. I turned the radio on and scanned for stations. On came a Weakerthans song, and I felt good. Apparently they hate Winnipeg. Must be about winter.

When you drive one of these big trucks, everyone gives you room. It feels good to be respected, or feared. I drove on, completely enjoying the freedom and my new truck. I saw a sign for a rest stop ahead and as I got closer I steered off the highway into a small parking area nestled among trees. In front of me was a small meadow, and across from it, about fifty feet or so, was a babbling brook. I hopped down and crossed the meadow.

It was a pretty sight. I knelt down and pressed my fingers into the water. Man, it was cold. I saw the silhouettes of a few fish dart away from me. I soaked in the sounds of birds chirping and the rippling of water and even a grasshopper flitting from grass stem to stem. This was the land. This was the earth, a film of life resting on the crust of a planet rolling in space.

Why didn't I ever notice this before now? It must have been ten years ago I last appreciated the land. For a moment, I had a fear that some wild animal might emerge from the thick trees on the other side of the brook and discover me. That was how out of touch I had become with the land. This trip was a good thing. I could learn so much by experiencing life.

A car pulled into the parking area and seated itself near my truck. It was a big old car, maybe late 80s or 90s. A man and woman stepped out from the front and two kids, about the same age as each other, emerged from the back seats. The kids ran into the meadow and crossed to the creek where they both immediately dipped their hands in the water, just as I had done. I suppose there was still a kid in me. They shrieked with delight and one jumped back, turning and chasing grasshoppers in the grass. They must have been about ten years old or so, one a boy in jeans and a blue jacket, and one a girl in a pink dress with a red jacket over top. The two kids jumped up and down yelling "Bangoshee! Bangoshee!" I have no idea what that meant, but they were having fun.

The man grasped the woman's hand and they walked around the kids, sitting down at a picnic table. The kids looked happy. The woman looked out over the brook as she talked to the man. This far from town, they must have been travelling for hours in the car. What could she be talking about? What more could she have to say after sitting in a car for so long with him?

Well, they seemed like a nice family. It reminded me of when I was ten and we would go on car trips. I bet I was carefree like those kids. The woman looked over at me and smiled. I smiled back and gave a small nod. Then I rose up and walked back to my truck, satisfied that I had just accomplished a new task; regaining a sense of attachment to nature.

I continued on down the road toward a town called Merritt. I thought it would be ironic if I got a ticket in Merritt and lost demerit points. I wonder how often the police heard a joke like that around here. As I neared Merritt, I saw a gas station with a diner attached, so I pulled in.

I had been on the road for about three hours and yet still had half a tank of gas, but thought it prudent to fill up anyway. I pulled up to pump some gas, or more rightly, let the attendant do it for me. A red-headed girl in her mid-twenties wearing dirty overalls and a red checked jacket came around the pump and stared at me.

"Can you fill 'er up, please?" I asked.

"OK." was all I heard from her. She stuck the nozzle in the tank and began to pump. She stared at the ground and leaned against the truck.

"The food any good in that diner?" I asked.

"It's OK. Nothing fancy," she replied.

I wonder what she thought of me. I did not look like the typical pickup truck guy out here. Probably thought I was some kind of yuppie getting my thrills by owning a truck.

"You been up this highway before?" I asked.

"Yeah, lots of times." She was not a wordy person. "Where are you going?"

"Fort Simpson. Ever been there?" I kept prodding.

"Fort Simpson? Where's that?" she asked.

"In the Northwest Territories, on the Mackenzie River," I replied.

"Oh, no, never been there," she said. "I went up to the Yukon. I spent a couple summers tree planting. It's nice up there. Wouldn't mind moving there. I was near Dawson City, but in the bush," she elaborated.

"What's the highway like, going up that way? I'm going through Prince George and Fort Nelson." I inquired.

"Not bad, but watch out for truckers, especially logging trucks. They're maniacs. What are you doing up there?" she asked.

"I'm looking for a house," I said.

"Hmm, you working in a mine?" she asked, looking puzzled. I did not look like I belonged in a mine, or any trade, or up north.

"No, I'm a scientist." It was all I could think to say. I'm sure she was even more puzzled by my mysterious trip now.

The nozzle clicked off and she put it back in the pump. "That'll be $54.35."

I showed her my visa and we walked into the shop where I paid. "Thanks for the gas." I said.

"OK. Have a good trip," she replied.

I drove the truck around in front of the diner and went inside. It was nothing special, on the outside or inside. It was not much more than a white, clapboard house with extra windows and some awnings. I looked around and found a booth by one of the windows.

In the diner was an older man at the counter chatting with a waitress who seemed completely uninterested in the conversation. I could only see his back, but he was broad, wore a dark checked shirt, boots and a cowboy hat. At a table near me were two men having coffee. They both wore cowboy hats and boots. At another booth was a woman with her two, well behaved kids having lunch.

The waitress approached my table with a menu. "Hello," she said, "how are you today?"

"Fine thanks. How are you?" I replied.

"Not too bad. Here's a menu. Would you like me to get you a drink while you think about that?"

"Sure, can I have a milk, please?" I asked.

"Of course you can," she said, smiling. "I'll bring that over to you right away." And she smiled again.

She was a pretty lady, about thirty five years old, medium height, slim, light brown hair spun up into a twirling bun atop her head. I have no idea how she kept it in place. She had very natural features, like high rosy cheekbones, a pointy chin, small nose, and dark full lashes. Or maybe she just had a natural flair for using makeup from the drugstore. Either way, I could see how a lot of truckers would want to stop in here for a bite to eat and chat with her.

She did indeed bring me that milk in a hurry. After ordering it, I felt a bit foolish. Milk? I'm pretty sure no one else was ordering milk here, except maybe the kids.

"I'll have a bacon lettuce and tomato sandwich, please." I told her.

"You betcha. That won't take long." More smiles. Either she's a very happy lady or the smile is an automatic reflex after each sentence.

I sat and listened to some of the conversations. The two cowboys near me were discussing skidders, whatever that was. Sounded like a bulldozer. Apparently it's hard to change a tire on them. I couldn't hear what the cowboy at the counter was saying, and it's just as well. If he bored the waitress, he'd likely bore me. The mother and kids talked about schoolwork.

When my sandwich order was delivered, the diner door opened and in walked two young guys, maybe about eighteen or nineteen, wearing, you guessed it, cowboy hats and boots. I am definitely in cowboy country. I'm really out of place here. I have got to get me a cowboy hat and boots, and jeans, and perhaps a buckle. Maybe I wouldn't need any of that up in Fort Simpson, but it would be fun to have.

The sandwich was fine. There was no shortage of bacon in it. I'm sure if you skimped on bacon in this part of the world you'd be run out of town. This was meat country. The milk on the other hand was lukewarm. They probably left it out on the counter for coffee.

The waitress bellowed over to the two cowboys that just came in, "You boys want coffee?" They nodded yes. Then she shifted her gaze to me and raised the pot. "How 'bout you, hon? Want some more milk?"

Well now, that couldn't have been more embarrassing. As much as I liked milk, I wish I had ordered something else.

"No Thanks," I replied with a shake of my head. When she came over, I asked her if she could wrap up the remaining half of my sandwich for me, to go.

"Not as hungry as you thought?" she asked, seemingly insulted that I didn't finish.

"Oh I was. I just didn't expect such a big sandwich. It was great though. I'll finish the rest tonight. Who knows what I'll get for dinner, eh? At least this way, I know I'll have something good." I smiled first this time as I explained.

"Well I tell you what. I'll sneak a couple cookies in with that so you have some dessert tonight as well." And then, the smile again.

"Thanks, that's very kind of you." I have always been polite, but never knew I had charm as well. I had been, after all, a veritable social hermit. But I was certainly enjoying this banter. I collected my sandwich and cookies, said goodbye and left the diner.

I was confronted with seven pickup trucks out front. At least my vehicle was appropriate for the area. OK, full tank, full stomach, and full of vigour. I was ready for the highway again. I needed tunes. Up and down the dial I went until I landed on a country song. Apparently it was Merle Haggard, and it fit this country like a leather glove. I barreled down the road experiencing another new thing, country music.

The drive went well. There was nothing boring about the scenery; mountains, deserts, rivers and lakes, and lots of pointy trees. I was surprised to see the deserts, especially as they seemed close to rivers and lakes. I had to turn before Kamloops, so never got to see that town. After that I hit Cache Creek and few other small towns before rolling into Williams Lake at 4:42. That was a long drive, but I made good time. I've never driven so far at once before.

As I drove into town I looked for a motel or hotel. I passed a few dodgy looking places and then saw a sign for the Sandman. It looked OK, had an indoor pool and a restaurant attached. There were lots of cars in the lot and it looked well maintained. So I turned in there and found a spot to park. It was surprisingly warm for an early October late afternoon, and the sun felt good. Maybe just the lack of wind made me feel warm. At the front desk a middle aged woman greeted me and I asked for a room.

"Yes sir, we have a room. It is $122 per night. Would you like a king or two queens?"

"Either is fine with me, thanks," I answered.

"OK then, I'll give you a king. There is a mini fridge for your convenience, an ice machine at the end of the hall, the pool closes at 10:00 PM and opens again in the morning at 7:00 AM. How would you like to pay for that?" she asked politely.

I took out my credit card and handed it to the lady.

"Where are you from?" she asked, seemingly making small talk.

"Vancouver. I'm heading up to Fort Simpson, in the Territories," I explained.

"Oh my," she said with a surprise, "you have a long way to go. Business?"

"Yes." Yeesh, again I was stumped for how to answer that question. If I had said I was moving there, it would have become a long, complicated, as of yet still unknown answer. "By the way, is there a good hat store in town?" I asked.

"Hat store? What kind of hat?" she said.

I was afraid she would ask that. "Western hats." I gave her a simple answer with no embarrassing explanations.

"Oh, I see. Yes, you can get hats at either the Stagecoach Saddlery or at the Feedstore just outside town along the highway. The Feedstore might be closed now, but they open early. The Saddlery will be open until 7:00 PM, I believe. You can walk there from here, just keep going down the main road here two blocks, turn left and go one more block. It's right there on the corner. They have a good selection." If I didn't know better, I'd think she was a salesperson for the saddlery.

"OK, great. Thanks very much," I said.

"So you're in room 109. You can pull your car right in front of the room. It's just down this way." She pointed with a sweeping motion at the side of the building. "Here is your key card and the Wi-Fi password is on the back of the envelope. Have a nice stay."

She handed me the envelope. I thanked her again and left. The room was big, clean and bright. I dropped onto the bed and sighed. I just needed a minute, but that minute became a few, and then a few more. I suppose I was more tired than I thought.

****

I rustled myself up. Must get to the saddlery and see what they have. I found my way out onto the street and followed the directions, dodging cars and trucks along the way. There it was, the Saddlery, just as I imagined it, rustic and wooden like a small barn. Inside was a thousand hats hanging from the rafters? Wow! How would I ever pick one from so many? The wall was lined with boots and there was a case of belt buckles.

I wandered around the store picking out hats and trying them on. Seems my size was seven or seven and a quarter, depending on the style or make. I selected one called the 'Stampeder'. It was black felt, not overly big nor too high. I liked it.

A girl came over and asked if I needed a hand. If she only knew. She was young, probably eighteen, and very healthy like a real country girl. She looked like she grew up riding horses and helping out on the ranch. She wore a tank top and shredded cut-off jeans. Seriously, who wears that kind of thing in October? Her name tag read Dawn.

"Yeah, I like this hat. What do you think?" I asked her.

"It looks good. How does it fit?" she asked, jostling it around on my head.

"Maybe a bit loose." I answered.

She took it in her hands and turned it over. The tag read seven and a quarter.

"Let me get a seven out of the back," she said, and with that left the room.

I continued to shop, browsing the selection of boots. There were brown shiny ones, black shiny ones, brown suede ones, square toe, round toe, extra pointy toe, and even pink ones with rhinestones. I liked the look of the shiny black pointy ones. They had a nice pattern of threads along the sides and holes at the top, which I assumed were used to help pull them on. Regular $169 on sale for $99. Not bad. I took a size nine. I looked for a box on the ground beneath the model pair and found what I wanted. Before I could grasp it, Dawn was back with a big box, the lid placed underneath revealing a nice, new crisp black hat.

"Here, try this one on," she said, lifting it out of the box for me.

"Uh-huh, that fits better. Not tight, not loose. I think it's good," I said.

"The style suits you," she said. I am confident she did not really mean it. "Do you want to look at those boots?"

"Yes, if it's OK," I replied.

"Of course. Here, let me get it for you. Sit down." She gestured to a small stool.

I did as I was told and removed my shoes. Oh geez, I hope my feet don't stink. I was in the car all day. She removed the boots from the box and slid the right one on. I stood up. It was the right size, for sure. I moved it around and walked a bit.

"Let's try both on," she said.

So they both went on and my polyester slacks slumped over the top. I walked down the aisle and back. It might take a bit of getting used to, with the pointy toe and the high sides. I'm sure my feet will hurt if I have far to walk. But otherwise I liked them. They were not so different from what I observed on other people today.

"OK, they're good. And I like that price." I stated.

She cracked a smile and laughed a bit. "Yeah, I know, eh? I should get a pair for myself." Yes, I agree, because I don't think the pink rhinestone boots would suit her.

"I will need a belt and buckle. Any suggestions?" I was leaving this in her capable hands.

"Come on over here. I'll fix you up. What are you, a truck driver, cowboy, or farmer?" Not sure if she was making fun of me or simply humouring me.

"I don't know. What do you think I should be?" I let out a good laugh. "I just want to fit in with the other good old boys around here."

"Well, first get rid of the slacks. They aren't helping you. And that shirt too. Wear jeans or work pants, and get T-shirts or checkered long sleeved cotton shirts. Now, I'll get you a simple leather belt and..." she paused while looking in the buckle cabinet, "how about this one?" She pulled out a silver buckle with a turquoise eagle on it. I liked it. I really did. Not ostentatious, not fake looking, notably attractive and contrasting.

"How much is that?" I asked.

"$24.95. That's a good deal considering the materials and craftsmanship. Most of the others are close in price and don't look as good," she stated.

"Alright, ring it all up. Do you know where I can get some jeans and shirts around here?"

"Well," she said, "we have shirts, but they're more like fancy duds than work shirts. You're better off going to the discount store right down there on the main drag. You can get what you need and it won't cost much."

"Perfect." I felt a great sense of accomplishment, not in a scientific way, but in a social way. Look at me, interacting with people, changing my style, listening to new music. I can't believe how one day has made this difference.

"Listen," she started, "why don't you leave this stuff here, go get your clothes, come back and we'll put it all together. You are NOT going out there with these clothes," she gestured to me, up and down, "and these accessories," she then gestured to the new items I just bought.

I smirked, knowing full well she was right. I needed help with this transformation. "OK, I'll be back in half an hour." And true to my word I dashed over to the main road, found the discount store, bought some straight leg jeans and a few shirts of different styles and dashed back to the store.

"Here, go in the back room and get dressed. Wait! Show me what you got, first," she said, obviously taking charge of me. I lifted out 3 pairs of jeans, one pair of work pants, 2 checkered shirts, one plain button down shirt, 2 T-shirts, and a dark beige, short work jacket. "Hmm…," she scanned the clothes, "put on these jeans and this shirt."

I emerged from the back room looking half ready. The boots went on, then the belt and buckle, and then the hat. Voila, I was dressed. I looked in the full length mirror. I liked it. I fit in. I put the jacket on and felt complete, like the album cover of a 1960s country music singer.

"You've got style," I said to Dawn, as I continued to stare at myself in the mirror.

"Hey, you picked most of it out. I think you know what you're doing. It will take a while to get used to walking in those boots. You'll probably feel a bit stiff until then. Just keep at it."

"OK, thanks." I genuinely meant it. She was very nice, and she took an interest in me. A guy who spends all his time doing science experiments does not get much attention from girls, even sales girls.

I scooped up my old and new clothes and left the store, bound for my hotel. She was right, it was hard to walk in these boots. They were stiff, and different from anything I had ever worn before. But I would tough it out, for the greater good of my social soul. I lumbered back to the hotel. I was sure people who saw me thought I was a drugstore cowboy; a fake dude. But I didn't care. I would grow into it in time. I grabbed the old sandwich out of my truck and headed into the room for a bite to eat and a good night sleep. I didn't want to take off these clothes and go to bed, but I was dead tired and had no choice.

****

I slept well, considering the highway noises and a strange bed. I awoke to the static sounds of a clock radio at 6:45. I hadn't set the alarm. I probably should have. But that was fine. I got up, turned on the TV and showered. After my shower I stood at the foot of the bed for a while watching the news and weather. Then, with great anticipation, I dressed up in my new clothes and admired myself in the mirror.

No time to lose. I dropped by the office and left my key card. I went next door to the restaurant. As I walked in a waitress greeted me and asked if I was alone. I replied yes and she took me to a small table in the middle of the room. I looked around. There were about a dozen people eating, and no one wore a cowboy hat. Not one. Well how about that, I'm finally in style and the style was out. I didn't care. I was proud of my new look. I'm sure, at any moment some big truck driver will walk in with a western hat and boots, and he'll look over at me and know this is the right place to be. Is it possible cowboys don't wear hats in the morning? Maybe this is one of those establishments that working men avoid. That's probably it. I could see a waitress heading my way. She's probably going to tell me they don't serve my type in here.

"Good morning, my name is Kelly. I'll be your server today. Can I get you something to drink?" she asked, knowing what 99.9% of people would order. I wasn't going to make that mistake again.

"Hi. Yes, can I have a coffee, please?"

"Of course, sir." Yes, of course indeed. What else would a cowboy order, milk? Sheesh.

"Do you have a regular breakfast, like 2 eggs, sausage, and toast?" I asked.

"Uh-huh. We call it the Rancher. It comes with coffee and beans as well." she answered.

"That will be fine," I replied.

As much as I am a loner, I am not used to sitting in the middle of a restaurant, at a table alone. Where do I look? What do I do? I wish I had a paper to look at. I peered around and saw some at the cash. I slowly ambled over and picked one up and went back to my table. The headline read 'BC Lions are destined for the Grey Cup!' I guess this was just the sports section. No wait, this is the local newspaper. Probably not a lot of news here.

My coffee came in a tall white mug. I blew some steam off of it and took a sip. Good God that is bitter. OK, I had not drank coffee before. Chalk this up to another first. Was it always supposed to be bitter? I've heard about how good it is, but this wasn't too good. Oh well, another thing I should get used to. Must be an acquired taste. At least I felt like I was ordering adult food now.

At a booth, parents were urging their kids to get along and eat up. The kids were not being especially well behaved. In fact I saw generous amounts of food leave the table and fall to the floor or land on laps as the kids fooled around. Glad that wasn't my problem. My phone rang.

"Hello?"

"Johnny, it's your mom."

Oh no. I had completely forgotten to call my mother yesterday.

"Mom. I'm so sorry I forgot to call you yesterday. I was so busy driving, and then I crashed at the hotel and fell asleep." Probably using the word crashed was somewhat inappropriate, under the circumstances.

"That's OK, John. Where are you?"

"I'm at Williams Lake. The drive was good, but very long. I stayed at a nice motel and I'm just having breakfast at the restaurant next door. I..." Before I could continue, my mother cut in.

"Are you eating well?"

"Yes, I grabbed a club sandwich for lunch yesterday at Merritt. Hey, I'm trying coffee this morning at breakfast. And I'm having a full breakfast. It's on its way," I said with some excitement.

"Oh, that's good. Is the truck running OK?" My mother asked.

"Yes, perfectly. Can you believe I drove 7 hours yesterday? Of course I shouldn't brag, I still have twenty-two hours to go. I'll be exhausted by the time I get there. I might have to take a break for a couple days when I get there just to regroup. How's Dad doing?"

"Your dad is fine. He's still sleeping. He misses you. So do I. I really wasn't prepared for you to leave so suddenly. But I guess this is something you need to do," she said.

"Yes. Yes it is, and so far it's great. I'm trying things I never would have tried at home. Even if I don't make it and I come back home, the trip will teach me lots of new things. My breakfast is coming, I should go. I promise to call later."

"Alright. Promise me you'll be careful," she said, with concern.

"I promise, Mom. Good bye." I hung up and put my phone away while the waitress placed my food down. It was huge. I don't think I ever ate a breakfast that big before. Well, I didn't plan on making myself sick, so I just ate what I was comfortable with. Still felt uneasy eating alone. Not sure if that's something anyone gets used to. I feel like everyone's watching me, of course that could be because of this costume I'm wearing. Time to gas up the truck and hit the Cariboo highway again.

Most of the morning was uneventful until traffic slowed and eventually stopped. Nothing was moving. I looked ahead as far as I could and saw nothing but cars. Eventually those cars started edging ahead. I was getting a little impatient. I tapped my fingers on the steering wheel and bided my time. Finally, I could see flashing lights down the road. That's it, an accident. I wish people were a bit more careful.

As I approached, I could see there was a small car off the road with serious damage. Geez, it looked really bad. I couldn't see any other cars though. The line of traffic ahead of me was going around something in the road, but I couldn't see what; maybe that was another car. As I approached, a policeman held up his hand in front of me, halting traffic. Now I could see it. There was a moose in the lane, sprawled out and bleeding. I hoped he was dead and not suffering. There appeared to be far more damage to the car than to the moose.

I strained my eyes to make sense of the tangled mess. Was it upright, on its side, or overturned? I couldn't tell. There, by the car was a plaid blanket. It covered something, something long. Could that be the driver? How sad, to be killed in a flash as you drive down the road. A fire truck sat at the scene ahead and a couple of firefighters walked about. I thought I saw movement down in the ditch ahead of the tangled car. Two firemen brought a person up on a stretcher and rested it at the side of the road. I was glad I had a big Ram truck.

A policeman was directing traffic around the accident. Sometimes it was northbound, then switched to southbound traffic. As I waited for the southbound lanes to clear, I stared at that massive animal. His antlers were like tree branches. There was little left of the small car. Definitely a total write-off. An ambulance came from the other direction and pulled over in front of the mangled wreck. The medics hopped out and went to the side of the person on the stretcher.

I couldn't help wonder what drives a person to become a medic, or firefighter, or a cop. The terrible things they have to deal with. My nerves would never withstand it. I had trouble just witnessing this scene at a distance from within my truck. I don't deal well with pain; mine or anyone else's. The policeman then waved us through and northbound traffic, me in the lead, pulled out around the dead animal. A sight like that sobers a driver. Tension and fear was growing in my mind.

Up ahead was the town of Prince George and I needed gas and food. I didn't want to lose any more time, so just filled up the tank and grabbed a bag of chips for the ride. I thought of calling my mother but decided I better wait a bit and not mention the accident. I knew that would make her worry. So I kept on driving all the way up to Dawson Creek and stopped at the first motel I saw, the Peace Villa Motel. After checking in I drove further on and picked up a sandwich at Tim Hortons, then bee-lined it back to the motel. A quick call to Mom, a shower, and into bed. That was a long haul, slowed down by the accident. The next leg of the trip would be no shorter.

****

An early morning led back to Tim Hortons for a quick breakfast. Coffee was becoming a necessity on these long days. The drive Up the line to Fort Nelson was long and dull, even the scenery paled compared to the previous drives. One stop was made at a gas station about half way up the line at the Mountain Pass Lodge. It was a great place to stop because there was a bistro, of sorts, and a gift shop.

I browsed around at all the crafts, some with small stickers on the bottom claiming 'Made in China', others clearly local. I bought a few postcards, and then it dawned on me that I didn't have a good camera, just the smart phone. I would have to buy one at Fort Nelson, the last town to have any decent shopping. I should have gotten one before leaving Vancouver.

I hit the road again and made it all the way up to Fort Nelson. With few exceptions, most of the way was rather flat and unscenic. There were trees, plots where trees had been cut out, swamps and bogs with stunted trees, burns with dead trees, and more trees. The gorgeous mountains, canyons and deserts had disappeared. I must have been travelling for hours up through a long low valley, because I knew from the maps that there were Coastal Mountains far to the west and Rocky Mountains at the near west, and plains to the east. This was kind of like the armpit.

As I entered town, I saw lots of logs and warehouses. Everything was so spaced out. The highway was obviously the main drag in town, littered with fast food joints and poorly built strip malls. I saw an average looking motel called the Fort Nelson and pulled in. It was nothing special but perhaps better than some other motels along here. I was just stopping over, so I didn't really care, but might as well have a nice room for the few extra bucks. It was close to food and other nearby stores. I had had enough of sitting in the truck. A good walk around town would feel good, even though the temperature here was quite a bit cooler than Vancouver, or even Dawson Creek for that matter.

I checked in and then wandered down the street. I grabbed a burger and took it with me as I walked along the highway. There was a small strip mall with a business supplies store, a tax service, a barber and an office. Next door was a Re Max real estate office. The windows were plastered with houses for sale. I counted about 12 small bungalows, a couple of big homes, and several mobile homes, all in town by the looks of it. At the bottom were three rural properties.

The first was a very nice house set along the highway for $655,000. The second was just property, no house. The third was a small log home on a river with a barn and a two-story garage slash workshop. It had forty acres, mostly treed, twenty acres of field and one acre of garden. I could see what looked like a mountain behind the property. The house listed at $147,000 and came furnished. That seemed pretty cheap.

I checked the location. It was off highway 97 along the Tetsa River. I wondered how far that was from here. It looked great. It looked better than Fort Simpson, which I was starting to have doubts about.

The office was closed, but would open again at 9 AM. Maybe it was worth sticking around for another day here and checking it out. I pulled out my cell phone and made a note of the agent and phone number and listing. I'd call in the morning and see if I could check it out.

I wandered around a bit more and then spotted a pub. I was not much of a drinker, though I did enjoy beer. So I dropped in to see what it was like. It was more of a cafe than what I would call a pub, but there was a counter, a few tables, a big screen TV on the wall behind the bar playing a hockey game, and plenty of newspapers sprawled around. The place was rather dimly lit and not especially decorated in any way. I sat at the bar ready to order a beer.

"What'll you have?" A middle aged man in a T-shirt with a tea towel draped over his shoulder asked. He had a deep, almost scratchy voice.

"What do you have on tap?" I inquired, squinting a little as the TV seemed overly bright as I looked up.

"Guinness, Kilkenny, Bass, Kokanee, and Driftwood."

To my surprise, they had some of my favourites. I asked for a Kilkenny and he poured it slowly from a keg. There were a couple of other guys at a table and a fellow down the end of the bar. This wasn't so much a cowboy town but definitely a working man town. Most guys wore ball caps, thick checkered shirts and construction boots. I suppose that's the style for logging. But I did not feel out of place. I would have felt much more out of place wearing my navy slacks and running shoes.

"There you go. That'll be $6.50."

I pulled out a ten and dropped it on the counter. He made change and placed it in front of me. I scooped it up, leaving a loonie behind.

"So what do people do for fun here?" I asked, jokingly.

"Go down to Fort St. John." The man laughed. "Are you just passing through or coming to stay?" he asked.

"Intending to pass through, but you never know, I might stay."

"Which way are you headed?" he asked.

"Going to Fort Simpson. Was looking for a house up there." I answered.

"Doesn't sound like you have a job. Just poking around?" That was said as a question, I think.

"You are right. Just looking for a good place to live."

"Well it ain't Fort Simpson, I can tell you that. You probably won't find a job there, and it's not pretty country. It's pretty harsh country. You're talking north. It's bad enough here in the winter, but it's a lot worse there. My advice... head back south. More work and better towns to live in. Stick around here if you want a job in logging."

"Well, the thing is I wanted to get a place with a bit of land and off the beaten track, away from any city. Maybe you're right. The territories might be a bit too extreme. I don't really care where I am, just as long as I find the right place."

"Them boys over there," he gestured to the two men at a table drinking from bottles, "are truckers.

They haul logs out of the bush into the yards here, and then haul lumber down to Calgary. They put in long hours doing hard work. You don't want that, and that's all this town's got, hard labour. Unless you own a bar." He laughed loudly.

I grinned. I wanted to tell him my whole plan. He seemed like a good sort. But I knew better. I didn't want anyone knowing what I did or what I wanted to do. I just wanted my work to be a secret.

The Leafs slapped a shot from the point, deflecting off someone else's skate in front of the net. The goalie dropped down and covered up. The man at the bar stared intently. A moment later a Leafs player cross-checked a Canuck into the boards. The man grunted, "You burken guy!"

"Burken guy? What's that mean?" I asked the bartender.

"Well, many years ago there was a crotchety old man in town called Joey Burken. As the story goes, and my brother was there to witness it, one day at a town meeting, a policeman asked who was making all the anonymous complaints about people in town. There were complaints about drivers, businesses, garbage pickup, etc. It was annoying. One person stood up and said 'I'll bet it's that Burken guy!' Another stood up and said 'I'm sure it's that Burken guy!' In fact everyone was annoyed at his antics in town. And that became a catchphrase. Anytime someone was a jerk, he was called a burken guy. Old man Burken died a year later, but as you can see, his legend lives on."

"Ha ha ha. I like that. I'm gonna use that from now on," I said with a big smile.

"Do you like hockey?" The bartender asked, looking up at the TV screen for a moment.

"I remember watching it and wishing I was a player when I was a kid. I can't say I've watched any in years. How are we doing this year?"

"You have to be careful when you say 'we'. There are lots of Oilers, Flames, and Canucks fans here. I was born and bred in Fort Nelson, so I'm a Canuck's fan. I take it that's what you mean by 'we'?" He paused for a response.

"Yes. I'm from Vancouver. My dad is a big hockey fan. Kind of wished I'd spent more time watching games with him."

"I see. So you're kind of leaving home, starting fresh, being your own man now. Am I right?"

"You nailed it. I've lived a quiet life. I haven't experienced much. I just decided to take the opportunity now. You know what I mean?"

"I do. When I was 17, I left home. I went to work on the oil rigs over in Fort Mac. I spent two years there, three years in Peace River, and then another year in Edmonton before coming back. I saved up enough money to start this bar, and I've stayed put ever since then. I'm glad I did it. I wish I'd gone further. You know I've never left the country. I've never even been east of Regina. But I learned a lot in those few years on my own. Some of it good, and some of it bad. You take the good with the bad. I've been up to the Territories. That's no place to be alone. I loved the Yukon though. I'd go back any day. But

I'm happy here. I don't need no big city. I love to hunt and fish and curl in the winter."

"Well, cheers to Fort Nelson." I raised my glass and he nodded. "Maybe I'll stick around a few days and think about my future. I'm not in any rush to go further north now." I smirked and we both chuckled. I gulped the last swig of beer down, thanked him for the advice and headed out the door. On the way back to the Hotel, I dutifully called my mother and told her I was planning to stay a couple days in Fort Nelson. My upbeat voice must have reassured her because she seemed quite perky by the end of our conversation. Back at the hotel, I advised the clerk I wanted to stay a couple more days.

****

A good night's sleep brought dreams of adventures one could only imagine. Waking up, I tried to remember the dream only to realize none of it had made much sense, with shifting objects and story lines. At one point, I was in a store and a customer who had apparently borrowed a sock from me returned it just as I was reaching up on a shelf for a blue jacket that was mine and had been lost. The jacket soon became a red book that I couldn't reach, unless I used a stick to get it, and then it was a banana muffin. How could such a realistic dream be so contorted? Needless to say, there was very little meaning in that dream.

I quickly dressed and went downstairs where there was a simple breakfast laid out in the lobby. Most of it looked unappealing, so I waited in line with others and just grabbed a coffee and, oddly, a banana muffin. Let's hope this did not change into something else, or I may still be asleep wrapped up in a bad dream.

I had slept in this morning, which was unusual for me, but I had no place to go before 9 AM. It was now 8:45 AM and I took my food with me out to the street and walked briskly down to the real estate office. I must have walked fast because I got there before it was open. There was quite a chill in the air and the coffee steamed in my hand. I really had not eaten well on this trip. I must make a point of having a good dinner tonight.

Time passed by slowly. An agent did not come to the office until 9:10 AM.

"Hi. I'm sorry I'm late. We don't usually have anyone show up first thing in the morning. Let me unlock the door here." She pushed in close to the door and twisted the key.

She was a middle aged lady with thick, somewhat frizzy brown hair, far too much makeup and wearing a black felt coat. She seemed to be the kind of person that rushed through everything. Once inside, she took her coat off and tossed it over the back of a chair. "Please, have a seat." She pointed to the chair in front of a desk where she was standing, and she then took her seat. "My name is Mindy Simpson."

"I'm John Biskit. Nice to meet you." I reached forward to shake her hand.

"Nice to meet you too. Did you have an appointment with an agent?"

"No. I was just passing by yesterday and I saw the listing for the log cabin out on 97. I wanted to ask more about that place."

"Oh, I see. That's the old Barnett homestead. That land is actually leased, so you wouldn't own it. But, it's a ninety-nine year lease, with sixty years remaining. At any time though, you can convert the lease into ownership at whatever the land's assessed value is. Let me look it up for you." She said, tapping away at her computer on the desk.

"Here it is," she said. "The assessment is currently $89,000. So, in sixty years, you would either have to buy the land at that current value, or vacate the land. The buildings do however belong to you. You can take them off the land then. It's actually a great deal. The taxes are low and you don't have to pay the full price of ownership until you decide to. That's why it's only listed at $147,000. And it's furnished. The old man that lived there died. He built the place. His two sons in Winnipeg are liquidating it and want to sell it fast, though it has been on the market for a while." I'm not sure she is supposed to reveal all this inside knowledge. "It is rather remote. You would be about 60 KM from town, and it's in the foothills of the Rocky Mountains. Unfortunately, there are no neighbours anywhere around.

"Can I go see it?" I asked.

"Of course. You can come with me just as soon as another agent arrives to handle the office. I'd offer you a coffee, but I see you already have one."

I gazed down at my hotel coffee. It was pale brown water.

"You know what? Let's just go. I'm sure another agent will arrive soon," Mindy blurted out. I was right. She was a rusher.

"OK. But do you mind if we stop somewhere for a coffee. This is from the hotel, and it is terrible. Is there any place we can get a good, strong coffee?"

"Oh my goodness, yes! I need one too. I usually go to Cup of Joe's. I'm sure anything is better than motel coffee," she said. She grabbed her coat and papers and locked the door as we left.

She drove a nice Nissan Altima with leather seats and a sunroof. She must be doing alright for herself. I wouldn't have thought many houses would sell in such a small town. She wasn't any slower moving in the car than she was on foot. We must have flown over some of the bumps we hit. She was a fast talker, too. By the time we got there, I knew all her kids names, interests, grades, and any scuttlebutt circulating in town. Most of it I zoned out on.

The ride was dull for the first thirty kilometres; flat and monotonous. There was no doubt this land was used for logging with patchy bush and small roads. Then the sparse trees reverted to tall, spiky spruce again and finally the foothills and rivers emerged. It was beautiful here.

The car turned into a small, one lane track that wound through the trees, then into a field and up to a cabin. I sat there in the car for a moment, looking out the window. It couldn't be more perfect; scenic, remote, convenient, furnished, and not way up in the Territories. Mindy looked at me for a moment, puzzled that I sat looking out the window.

TWO - The Homestead

"You don't like it?" she inquired, or exclaimed. Not sure if that was a question or a statement.

"Oh, no. I like it fine," I replied.

We exited the vehicle and I slowly walked the few steps to the cabin. It was the back door. The front faced the river, which was down a slight ravine that flattened out to a slab of grassy sand and gravel jutting into the river. It was indeed a log cabin. It looked pretty small from the back, and although a bungalow, it had a high roof with a window up above.

Mindy fumbled with the lock box on the door handle and retrieved the key, which easily opened the door. The meadow grew right up to the back door, which needed no step. Inside was one open room with a couple of large vertical timbers in the middle. To the right, a cozy sitting area with a big cast iron wood stove. To the left a kitchen. Beyond the timbers, the entire front was a living room with a dining table at one end.

"Well, this is it. It's not big, but for a single person this would be great. As you can see, it's all in one room. You have a kitchen over in this corner with a full size fridge, electric oven and stovetop, a microwave, a good size sink." She turned the tap on and showed the water pressure. Then shut it off. "There is a good eating area in front of it." We walked past the table and four chairs, and a small, old china cabinet to the front of the cabin. We rounded the corner into a spacious living area. Mindy turned and pointed up. "There's the bedroom."

Ah, I wondered where that was. I saw no bed downstairs. It was a loft taking up the upper back half of the cabin which is why there were vertical timbers. A ladder led to the upper room. The living room was sparse but comfortable with a couple of chairs and a chesterfield. All windows in the cabin were quite big and checkered with wood frames. The windows were tall, starting about one metre off the ground and extending up another metre and a half or so. The two windows at the front were extra wide, giving a nice view of the river.

I opened the front door, made of thick wooden planks, and peered out over the river. We continued to the other side of the cabin which had a separate room built in. Mindy opened the door to reveal a nice country style washroom, complete with an old tub, tiny corner shower, sink and toilet. Behind that, along the wall were two more doors, one led to a closet and the other to a utility room that had a water heater and a small propane furnace with a vent in the wall above. Finally back around to the cozy sitting area and wood stove. This seemed to be a den. There was a small desk and chair, a loveseat, and an easy chair. An old TV sat on a small table.

"I will not go upstairs, but I would encourage you to go up and look around." Mindy urged. I nodded and obliged. Up I went, climbing the ladder. The loft was quite spacious, except of course that the sides were very low. The bed was pushed up against the back wall, and the low roof at the sides wasn't a problem.

There were side tables on the left and right with small lamps, a comfortable chair on the far left and a dresser on the far right side. Drapes hung at both sides which could be drawn all the way across. I assumed they closed to give privacy to the loft. Looking down, I guessed the size of the cabin at 25 x 30 feet, maybe a bit bigger.

I crawled back down the ladder. "Should we check the rest of the place out?" I asked.

"OK, let's go. There's lots more to see."

We left the cabin and walked about fifty metres back along the road to a barn. The large doors opened out. Inside were two horse stalls and a few smaller stalls, all along the sides, perhaps for pigs or sheep. The middle was empty, except for an old tractor and garden tools. Above was a loft with a few bales of hay, or straw. It was strung with lights and I saw some outlets. This place would be useful for storage. On the other side of the lane was a two-story garage or workshop. Looks like the old man liked to work on cars and engines. There was a good place to park my truck if I wanted and upstairs was a nice, well equipped workshop with some table saws, drills, routers and hand tools. I stepped back outside where Mindy waited.

"So, does it fit your needs?" she asked.

"Yes. I like it. Do you mind if I take a short walk down by the river?" I asked.

"Go right ahead. I'll wait in the house for you." It really was a house. Cabin did not do it justice. I walked past the house and down the ravine to the flats along the river. I touched the fast bluish grey water with my hand. I turned and gazed up toward the house. The backdrop was a scattering of thin black spruce trees and a stumpy bulbous mountain in behind.

It was scenic. Considering the lack of lush forest, I would assume it was not a particularly rainy area. The flats were mostly gravel and sand, but with grassy intervals. I'll bet it gets flooded in the spring. This must be a low time. I knelt down and drew sand up in my hand, letting it sprinkle through my fingers. I had the money. I had the time. I had the research. But could I do this, all alone out here in the wilderness. If I couldn't do it here, I definitely couldn't do it up in the Territories.

The research would be the least of my worries. Loneliness and fear would be my greatest challenge. I've come this far, worst case scenario I give up, sell the place and go home. Best case scenario, I succeed. Those sound like good odds. With that logic cemented in my doubt ridden mind, I made a decision; buy it. I stood up, turned and resolutely walked back to the house, entering the front door which I had not locked after first opening it. Would have been a bit embarrassing if Mindy had locked it in the meantime. I smiled and said, "Alright, what do we do now?"

"Does that mean you want to make an offer?" she asked.

"Yes, I want to make an offer. Should we go back to the office for that?" I had to get these words out before I chickened out.

"Yup, we can go back, draw up the papers and see what they say. I take it you will need financing. I have the name…"

I had to interrupt. "No, I don't need financing."

Mindy looked a bit shocked. A young guy buying a house without a mortgage. There must be a story there. But she took it in stride. Maybe she had seen stranger things.

"OK, let's go," she said.

We drove back to Fort Nelson. I read all the papers Mindy had on the property. I studied the maps outlining the property boundaries. I read the terms of the lease and the buyout. I felt assured I had checked all the information. I was sure any lawyer would find a problem if it existed. After reading, I laid my head back against the seat and closed my eyes. I pictured myself sitting in the house at a table full of drawings and designs. I tried to imagine how I would set up the workshop.

It would be fun to have some animals in the barn, but I knew nothing about taking care of livestock, and who would have the time anyway. I opened my eyes and asked Mindy, "Have you ever raised chickens?" I will admit, that was probably a dumb question to ask a real estate agent driving a nice car with leather seats. But then again, this is quite a rural place, so who knows.

"No, I've never lived on a farm, but my husband's folks are farmers and I used to visit them often. I don't know much about raising chickens, but know they eat anything and don't take much effort. Did you want to get some?"

"It was just a thought. Seems a waste to have all that room in the barn and not use it," I replied.

"Well there is a feed store down near the lumber yard. They will source you chicks and can supply you with any feed you need. I do know there are basically two types of chickens, the ones you raise to eat and the ones you raise for eggs. If you want to produce more chickens, you'll need a rooster." Mindy spoke about everything with confidence.

"OK, I'll check them out," I said. "Looks like I don't have much to get. The house and shop is well equipped."

"When we get back to town, I'll draw up a map for you and put all the stores in town that would be useful for you," Mindy said, almost motherly.

"Thanks." It was only about five more minutes until we reached the real estate office. We went in and sat at Mindy's desk.

"Here," she said, "have a seat and I'll start the paperwork." Mindy went to a filing cabinet and pulled out a folder filled with forms. "The asking price is $147,000. What do you want to offer?"

"I don't know what's appropriate." I answered. "What do you think is a fair price?"

"Well I think, if anything, it's underpriced. However it's been on the market for quite a while and not budged. So you could try $140,000 and see what happens. You don't want to go too low or they'll just say no and get insulted." Mindy had to play a careful game, bargaining for me and the other side. "If you put the offer in unconditionally, that will help you."

"OK, try 140. What do you mean, unconditionally?" I asked.

"You don't need to put conditions on the sale, like financing or a house inspection. And I assume you want to move in quickly, so you don't need to sell a house or set a future date for possession. Is this correct?" she asked, or more correctly, led me.

"That's correct. I can move in right away. I assume if there were any known problems with the plumbing, etc., they would say."

"Oh yes, that's the law. They have to make a full disclosure. That being said, the old man died and the kids are selling his place. But it's not like someone is selling because they want to get away from an expensive repair. It's an estate sale," Mindy informed me, all the while madly typing on her keyboard and writing into the forms.

After she was finished with the first form, she handed it to me for a signature. I looked the paper over and then signed it where she had marked an X. A few more signatures and I was done. "By the way, you will need a lawyer. Here", she handed me a card with a lawyers name on it, "he takes care of most of my clients. He's very good and he's quick. And that's it!" She smiled and looked at me. "You are all set now. I just have to fax them this offer and then we wait for their answer. They may counter with another price or accept it. Why don't you give me your phone number and I'll call you as soon as I hear back from them?"

I wrote my number down on a notepad for her and stood up. "Thank you very much. I'll be around town." I told her.

"Oh, don't forget this." She handed me a page with the town's layout and a half dozen scribbled notes to show useful places in town, like a hardware store, laundromat, the pub I drank at last night, clothing stores, home furnishings stores, a grocery store, the feed shop, a pizza joint, the beer and liquor store, and an electronics store. I nodded and thanked her, shook her hand and left the office.

****

The fall sun was a bit warmer here in town than out in the mountains and it felt good on my neck. It didn't take long to walk back to the hotel. I was starving. It was just a bit past 2 PM. I already missed the variety of restaurants in Vancouver, even though I didn't eat out much. But now that I had to eat out, I wanted good food.

This motel, or hotel as they considered it, had a restaurant, so I went in and took a seat. Even though it was an off time for lunch, there were still a number of people eating and drinking. I suppose a lot of truckers move through here, and they have no set schedule. They are, where they are. Most of the people were older men in work clothes. There were a couple of families, no doubt just passing through town. A waitress walked toward me.

"Hi, do you want coffee?" She asked, and handed me a small menu.

"Yes, please." I answered out loud, but inwardly cringed at what this coffee would taste like. It's amazing how I became a coffee snob in all of a few days. I sat there, wondering how often I would come into town, just to be around people. I wondered how old the old man on the homestead was. What did he die of? Did he die alone? I was experiencing a range of emotions I had never been exposed to before. I suppose I was very fortunate and sheltered my whole life. Now I was confronted with death, anxiety, fear and loneliness.

I thought about the cabin. I would need to get new sheets, blankets, pillows, and towels. I don't know why that's important. I spent lots of time in hotels sleeping on their sheets and I was OK. Seemed like an odd requirement. Then I thought I should get new cutlery and dishes. Again, here I was eating at a restaurant on dishes used by thousands of people and I was alright. But it was how I felt. Perhaps because it would be my house, and I wanted my personal things. I would get them, and cleaning gear, like mops, buckets, soap, etc. I would also need washroom items, dish rags, paper towels and tea towels. I didn't want to forget anything and have to come back to town so soon. I glanced at the menu and chose the fish burger with fries. My coffee arrived and I handed the menu to the waitress.

"I'll have the fish burger," I said.

"Yes sir. That'll be about 5 minutes," she said, staring at her notepad as she wrote. She was late twenties, dirty blonde hair in a ponytail, a less than crisp, light pink dress and white apron. She never did make eye contact. She was somewhat plain looking, almost non-descript. Maybe it was the attitude that made her seem this way; no smile, no expression.

My phone rang. Uh oh, was it Mom again? "Hello".

"Hello, John?" I heard on the other end.

"Yes, this is John."

"Mindy here. I have some news about the house."

"Oh yes, what's the news?" I almost gasped. Did I buy it? Am I a home owner?

"You got it!" she said with excitement. "They were happy with the price and said the closing can be tomorrow if you want, as long as the lawyers can settle the money."

"That's great. I'll go see your lawyer after my lunch and hopefully we can wrap this up without any delays. Do I need to come see you?" I asked.

"Not now. Go talk to the lawyer. I'll take the papers over to him right now and explain the deal. Then tomorrow drop in before you head up to the cabin and we'll make sure everything is final."

"OK, that's fine. Thanks Mindy. You were a big help," I said, trying to gain some appreciation from her.

"John, it was all my pleasure."

We said goodbye and I hung up. I sat there, slightly numb, slightly dazed, and yet exhilarated. Shopping was a new thrill for me. It's good to have money. I began to smile. It was uncontrollable. I must have looked like a fool, sitting there all alone, grinning. But I didn't care. An old country music song quietly played from above and I felt as though I had been transported to a different world, a different time.

I both liked it, and feared it. I did miss my parents, and my home, and Vancouver. I was now in a diner in a straggly northern town wearing dudes duds, surrounded by truckers, country music and spindly trees. There was no skyline here, no cute bistros, no pretty lawns, cedars, palms or flowers. I never knew I was aware of these things before, nor did I think I would miss them. Part of learning about who you are is leaving the comfort of your familiar surroundings.

When the waitress came, I asked her if she would wrap it up for me. I had to go. She obliged. I paid quickly and started to walk to the lawyer's office, which was near the real estate office. I ate along the way. I was starting to get a feel for this town now.

I made my introduction to the lawyer, discussed the deal briefly, wrote a cheque for the purchase, signed off and was back out in the street. I practically ran back to the hotel. Tomorrow I would buy all the items I needed and a load of groceries. Tonight, I would celebrate.

Crossing the main road in front of the hotel, I pulled out the cell phone and dialed my Mother. "Mom?" I asked as she answered the call.

"Yes. Johnny? Is everything alright?" she quickly asked.

"Yeah, everything's fine. I have some news. Is Dad standing by?"

"Yes, he's right here in the kitchen. What's going on?" she asked.

"I bought a house. I mean a farm... in the mountains. It's 40 acres, on the river with a log cabin, a barn and a garage, and it's right at the base of a mountain in the woods. And it comes with everything, like furniture and a tractor." I could hear my mother relaying every word to my Father. I heard him in the background ask how much it was.

"John, your father wants to know how much it cost."

"Well, it was $140,000 but the land is a lease. That will cost an extra $89,000 if I want to buy it. But I don't have to for another 60 years. I wish you could see it. Hey, actually you can. I took a couple of pictures with the phone. I'll email them to you."

"Johnny, your father wants to know where it is."

"Oh, yeah, it's near Fort Nelson, on the Tetsa River. I never went up to the Territories. I saw it in the window of a real estate office and they took me out to see it. It's perfect. It has everything I need, a nice place to live and I don't have to go as far away," I explained. I wanted them to feel as excited about this as I did. I wanted their reaction to endorse my purchase. I have enormous confidence in science, but very little confidence in my new found life decisions.

My father came on the phone. "Johnny, how are you?"

"I'm doing fine, Dad. How are you doing?"

"Not too bad. So you bought a farm, eh? Congratulations. That sounds like a good deal. I hope it has electricity and water. I'm glad you didn't go all the way up north. Fort Nelson is a long ways up there, but Fort Simpson is a whole different world. How far out of town is the farm?"

"It's almost 70 KM, but it's a good highway. Takes about 45 minutes. It's like a morning commute in

Vancouver." We both laughed at that. I went on, "Seriously Dad, you would love this place. I can only imagine what the fishing will be like. I might even get some chickens for the barn."

"Is this really John? John Biskit, the brainiac of Van? Have you bumped your head? Been breathing in too much truck exhaust fumes?" My father goaded me.

"I know eh? You should see me. I don't even recognize myself. You'd be shocked. I wear a cowboy hat and boots now." I laughed.

"I have got to see that. Send us a selfie, would ya?"

"OK, will do. I'm gonna go. Say bye to Mom. I'll call later," I said.

"OK Johnny. Take care. We'll talk to you later. Bye."

"Bye Dad." I hung up and walked on into my hotel room. I am not a big sleeper. I only sleep about three or four hours a night usually. But this trip has been exhausting. Between the driving and mental stress dealing with things I've never had to worry about before, I was sleeping a solid eight hours at night. Now it was 4:00 PM and I didn't know exactly what to do with myself. Too early to party, like I would even know how. I cannot sit alone in a restaurant again. I know no one in town. I checked the hotel directory to see what I could do. There was a pool and hot tub. That might be a good start. I could swim a few laps and soak in the tub.

I put my trunks on and wandered down the hall, looking for the pool. I will admit, my choice of trunks and cowboy boots were oddly matched. Despite being rather sedentary, I was not in poor shape. Perhaps because I ate well and somewhat sparingly, and I often took walks to think, I stayed in shape. So I should not have been embarrassed by my unclothed torso, but it did feel inappropriate.

I strode down the hall looking for a sign pointing to the pool. I must have gone the wrong way. There was no sign and I reached the end of the hall. There was a door leading into the front office, so I opened it to ask the desk clerk. To my surprise, there was a family with two teenagers standing at the front desk speaking with a young lady. They all turned and looked at me. It was perhaps one of the more embarrassing moments I can ever recall. One of the kids looked me up and down and then began to smile, obviously tickled by my appearance. The desk clerk had a rather shocked look on her face. I could only imagine what she thought and how my appearance may affect the reputation of this hotel.

"Sorry, I was just looking for the pool," I said, sheepishly.

"It's down the far end of the hall, sir," she replied.

"Thanks." With little time to spare I had the door open and was bolting down the hall. I got to the end and saw a small sign announcing the pool. This time, I carefully opened the door and peeked in. No one was there. Whew. I entered the room and went over to a lounge chair where I picked out a neatly folded towel from a box. I placed my boots at the end of the chair and sat at the edge of the water. It was surprisingly warm. I slipped down into the water and leisurely swam to the other side.

I swam now and then at the university. It was a convenient activity, just a short walk from the lab. Another couple laps and then over to the hot tub. You had to press a button to activate the jets. It frothed up with a roar. I sat and enjoyed the swirling water. I shut my eyes. I think I could have fallen asleep.

The peace was interrupted by the door opening and three young ladies entered, chatting away to each other. They stopped short for a second as they spotted me in the tub, and then carried on, speaking more quietly. I felt a bit cornered. They slipped into the pool and played like kids. Once again I felt awkward and stayed hidden in the tub. A few minutes passed and the ladies, in their late teens, came over to the hot tub and stepped in. This was even more awkward. I smiled at them.

"Hi," one of them said.

"Hi. How are you?" I asked.

"Good," they all answered, and then giggled.

"I'm John." I introduced myself. I resisted the urge to shake hands. It just didn't seem like the right place for that.

"I'm Tina," said the girl on my left with long flowing brown hair, "and this is Lizzie," she pointed to the blonde beside her, "and that's Alison over there." Alison had short dark hair, almost like a bowl cut, but a bit longer.

"What are you doing in Fort Nelson? I take it you're passing through," I said.

"We have a hockey tournament here. We're from Fort St. John. What do you do?" the blonde asked.

"I'm a scientist," I replied.

"How old are you?" Alison boldly asked.

"I'm twenty-one," I answered.

"That's pretty young for a scientist. Did you go to university?" Alison continued.

"Yes. UBC. I have a PhD." I was proud to say.

"What are you doing up here?" Alison was quite inquisitive.

"Ah, well, I kind of blew up a lab, and lost my job in Vancouver, and so I'm... exploring new opportunities," I said, slyly with a smile. All three girls laughed. "But it's OK. I just bought a house, so... I guess I better find something to do around here, or I'm in trouble, eh?"

"That sounds pretty risky!" Said Lizzie, obviously the conservative one.

"How old are you ladies?" I asked. They all replied seventeen at the same time. "That's a shame," I said. "I guess we can't go out drinking tonight to celebrate." The girls giggled.

"We can't go out anyway. We have a curfew," Tina said with disappointment.

"Well sitting in a hot tub with three girls ain't bad!" I said, laughing. When did I start saying 'ain't'? I really was turning into a cowboy. "I just hope your coach doesn't walk in here and catch you sitting in a tub with.... a scientist!" Oh my, I was like a comedian. I could start a Seinfeld routine and kill!

"You're bad!" Alison said and smacked the water in front of me. I laughed. "We have to go. Team dinner at 5:00 PM." Sounded like a command.

"Alright. Good luck in the tournament. May science be with you."

"Thanks," they all replied. "Bye."

"See ya." I waved at them.

That was fun. I'm as wrinkly as a prune now. How long was I sitting there? I got out as soon as they left, dried off and went back to my room where I took a shower and changed clothes. Maybe I would take out a pizza and buy some beer, and just eat in the room with the TV on. Life is boring without work. At least when I had a job I always had a place to be, something to do. Now I was in limbo. I was in between. I had trouble knowing what to do with myself or where to go. Ironically, I had all this freedom to do anything, and yet had nothing to do. Well that clinches it, I'll get pizza and beer. Again, I was on the run, so to speak.

Into the truck, I dashed off to get what I wanted. It didn't take me long and I was back in my room. Party night was quiet night. I watched TV until I fell asleep.

****

The next morning, I reported for breakfast at 7:00 AM sharp. My friends from the hot tub and the rest of their team were already eating. They ran over to me. "Hey! How was your party last night?" Alison inquired.

"Awesome!" I answered.

"So, what did you do?" Asked Lizzie.

You mean after the pool party with three hotties? I spent the night with another three beauties... pizza, beer, and TV. Woo!" We all laughed. "Today's my big day. I move in."

"Exciting," said Tina.

"When's your first game?" I asked.

Lizzie answered, "We play Cache Creek Wolves at 9:00 AM over at the Community Centre."

"Hmm, maybe I'll try and catch the game. But hey, I'm all about the action, so bust some heads out there, eh?" I replied with a smile.

"We can play rough, don't worry about that," Lizzie said, though you would never expect her to be tough.

The coach, I assume she was the coach, called the girls over. I said goodbye. I grabbed a coffee, a bagel and a banana and left for the front desk where I checked out. I headed back to my room to pack. I would leave just before 9:00 AM and go to the arena until the game was over or the lawyer called. I could shop after that.

There wasn't much to pack in my room, just a few clothes. I tossed them into the truck and drove around looking for the community centre. Things aren't hard to find in small towns. I drove up the highway to the edge of town, turned around and back the other way. There was a sign that indicated Arena, and so I followed the arrow which led off the highway onto a secondary road. It only took a few minutes.

I parked much further from the door than anyone else and entered the arena with a group of adults and children who were streaming in from cars, and others coming off the street. We were greeted by the smell of deep fried things from the canteen, conveniently located just inside the doors. I passed by a small lineup of customers and went straight into the arena bleachers. The Zamboni was just finishing the ice; one more strip to do.

I could see the players standing down at the boards waiting to get on the ice. I didn't know which side Fort St. John was, so asked a lady sitting in a front row seat and she told me Fort St. John was the home team for this game, right where I was standing. So I went up the steps to the last row and stood along the rail. There were about twenty other fans for the team, but must have been forty or more fans for the other team.

It was a nice looking arena. The rink was surrounded by boards topped with glass and then netting. The doors opened and the players hopped onto the ice, skating around in their own respective ends. They were great skaters. The coach on the other side threw a few pucks out on the ice for them to warm up with. I couldn't recognize anyone. They all had helmets and face cages. One girl motioned to another and they spoke, and then motioned to another. Then the three girls skated over to the glass and waved up at me. I smiled and waved back, and gave them the thumbs up sign. I made note of their numbers.

They returned to practice. A moment later the referee blew his whistle. The faceoff was a battle. I learned their team name from a woman who yelled "Let's go Grizzlies, let's go!". It's hard to see the three young ladies in the hot tub with me yesterday as Grizzlies. Somehow it didn't fit. But here on the ice, they fought hard. It was to and fro for five minutes before number 37 of the Grizzlies slapped the puck from the point to whiz past the goalie and score the first goal. Number 37 was one of my girls. I think it was Lizzie as I could see blonde hair below the helmet. The crowd cheered and number 37 raised her stick and hand up while circling around to head to the bench. I raised my arms and clapped.

The game continued without more goals through the period. The teams changed ends and started up right away without a break. Seven minutes into the second period one of the wolves who was loitering near centre ice took a pass and had a breakaway. A fast deke and she slid the puck right through the five hole. The other side roared. A few minutes later, one of the wolves took a whack at number 4 and the ref blew the whistle; two minute penalty for slashing.

The Grizzlies had a power play with only one minute left in the period. At the face off, number 19 passed to 44 who shot the puck into the end zone. Number 65 raced into the corner and knocked it out in front of the net. Number 37 flipped the puck at the net, which deflected off the goalie's blocker and the rebound was immediately pushed back in by number 4, right passed the pad. It was a goal! The Grizzlies were up by one.

I felt my pocket buzz. The noise in the arena was too loud to hear the ring tone. I ran down the steps and out of the rink to answer the call. It was the Lawyer and he wanted me to come over. I hated to miss the end of the game, but I wanted to get the house key and ensure everything went through fine.

I hopped in the truck and sped over to the lawyer. It took very little time and all was complete. I walked out with a set of keys for my new house. I couldn't have been prouder. I decided to race back to the arena to see who won the game. By the time I got there the game was over. The Grizzlies had won, 3-1.

There was a small ceremony in which the players lined up and a player of the game was announced from each team. For the Grizzlies, it was Lizzie. I would never have guess it yesterday, sitting in the hot tub. I suppose you can never judge someone by appearance. I raised my hands and clapped when the ref placed the medal over her head. The players left the ice and I left the building.

Now to shop. I headed to the home furnishings store where I picked out linens and towels, blankets, dishes and all the things I did not want to use in the house. Next was the hardware store where I found cleaning supplies. After that was the electronics store. I bought a satellite dish, a twenty four inch TV, and a cordless phone. They only had little point and shoot cameras which weren't much better than my smart phone, so I skipped them. I signed up for a basic satellite service and satellite internet. Finally I went to the grocery store where I filled a cart with enough grub to last a week. With everything stored safely in the truck, I blew a kiss goodbye to Fort Nelson and drove on down the highway along the Muskwa River.

Forty minutes later down the winding highway I reached my laneway. I had not considered what plowing would be like on my long laneway into the house during the winter. I'd have to see what the old man had. I'm sure the tractor could do it, if there was a plow I could attach. The laneway was about one quarter of a kilometre into the house through the spiky spruce trees. That is certainly far enough for privacy, but not too bad for maintenance. It was a natural, hard packed gravel with weeds growing along the sides and up the middle, leaving two tire tracks to follow.

As I entered the clearing, I could see the barn and garage ahead, and then my log house. It took all day to clean the cabin, top to bottom, strip out what I didn't want, unload the truck and put everything away in the proper place. By 5:00 PM I had the house in order, the satellite dish installed, the new TV hooked up, and my clothes put away. I don't know why I was holding on to the old clothes I brought from Vancouver. Looking at them now, they seemed pathetic. These were the kind of clothes that got kids beaten up over in school. I decided to turn them into rags. I would continue to get new clothes whenever I went to town, like jeans and maybe overalls.

The propane tank at the side of the house had a gauge that read ¾ full. It was just a regular size tank. I noticed another tank out in the garage attached to a heater, and a third in the barn attached to a barbeque. I should get a few backup propane tanks for the winter. The house was reasonably warm. I really hadn't noticed because I was moving around so fast. I wasn't at all cold. The temperature would fall tonight, so I grabbed some split logs at the side of the house and started a fire.

The stove crackled and hissed while the flames began to grow, Soon there was good heat radiating off the metal. This is why the old man had his sitting room or den here. It would be the warmest part of the house. The stove pipe ran straight up into the loft and out the roof. One thing I had noticed before and neglected to look closer at were the shutters on all the windows. Were they decorative or functional? I went out and checked one set. They were indeed functional. They could be tightly closed, blocking out sun, cold or wind.

I reached up toward the rafters in the kitchen and slipped a pan off a hook. I cut up a few slices of cheese and laid them on a plate, buttered two slices of bread and began to fry them In the pan. When I turned them over, I placed the cheese on one slice, fitted the sandwich together and continued frying till the cheese melted. The toast was ever so slightly burned on the edges. I twisted off the cap of a cold beer from the fridge. I had bought a two-four the other night, drank just one beer with my pizza, and was left with twenty-three more to consume. Now twenty-two were left. That should last me a long time at this rate.

I settled into the easy chair by the wood stove, reclined and turned on the TV. It was a nice crisp picture, thanks to satellite and high definition. With my feet up, I gazed around me. This was no longer just a cabin, nor a house. It was my home, with warm lighting, honey coloured log walls and plank floors, trees and a river out the window, and a crackling fire. It was ideal.

THREE - The Prototype

It should not come as a surprise that I nodded off later that evening, warmed by the fire and lulled to sleep by a chattering TV. I slept about two hours. I awoke to more chattering on TV, glanced at the clock and saw 7:21. Call it a catnap if you will, I was not a long sleeper. I usually went to bed for three or four hours, then arose and worked. I was eager to restart my research and pick up where I had left off. I had already accomplished many things, so it wasn't like I was starting with a blank slate. I rifled through a box of papers and began to read. I read until midnight.

Then I opened my laptop and began searching for news on astronomy. I clicked on a link to a story about a possible Earth sized planet within Alpha Centauri, so I did some research. Alpha Centauri System: some call it 'Rigil Kent', sits in the Centaurus constellation in the southern sky. It's about four light years from Earth and is made up of two stars closely bound together, the Alpha Centauri A and B. A third, less important star called Alpha Centauri C also exists. It's hard to imagine this odd solar system with three stars.

The possible planet is Alpha Centauri Bb, though quite likely there are others, just like our own solar system. These stars are similar in age to the sun. According to some scientists, Alpha Centauri B could possess a planet considered even more habitable than Earth. Seems like a bold statement, I thought, based on what little verifiable evidence exists today. But with three stars in the system, I can see a good chance that a habitable planet might be found someday. It all sounded fascinating. Would be nice to see that far away.

Normally I would continue reading all night, taking a nap in the morning, but this night I decided to try out the bed. I threw a couple more logs on the fire, turned off the lights downstairs, put on the loft light and climbed the ladder. It was even nicer up here. The lamp by the bed was controlled by either a switch downstairs or the switch upstairs. The loft had a rail all the way along except where the ladder rested. I pulled the fresh sheets back, undressed and crawled into the comfortable double bed.

It was nice and warm in the loft, and the new blanket was heavy. I rested my head against the feather pillow and drifted off. I can't tell you it was a restful night. It was not. I am not used to sleeping all night, even in my own bed. Occasionally I awoke, tossed and turned, and tried forcing myself to sleep. Maybe I would get better at this. My mind raced, as it often does, working out formulas, testing theories, calculating with my mathematical brain.

Eventually I awoke with the faintest of light breaking through the front windows. Birds sang, breaking the silence. I rose and dressed. It was cold. I went downstairs and added wood to the fire, which still had coals. In no time the cabin began to warm up. I checked the propane furnace and there was a thermostat, but it was turned all the way down and the pilot light extinguished. I would have to fix that so my early mornings would be warmer.

Before making breakfast, I stepped out the front door, tentatively, worried about bears and cougars, and after looking around strolled down to the river. Something kept drawing me to the water. Maybe it was the animation. It was like a tea party at the back of an empty room. It's where you want to be. I'll get around to throwing a fishing line in here eventually. I looked up and down the river only to see silhouettes of hills and trees. I was alone here.

I crawled up the bank and entered the warm cabin. In the kitchen, I flipped the switch on the radio and a country song bellowed out. Roaming up and down the dial, I found only a few stations, and I ended up back at the first. I tried humming along to the tune.

A hearty breakfast was in order. I selected eggs, bacon, and butter from the fridge. I opened the bread box and retrieved the bread. I began to fry the sausage. As I picked out two eggs, I remembered my thoughts on chickens. These could be my eggs. I have to try that. Next time I'm In town, I'll get some.

I cracked the eggs and gently fried them. I toasted the bread in a small toaster oven, and brewed a pot of the best coffee I could buy in Fort Nelson. It was good, though my poor knowledge of coffee could have been a limiting factor in my taste. It was, to say the least, far superior to that motel swill. I thoroughly enjoyed this breakfast, sitting at my table, with a song on the radio, hot coffee, and the sun breaking the horizon out front. There were curtains on all the windows, but all were simple lacy things, and all were drawn back, not that they would cover much. They added a nice touch though.

Breakfast done, I spread some paperwork out on the table. I opened the laptop and started working. I was making calculations for the battery pack I invented. I don't actually like the antiquated term battery for these things. I prefer to call mine a power pack, or more aptly the power-puck, because it looks exactly like a hockey puck, except for the outlet in the middle. So far, I could recharge the battery with a 110 amp extension cord.

I wanted to try and build a small, but powerful solar generator. I knew if I could make the solar cells with organic semiconductors, the efficiency would be very high. I had already tested several compounds and configurations and found that I could generate 24 KW of electricity per hour from a solar generator the size of a dishwasher. It could be crudely made. With refinements, that could be shrunk in size considerably. The manufacture would be tedious and complicated, fusing organic molecules with chemical gases that could bend and magnify light. Placed in columns under solar collectors, these could pack an enormous amount of energy. I would put this idea on my list, but for the future. There was too much to do before engineering power supplies.

The power-pucks were equally complex to make, though not terribly difficult to conceptualize. They were comprised of tightly wrapped, silver plated carbon tape made with energy retentive microchip capacitors and antimony micro-chains that are wound around and around into a solid disk surrounding a hub of microchips to organize the energy and a central outlet. The energy is stored as mass resulting in density so thick that a single puck at maximum electrical capacity would weigh three kilograms. To be fair, it held what I called hyper electricity. This power is almost stagnant until released, then it excites exponentially. Hence the explosive nature when not harnessed or released properly.

The taped puck would then be coated several times in a highly resistive barrier to prevent any loss or damage. The result, a hockey puck of power, the source of my expulsion from UBC. This was the cause of the explosion; a badly formed puck with a weakness that allowed all energy to push out upon rupture. I never did find that puck. I can only imagine it blew to pieces. The puck however was vital. This can store the enormous amounts of power needed for any device that is unable to be connected to a regular generator. Imagine driving your electric car around the globe, many times, with nothing more than a hockey puck. That's what I wanted to achieve.

****

The day progressed slowly, as did the next day, and the next. The days dragged on as I setup my lab, continued my research, and ordered testing tools and supplies. A week had passed and, although progress was good, I was feeling lonely. The post office in Fort Nelson called to let me know that several boxes had arrived for me. I was low on food, so it was good timing. I looked forward to seeing people and chatting. I took the truck into town and first hit the post office, collecting seven boxes. Then I hit the grocery store, and finally the pub, where I first had a beer in town. I opened the door and stepped inside. Holy mackerel, the place was hopping. It was only 3 PM. I walked up to the bar.

"What can I... hey, I remember you, the scientist. How ya doing?" the bar man asked.

I smiled. "I'm doing fine, thanks. How are you?" I asked back.

"Same old me. What are you still doing in town? Thought you were heading up north?"

"I was," I answered. "But took your advice and decided to stick around. Bought a place not far out of town. Guess you're stuck with this science geek."

"Ha ha ha," he laughed. "A cowboy geek? Now I've seen everything in this old town."

"What's going on?" I looked around me at the crowds and back at the bartender. I had to speak up to be heard.

"The mill sponsored a curling event this morning and everybody came here afterwards. It was a surprise to me, but I'm happy about it," he said. "You never told me, what's your name?"

"Johnny."

"Well, Johnny, the cowboy scientist, I'm Mac. What can I get for you?" he asked.

"I'll have a Kokanee," I answered. "On tap, please." I like draft beer. Some people don't care, and some people like drinking from a bottle. Not me.

"You got it," he answered. I looked around the place at all the people. Most were men. A few were accompanied by women. All were middle aged or older. All looked like lumberjacks. Even the women. I wouldn't want to tangle with any of them, especially the women. But they all talked and laughed. I don't think I'd ever been in a place like this down south, with regular blue collar people out for a good time. I liked it. I wanted to be a part of it. I swept up my beer off the counter and paid the bartender, then wandered out into the room. One man was standing alone, so I walked over and asked how he made out at the curling rink.

"Oh, I did OK, I guess. I didn't see you there."

"No, I wasn't there. I didn't even know about it. Sounds like fun. I've never curled before," I said.

"Well you ought to come out some time. I can show you around. I've been curling for years. I was one of the organizers of the event today, and I help organize the leagues. Are you with the mill?" he asked.

"No. I just moved to the area a week ago," I replied.

Another older man wandered over to us. "Hey Charlie, who's your friend here?"

Charlie looked at me. "I don't know," he exclaimed with a laugh. "What's your name?"

"John. And you guys?" I asked.

"I'm Charlie", said the first man, "and this is Bob. Bob's an ace curler. You gotta watch out if you're up against him. He'll knock your stone clean off the pad."

"Do you curl, John?" Bob asked.

"No, I've never tried. Can't say I play any sport, or haven't since I was a kid."

Charlie turned to Bob and said, "I suggested he come out sometime and we could give him a lesson or two." Charlie turned back to me. "It doesn't take long to catch on. You just need a soft touch. Unless you're Bob, then it's all about brute force." We all laughed.

"Hey, you guys ever fished in the Muskwa?" I asked.

"Sure," answered Bob. "There's grayling, catfish, pike and pickerel. I haven't fished there much, but enough to know there's good fish. You like to fish, do you?"

"I guess. Last time I fished was with my father when I was ten or so."

Bob looked at Charlie and said, "how about we take him fishing with us some time. Seems he's missing out on all the fun things."

"What do you do with all your time?" Charlie asked.

"I… work. I do research. I haven't had much time for anything else since I was a kid. I'm just discovering things now. Seems I missed a lot."

"Come on, let me introduce you around," said Bob.

We walked around the room under the songs of Buck Owens and Bob introduced me to half a dozen people. They all seemed nice and were interested in who I was and why I came to Fort Nelson. I, of course, had no clear answer for why I came here, but that didn't seem to matter. People wanted to know the new man in town. Not sure they were going to see a lot of me, as I would be tucked away in my wee farm most of the time. But I wanted to know them. I wanted to say hi to familiar faces now and then when I came to town. And I was enjoying this local, social gathering. Bob even challenged me to a game of darts, which I happily accepted. How hard could it be? Aim a dart at a disk and throw. Well it was easy enough to hit the general area, even the board, but a lot harder than I thought to hit those little pie shaped point zones. I lost, obviously, but we talked and kidded each other.

Long after I finished my beer, I walked around and shook a number of hands to say goodbye to all my new friends. Bob and Charlie asked me if I wanted to meet them at the river to fish one day. I told them I'd be glad to. They proposed October 21 and explained where to go. I told them I'd be there. I went to the bar, shook Mac's hand and told him I'd see him again. It was an enjoyable afternoon.

I was both eager and sad to return home to my cabin. I loved the farm, the log house, my workshop. But I would miss all the cars and people in town. Maybe next time I'd book a hotel room and stay a night. I decided to stop by the feed store and check on chicks. It was as you might imagine; a long warehouse filled with sacks of oats, soybean, corn, hay, barley, and special feeds. Inside was a bounty of horse tack. I asked the lady behind the counter, "Do you carry chicks, for eggs?"

"I do. I have a batch in the back room. They are a few months old. Didn't think I was ever gonna get rid of them. How many do you want?" she asked.

"I don't know. I just want eggs for myself. How many do you think I need?" I asked.

She must have thought I was completely stupid, buying hens and not knowing how many I wanted. She must have also thought, quite correctly, that I was unprepared to raise them.

"I should think four is plenty. You'll probably get more than enough eggs from them." she answered.

"OK. How much are they?" I asked.

"$1.50 each. Do you have a cage?"

I hadn't thought of that. "No, I guess I'll need that too, and a bag of feed that can last me a week or two," I said, as if I was thinking aloud.

"Yes sir. That'll be $48.50." I handed her a fifty and collected my change. "Just pull around to the back lot, second bay. They'll load the feed for you and I'll bring the cage of chickens over to you," she said. "The bag of chicken feed will last you a month."

"Great. Thanks." I left the room and drove over to bay number two, backing up where a young fellow was waiting. I explained what I bought and he loaded a big sack in the truck bed. The lady came through the bay from inside carrying a cage of hens.

"You do have a barn or coop for them, don't you?" she asked with some concern.

"Yes," I answered with a nod.

"OK, feed them one cup of feed a day, for all four. Just scatter the feed on the ground. Make sure you have a floor of sawdust or straw and a ledge for them to make nests. Good luck. Come on back if you have any questions." She was very helpful.

"Alright, I'll do that. Thanks," I said with a smile.

I had just become a farmer.

Back home - I called it home now - I unloaded all my gear. There were several large boxes containing scientific equipment, including a good telescope, boxes of chemicals and materials, groceries, and clucking chickens. I took them into the barn and prepared one of the stalls for them. I laid a whole bale of straw down on the floor and a second bale spread along the back wall for nesting, then opened the cage and let the smelly birds out. They ran around flapping and clucking before settling down. I left the stall and unloaded the incredibly heavy sack of feed. I thought I might give them some feed now and took a big handful to spread out on the stall floor. I found a dog's bowl in the barn, filled it with water from a faucet and placed it in the stall for them. Geez, I thought, they are easy to take care of.

****

I spent the rest of the day setting up equipment in the workshop. I should stop calling it that. It's now a lab. My new lab. I was missing a few things that UBC had, but I could get by. I'm sure if I get stuck I can send samples out to a school or go borrow their equipment. I would have to brush up on my knowledge of mechanical engineering. I had great software to design with, but my actual fabrication abilities needed some work.

I could now get down to work making new power-pucks. My goal was four. My second project was motion. I had already proven, in theory, the ability to move an object through pulsating rings of enhanced electromagnetic waves. Think of it as a hula hoop shot out of the jet. The key to lift is oscillation. The key to thrust is the pulse. The pulse is a wave. The oscillation is another wave, always connected to the craft's jet. So the pulse is a wave within a wave. You can imagine this like a coin, spinning or oscillating, with the craft atop it. Essentially it's like a series of vibrating strikes on the ground or through the air or space, pushing the source away.

The main jet providing thrust can be oscillating for hover or high energy bursts to add thrust. This, if strong enough is like a fish tail creating a disturbance in the water and launching the fish ahead. What makes this so useful is the lack of combustion. There is no need to burn fuel. A well timed series of pulses could lift and push a vehicle, in air or in space. There was a time when light was completely benign. Then light was focussed through crystals in lasers, and that power was translated into heat powerful enough to cut steel. Electromagnetic waves could be converted to kinetic energy, rather than heat. That was the gist of this theory. I would have to build a small droid and affix pulsar jets to it so I could test it in the field. I could easily just borrow designs of rockets or planes and miniaturize them.

I started the design and manufacture of one power-puck and then looked at designs of rockets. I didn't really need aerodynamics, so aerodynamic wings weren't a requirement. My choice was a rocket pipe with four small rudders, or more correctly fins. On two fins I would affix small pulsar jets facing down. On the top two rudders I would affix small pulsar jets facing forward and backward. That way I could rotate the rocket in any direction. I would put one pulsar jet on the back end of the rocket body to push it forward at high speed. A-shaped arms and legs would be attached to the body so the whole rocket could stand, horizontally, and if fitted with spring loaded pads, could land with some force, if needed.

Within a week, the first puck was built. The design for the rocket fully spec'd out in a cad program and the chickens laying more eggs than I could eat. These hens were serious producers. I started baking cakes and pancakes, making eggnog and bottling pickled eggs. I planned to take some to town and hand them out so they weren't wasted.

I decided to take a day and explore the property. I had a map in hand of the boundaries and was determined to see it all. I set out from the house down to the river. I followed the river north, looking at the contours on the map and trying to match them to the land. At some points the river bank was narrow and steep making it hard to follow. I climbed up the bank so I wouldn't get wet and I could see the topography better. I reached a bend in the river that matched my property corner. I turned in from the river and walked into the forest toward a hillside slope. The bush wasn't very thick, mostly made up of black spruce. There were a scattering of poplars, mostly down by the river, their leaves changed to yellow.

It was a peaceful property. I followed the direction away from the river up a hill, about halfway. From there I turned south along the side of the slope. I could see my farm down below. The hill sloped down and I kept walking until I reached my lane. I was not quite where the lane meets the highway, so I was off by a bit. I wandered into the woods across the lane and the land sloped uphill again. I followed it up and along the face where a broad rocky area opened up.

I sat down on a boulder and stared out over the river and farm. I could see a long way from up here. Mostly to the east, across the river, it was low and flat with thick forest. I could see far, but not all the way to Fort Nelson. Little Chickadees flitted around in the spruce trees behind me. They didn't seem the least bit afraid. I felt more comfortable out here now that I walked the land. I could see that it would be hard to get lost. Either I can see the river from the hills or I would run into the highway if I went too far over the hills. I still had a fear of bears and mountain lions, wolves, wolverines, and any other wild creature I knew nothing about. I headed back down the slope to the river and followed it back to the house.

I turned on the TV and watched the news. There was a well-groomed anchorman discussing the Middle East and oil prices. Then he said something that completely took me by surprise. He said, "Happy Thanksgiving." I had completely lost track of the date. I ran to the kitchen and opened the fridge. I had a chicken, some carrots and mushrooms. In the pantry was a container of potatoes and a container of onions. I had bread. I looked up some recipes on the internet and went to work putting together a patchwork Thanksgiving dinner.

It would take about two hours for the chicken to roast. I boiled the potatoes, fried the carrots and mushrooms, and mixed some onions, bread, egg and herbs to make a stuffing. Cooking is easy, but exhausting. I turned on the radio and sang along with an old song. By 7 PM the dinner was ready. I set the table, placed all the food out on dishes, and lit a candle.

I took a few pictures with the cell phone and sent them to my parents. I should have gone to dinner in town. I bet there was a community dinner somewhere. In any case, I had a great feast, a cold beer, and lots of leftovers for the next day. A little while later my mother called to wish me a happy Thanksgiving. We talked about our dinners, describing what we had. I knew what hers was like. I ate it every year for 20 years. Mine was much simpler. Mom was impressed, none the less, by my attempt.

****

By late October, I had the rocket finished. I made some enhancements I thought would come in handy. It was made of reinforced aluminum with a coat of carbon fibre made from graphite and tungsten. The carbon fibre could act as a heat shield, however this rocket would not need it. With the jets, I could slow the rocket down before re-entry, preventing the friction normally experienced by other rockets and the space shuttle. A globe window was added at the front with a mini video camera mounted inside.

A cargo hold was added in the middle, with a mini camera and tiny light. The rocket was insulated and a heating element added to maintain temperature. A mini oxygen tank was added to supply oxygen and a filter to recycle the air. It was made to be radio controlled at near range and able to take commands through satellite, which I could bounce signals off from the smart phone. The power-puck would fit in a slot just in front of the rear pulsar jet to add balance and lower body weight. The only thing left to do was take it for a spin.

I sat at the table holding the rocket, examining all parts. I wanted to be sure it was complete and ready for a test flight. I stood up and carried it outside to the field by the house, then walked back inside. On the laptop I started tapping my keys to set up the flight details. I would send it up off the ground, tip the nose up, and then shoot the main jet to push it up and forward. I wanted it to zip around in a wide circle, hover and land back where it started. After all the details were entered, I looked out the window at the rocket. I used my laptop keys to control the jets.

Firstly, I fired the lower jets, slowly. The rocket bounced up about five metres. Woops, that would have to be calibrated better for an easier liftoff. I continued to raise the rocket up to 20 metres. I decided to test the edge jets. I tried rotating the rocket left, then right. That seemed good. I rolled the rocket counter clockwise. It started to roll, then lost control, wobbling and falling. I quickly shut off the rockets and deployed a small parachute. The weight of the power-puck righted the rocket and it fell to earth. I could see it bounce as it hit. Despite the parachute, it hit pretty hard, certainly not as hard as it would have if it had fallen a thousand metres or had no parachute.

I went out and checked the rocket. It landed on its feet and everything looked to be intact. I went back inside and made a note to alter my design. Not sure why I didn't see that rolling the rocket would remove the upward thrust from the base jets. I could see rolling it if it was pointed straight up. Then the main jet would always be facing down and keep the rocket up. I tried again, lifting the rocket up to twenty metres, turning the rocket clockwise slowly and then firing the main jet. As it flew, I turned it in a wide circle. I could watch it from the window. I had a small GPS unit in it that sent me location information that plotted on a map. After bringing it around and maneuvering it, I lowered it back down. Again, it dropped abruptly in the last 15 metres, this time bending a leg without the use of the parachute.

I retrieved the rocket and brought it back inside. Immediately, I started dismantling the upper jets. A redesign was in order. So the test flight was a success, sort of. Maybe not in a traditional sense, but it taught me that the design was flawed. I could figure out a better approach. I was happy with the RF software controls and the GPS. I hadn't connected the camera feed yet. For my next flight I would.

I dampered the jets and reattached them, then altered the firmware so that the lateral jets could only be active if the rocket was vertical. I replaced the tiny camera in the front and hooked it up to the satellite transmitter so I could watch online. The bent leg was straightened out. The lower jets had to be calibrated so that they would fire more smoothly, rather than popping right away. That would solve the leap up to five metres at liftoff. Once again, I took the rocket outside and placed it on the ground.

Back inside, I started the ascent. This time the rocket gently lifted off, gaining only a metre at a time until it reached 20 m. I lifted the nose to fifty degrees and fired the main jet. The rocket took off. I looked out the window and saw it steak upward. It did not take long to disappear.

I turned back to the laptop and watched the camera. I could see a few wisps of cloud pass by and then grey sky. It was a black and white camera. I checked the speed, 300 km/hr and climbing. I expected nearly 1000 km/hr. It took about seven minutes to reach that speed and then maintained it. It would be a full twenty minutes until it reached 300 km, the distance of near earth orbit, the same as the International Space Station. I kept an eye on the speed and camera and watched the clock. To pass the time, I walked outside and stared up. Of course I didn't really expect to see the rocket, but it seemed more real to actually look into the sky. It's like being at a hockey game, but in the back seats. You can see much more on the screens, but you still want to see the real live action, no matter how tiny the players are.

I went back inside. At twenty minutes all I could see was a dark screen. I sent a signal to fire a side jet and tilt the rocket. At the edge of the screen I could begin to see some light, and then the round bright edge of the earth. There it was. I was in orbit. I turned off the main jet and watched the turning edge of the planet. I let it go until I recognized the Pacific Ocean. I turned the rocket to face downward and then fired the main jet. The rocket began to dive. I quickly shut down the main jet, swiveled the rocket 180 degrees and fired the main jet again, slowing the descent to a gentle tumble. As it hit the atmosphere, I maintained the speed at 1000 km/hr.

After ten minutes I shut down the main jet again and swiveled the rocket so it would be nose down. This way I could see where I was going and guide it back home. I was still over the ocean, but at an altitude of 26 km. I could see the coast. I aimed the rocket toward the mountains and fired the main jet. As it got closer I could recognize landmarks, thanks to Google Earth. This is where a second design flaw became apparent.

Every time I wanted to slow the rocket, I had to reverse it and fire the main jet. I needed a forward jet. It was coming in much too fast. I swivelled the rocket one more time and fired the main jet to slow it down. It was headed my way. I should see it go overhead soon at about 140 km/hr. It was off by a kilometre or so, but I saw it. Accelerating the main jet and firing the lower jets, it slowed to a stop, dropping slightly, and then returned. I was able to turn it so that it came over the farm at a slow pace. I stopped the main jet and eased off the lower jets, letting it down gently.

I had done it. The method was far too error prone and complex, but I did it. I would have to completely rethink the design. I needed aerodynamics and fewer, but adjustable jets. It will need good handling if it is to be useful. My next prototype would be plane shaped so it could glide in air.

That was enough excitement for the day. I typed out notes from my learning experience and collected all the data from the flight. I looked up the Canadian Space Agency's web site and navigated through their pages. I looked at their projects and the scientists involved. One lady named Dr. Jane Pearce was the director of Laboratory Sciences. A man named Dr. Peter Manning was director of Space Exploration. I checked the National Research Council in Ottawa and perused their projects. I Googled Dr. Manning and found a number of references to papers he had written on propulsion and aeronautics. I found an email address for him and decided to send him a note. I thought it might be useful to see what the CSA was working on. So I sent a short message:

Dear Dr. Manning.

I saw your name on the CSA website and thought I would drop you a line. I am researching space travel and would like to know what activities the CSA is currently working on. It sounds like you have an interesting job.

Hope to hear from you.
John.

I really couldn't divulge too much of my research. I was already far ahead of any others working in space travel. And my next invention, which was only theory, would blow away anything ever devised or developed in the history of mankind. Although rather elementary in principle, like Einstein's theory of relativity and the notion of bending space, my idea was something I could easily imagine, even if others could not; that of travelling faster than the speed of light. Oh yes, I know it's possible, but was it practical? That remained to be seen.

I had no idea what would happen to an object or being while travelling faster than light. You see, in the universe you can't actually travel faster than the speed of light through space. But like bending of space, I theorized breaking space, or ripping it. I liked to call it rifting space; creating a small rift that permits travel, not through space, but between space, like a void in a void. In fact, I don't really believe in voids. I believe there is always something there, even if we cannot detect it.

I remember when I was a kid, my friend lived in a house on the street right behind us. The quickest I could get to his house on foot was eleven minutes, following streets around the block. It really annoyed me because he lived right behind me, so close and yet so far. There was a thick cedar hedge separating our properties. One day the dog took a plunge into the cedars and created a small hole, just large enough for me to fit through. Now I had a shortcut. It seemed so easy. I could whip over to his place in seconds. The dog rifted the hedge. I followed his path.

Space is like a break through a quagmire; a pocket of air in the water. I can swim pretty fast, but my friend can run along the pool much faster. If I could rift the water and create a void, I would zip through fast. In fact, cutting a swath would pinch the ends together, so you really are not zipping, you are short cutting. It was elementary, but the math was not. I had to prove this with calculations and then develop a mechanism that could do it, at a reasonable energy level. This would occupy my time now. This would be my ultimate discovery.

****

The twenty-first day of October arrived. I was quite excited to go fishing with my friends from the pub. I took a fishing rod and some tackle from the garage, jumped in the truck and headed back toward town, stopping where Kledo Creek met the Muskwa River. Bob and Charlie were already there, sitting in a Ford pickup sipping coffee. They hopped out as my truck pulled up in front of them on this small dirt track by the river.

"Johnny, are you ready for some action?" Bob yelled out. He was definitely the more lively and talkative of the two. Charlie was more conservative and quiet.

"Hey Guys!" I called back. "How ya doing? What are we fishing for today?"

""Whatever bites," Bob kidded. "My money's on grayling. They give a good fight. Only good to eat though if you fry them with lots of seasoning and a batter or crust. They tend to be a bit mucky otherwise. Let's see what you got for tackle."

I opened the tackle box and both men kneeled down to see inside. "I just took what the old man left in his garage. Same with this fishing rod." I looked it up and down.

"I'm sure the rod's fine. Any rod will do. Here," Bob pulled out a small spinner from the tackle box and said, "This is good. You know how to tie on a lure?" I was embarrassed to shake my head no. "Look," he said, showing me how, "put the line through the eyelet, twist, slip the line back through the loop you just made and pull tight. You're all set."

"Thanks." I nodded to him. They had their lines all ready to go at the back of their truck. We walked over to the water's edge. This was a bigger river than the Tetsa, and faster. But there was a gentle pool in front of us.

We spread out a bit and started casting. Minutes went by. I was beginning to wonder if there were any fish out there. I sat down on the sandy bank, pushing my heels into the soft earth and watched small gravelly stones roll down toward the grey water. A moment later, Charlie yelled out, "I got one!" I saw his rod bend over and the line stretch tight. The tip danced as he fought against the fish. I don't know how long it took, but he reeled it in and finally I saw a splash near shore. I couldn't see what it was or even how big, though it made a considerable noise breaching the water's surface.

"What is it?" I yelled over.

"A fish, I think," Bob, who was in the middle, called back with a big smirk.

"It's a grayling," yelled Charlie, whose concentration was intense.

Charlie landed the fish and I ran over to see. It was a handsome fish, the likes of which I have never seen before; silvery grey sides with thin black lines and specks, a large fin on top and a sharp, yellowish tail at the rear. Charlie de-hooked it and placed it in a white bucket filled with water over by his truck. "One down, two more to go for me." I assumed he meant you could only keep three. "Well, what are you guys waiting for? Get yourselves some fish," Charlie said with a big smile.

We fished on. Bob and Charlie were pulling in more fish. Finally I felt that resistance. I thought I just hooked the bottom at first, but then felt the unmistakable pull and watched the rod tip dance.

"Bring 'er in easy. Don't pull too hard and don't give 'er slack," Bob yelled over.

It was a thrill. My heart thumped, praying I would not lose this fish and look like a failure. Bob ran over and waited patiently. As the grayling came to shore, Bob reached down and slipped his finger in the gill and swooped it up. "Nice one!" he said, as if I had actually chosen to catch that particular one. I felt pretty proud of myself. We carried on until noon. Charlie had his three grayling as well as a pike. Bob had three grayling and two catfish. I was happy to just have my three grayling.

"Well, let's call it a morning. I have to take the grandchildren to a birthday party this afternoon. Next time we'll make it a whole day and go for lunch. What do you say?" Bob asked.

"I'd like that. This was a lot of fun. I can't wait to do it again," I replied, with enthusiasm.

"Good," said Charlie. "And maybe this winter we can get you out hunting."

"Ha ha ha," I laughed. "I better get acquainted with a gun before I do that.

"Don't you worry, we'll teach you all you need to know. Load, aim, fire." Bob had a good quip for everything. We all laughed. It wasn't far back to the house where I cleaned the three fish and froze them.

****

November rolled in and through. The days grew shorter, the air colder and snow began to accumulate on the ground. I had bought several propane tanks and aligned most of them along the side of the house, one attached to the furnace. Another was attached to a heater in the workshop. Loads of wood were bought from a local man in town for the stove. I had not considered the amount of energy required to heat a place in the winter. On cold nights and stormy days, I closed all the shutters to keep the heat in. A solar concentrator might be a great idea, but not sure it was practical this far north with such weak sunlight.

I received an email back from Dr. Manning. He was pleased to meet me and asked what exactly I was interested in. I briefed him on my desire to launch an unmanned probe and test it in space. I think he probably considered me a nut, but he humoured me just the same. I sent him some requests about aerodynamics and best designs. It was a pleasure having someone to talk to again about science.

Days and nights of theory were slowly transposing into practice. December came and I had my first rifter prototype. It was a small cone, quite solid and coated with carbon. Protruding from this was a 60 cm long tungsten rod and zirconium nib on the end. The rod focused the rift and the zirconium nib pushed the rift. I could not test it in atmosphere, only space. The power level of this device would only be sufficient for one times the speed of light, roughly. That meant if I sent the probe up, I could rift for 1.3 seconds and reach the moon. I had great confidence in this, however I had no idea what state the computer, probe or any life forms in it might be like after a rift.

FOUR - The Visit

December 23 was a cold but bright day. The new probe was built and outfitted with wings, modeled after the Saab Gripen fighter jet. The main body and jet engine was maintained from the first prototype. After the wings and tail were added, three stubby feet with pads were attached, rather than the spindly legs. Two small jets were added, one at each end of the wings. These jets were rotatable through three hundred and sixty degrees. A small jet faced down at the front and another at the rear to lift the nose or tail. Five jets in all, 4 small jets for maneuvering and one main thruster for speed. This configuration, although complex to master would provide complete control of the probe. I built a control panel that attached to the laptop so I could work the controls more easily. It would take some practice with the simulated software to become proficient. It was in good shape. It could take off and land over and over. Cameras mounted inside could view the payload and the sky.

At 6:54 PM the phone rang. It was my father. "Hello, Johnny?"

"Yes, this is Johnny," I replied.

"It's your dad. How are you?"

"Dad! I'm fine. Is everything OK?" I was worried. Usually it was Mom that called.

"Everything's fine. We just took a little trip."

"Did you go south? Where to, California?" I asked, surprised that they went anywhere.

"No, we're in Fort Nelson!" he bellowed.

"Fort Nelson? Really?" I was excited. I hadn't seen them in months.

"Well to be exact, just down the highway from you. We should be there in twenty minutes or so, if the map is correct."

"Did you eat already?" I asked.

"We had lunch around 3 PM. But don't worry about us," he said.

"Well I haven't eaten dinner yet, so I'll get something started for us." I was excited to be making dinner for everyone. "OK, you know where the lane is, right?" I had shown them in an email exactly where the farm was and how to get here, so I expected them to know the way.

"I'll call you back if we get lost," said Dad.

"Alright, see you soon." I hung up the phone and looked around. Yeesh, it was a bit of a mess. I had papers and materials and parts all over the table. I scooped them up and put them in boxes and ran them out to the lab. I came back in and did a bit of sweeping and tidying. I opened the freezer and took out my three medium sized grayling. I dumped them in a pot of warm water to thaw out. I pulled out a bag of mixed rice, part brown and part wild rice, and measured out some water in a pot for that. In the fridge, I had green beans. They would be easy to fry, maybe with mushrooms. So I began to warm a frying pan.

I heard a car in the lane pull up behind the house. I put on my hat and opened the back door and leaned against the frame, grinning as they exited the car in the darkness. My mother was beaming. She could barely contain her excitement. She had been the one driving. I suppose my father had done most of the driving and she finished the last stretch. The lane was plowed and packed hard, but slippery in places. I stepped down and walked over to my mother, and hugged her. My father came around the front of the car and I hugged him.

"I just can't believe it," my mother gasped as she placed her hands over her mouth. "Look at you! Look at this place."

"Well come on in. It's cold out here," I urged them. They followed me in, wiped their feet on the small rug and hung up their coats on hooks.

"Oh Johnny, this place is charming," my mother said, looking all about her. The beans and mushrooms were quietly sizzling in the pan and the water for rice was beginning to steam. I took them to the living room and sat them down.

"I forgot," my father said with a start, "all the luggage is in the trunk."

"Relax. I'll get it. Give me your keys," I demanded. I went back out to the car and opened the trunk. I saw two medium sized bags and several well wrapped Christmas presents. I looked back toward the house and smiled. I grabbed up the bags, closed the trunk and went back inside.

"You have had an epic journey, coming all the way up here in winter. What can I get you to drink? Dad, a beer?" I turned to my mother. "Mom, tea?"

"You know us well, Johnny," my dad answered. I went to the kitchen and poured the hot water from the kettle into a small pot with a tea bag. I opened the fridge, pulled out a can of Guinness and slowly poured it into a tall glass. Everything was placed on a tray and carried to the living room where my mother and father were quietly chatting. OK, it was mostly my mother doing the talking. My father was more of a listener. I put the tray down on the coffee table in front of them.

"I'm just making dinner. I'll be right back after I put the fish on." Back in the kitchen, I floured the fish and laid them in the hot bubbling butter. I added the rice to the boiling water and turned the heat down to simmer. Everything was set. "It'll be another 20 minutes or so before dinner's ready," I called in to them.

I poured myself a Guinness and joined them in the living room. "So tell me about your trip? When did you decide to come up?" I asked.

My mother jumped right in. "We decided to come up the minute you told us you bought a house. I would have come sooner, but your father said we should give you some time and let you get settled first. You didn't call for help and you never told us you were homesick, so I agreed. But there was no way I was going to let us be apart for Christmas."

"Your mother is right. We wanted to come up and help you move in but you were doing so well on your own, I thought you deserved some space," Dad said.

"Well just to let you know, you're always welcome here. I would have been fine with you coming up sooner, and you can stay as long as you want. Consider this your home too. Dad, you would love it here. Remember going to the lake when I was a kid? It's just like that here. Well maybe not in the winter. I went fishing in the river a few weeks ago with some guys I met in town. In fact, the fish on the stove are the fish I caught," I said with some pride.

"I must say, Johnny, you are a completely different kid… I mean man. You have grown in so many ways in the last few months. You've grown up. I was always a bit worried about you. You worked so much and never cared about your life. You've built a new life here. I love your home. I wish it was closer to the city, but I'm very proud of you. Have you done any work while you've been here?" my father asked.

"There's really not much else to do here. Can you imagine staying out here and not having work to do? I built a drone and flew it around the world. I rebuilt it and am almost ready to test it. I'm glad you're here for this. You can watch, even help with the flight. I'll show the new drone to you tomorrow. In fact, I'll give you the grand tour. There's lots to see," I said.

My mother got up and walked into the kitchen. "Stay there," she said to me. "I'll check on the dinner." The motherly instinct never ceases. "What kind of fish is this?" She asked.

"Those are called grayling," I said. "They give a good fight. I don't really know what they taste like because those are the first fish I've caught. Just make sure they are crispy. That's what the guys from town told me."

"Grayling?" my father added. "You really are up north. What else is in the river?"

"Pike, catfish and pickerel, or so I've been told. I've seen the pike and catfish. They say there's lots of moose up here too, but I haven't seen any on the property. I have a good stretch along the river and all the way back to the highway at the lane."

My mother asked, "Where are the dishes, Johnny?"

"Look up over the sink," I answered. My mother started setting the table and my father and I went in to help. "I'll get the cutlery." I opened a drawer and pulled out a handful of forks and knives and placed them at each of three seats where the plates were set. I put my father's glass at the head of the table. The fish looked pretty good, as did the vegetables. I spooned the rice out onto plates. "Where did you stop on the drive up?"

"We stopped at Kamloops, Prince George and Fort St. John," my dad said.

"I never got to see Kamloops. I kept on going past it. I didn't want to tell you this before, but up past Kamloops I saw an accident. A little car hit a moose. Looks like the driver died. Pretty gruesome sight," I told them. "Other than that though, it was a pretty uneventful trip. I mostly grabbed fast food and moved along. You never said, what do you think of my new style?"

"I think it looks great," my mother barked. "But what on earth made you change?"

"I was stopping in towns and everyone looked like this. I felt out of place. So I went to a specialty shop and some girl completely outfitted me. I looked in the mirror and saw a new man. I became someone else, someone interesting."

"Johnny, you were always interesting," my mother countered.

"Yes, Mom, but not so much in a good way. Not in a way a stranger would appreciate. I looked like an antisocial nerd. I could see it as soon as I changed clothes. Maybe I'm still the same person, but at least I don't immediately broadcast it. I'm OK with being a scientist or an academic. But I like my new look. I'm just like others here."

"You had a lot of guts coming up here. I don't know what got into you. I thought you'd lost your mind at first." Sounded like the start of a lecture from my mom.

"I won't lie to you," I went on, "I was scared. I was so driven to continue my research, I didn't really think the plan through. I just knew I needed a place to work. As I drove away, I had to keep my foot on the gas to keep going. Halfway here I was tempted to turn around. As I got to Fort Nelson, I started to think I was crazy. Maybe I had changed enough. I didn't have to go further. I'm not sure I would have stayed had I made it to Fort Simpson. I had the biggest doubt when I made an offer on this house. That was a bold move that meant I couldn't turn around. But now, I'm glad I made the trip. I mean, I'm proud of what I've done, how I grew up, but I do get homesick. I miss you guys and the city."

"Johnny," my father changed the subject, "this fish is great. Well done. I wish I could have gone fishing with you. I must come back up in the summer."

"Well, I'm glad you're here now," I said. "You do realize we're going to have to get a Christmas tree.

We'll have to drop into town and get some decorations. We only have a few days till Christmas."

My mother made a request. "If you're going into town, I'll give you a shopping list of groceries. I want to make a proper Christmas dinner for us."

"I'm not going to argue with that," I said, and we all laughed.

After dinner we cleaned up the dishes together. The chesterfield in the living room pulled out into a bed. I brought out some brand new sheets and blankets and a couple pillows for them.

"Look, whatever you need, help yourself." I showed them the washroom, the TV, a laptop they could use, the closet and of course the whereabouts of everything in the kitchen. "Just make yourself at home." I pointed up above. "That's the bedroom. The only way up is by ladder, but there's nothing up there you'll need."

"We're fine John," my mother said. "Don't worry about us. I think we should turn in. Three days of driving takes its toll. I must say, this is far better than any hotel room."

"OK then. Good night. I'll see you two in the morning."

"Good night, John," said my mother, echoed by my father.

I gathered my laptop and papers and took them up to bed. I normally didn't close the long drapes that hid the loft, but I did this night. I knew I wouldn't sleep all night and didn't want to wake anyone when I wanted to get up and use the computer.

****

The next morning I waited until 8 AM to get up. I showered before the others were up. Then I started a pot of coffee. The percolator churned out a profuse aroma. I set the table in anticipation of breakfast while the folks arose.

"Good morning, sleepy-heads," I chided them.

"Good morning yourself," they replied.

"I laid out some towels and soap for you in the washroom. Go ahead and take a shower," I told them. They both disappeared into the washroom. My father shaved while my mother showered and then my father took his shower. Dressed for the day, I motioned to the door. "Mom, I have to do something and I could use your help." I looked at my father and winked.

"Uh-huh." My mother's response was apprehensive.

"Come on and put your coat and boots on." I put on my big rubber boots and coat. My father followed along and dressed for the outdoors. The three of us traipsed outside. I led them toward the barn.

"Johnny, where on earth are you taking us?" asked my mother.

"This way." I led them on.

With the big barn doors open, we walked forward to a pen. My parents peered over the gate at the chickens. "Good gravy, John. You are full of surprises!" my mother blared. I handed her a metal bowl from the wall, opened the gate and went in to retrieve the eggs. The hens shrieked and scattered. I placed the eggs in the bowl and left the stall.

"OK, now we have breakfast." I smiled at them. Actually I had plenty of eggs in the house, but wanted to surprise the folks. Back inside, I washed up the eggs and found a few more in the fridge. Together we made breakfast.

"Mom, why don't you sit down here," I placed her at a seat and gave her a pen and pad, "and make up that list of groceries you need. Dad and I can handle the breakfast. Dad, can you start frying up those eggs? Here's a pan for you." I lifted a pan down from the rafter and placed it on the stove. "The butter's right there." I pointed to a white, covered dish. "I'll throw some bacon in another pan." I pulled out a slab of back bacon from the fridge and sliced it up. "Mom, put down a separate list of things we might need to decorate the house with."

"This is exciting," my mother exclaimed. "If you had asked me a year ago how I'd be spending this Christmas, I would never have dreamed it would be in a log cabin up north."

"Me too!" I replied with a laugh.

Breakfast took all of a few minutes to eat. I suppose we were all very hungry.

"Johnny, those eggs were perfect, and so large. What do you feed those chickens?" my mother asked.

"I get a bag of special feed from town. It's a mix of flax and barley, I think. Totally natural. I also take some scraps out at night and leave in a small trough. They seem to like that as well. The eggs do taste good, don't they? Much better than those factory things in the city." I was proud of my hens.

"Last night, fish from the river. Today, your own eggs. I'd say you're living a very healthy lifestyle out here," my father chimed in.

"Yes, and I like it," I said. "Do you guys want to come to town?"

"I think I'll stay here and knit, if you don't mind. I've had enough car time for a while," my mother said.

"I'll come, Johnny." My father was not going to be left behind. "There's a few things I'd like to pick up in town."

"OK, Mom. Sorry, I'm just gonna dump the dishes in the sink here and get to them later," I said, gathering the dishes and putting them in the sink with some water.

"Don't worry about the dishes, just go have some fun. Don't forget the list I left on the table." My mother pointed to it.

I swooped up the list, got dressed for the cold and we headed out. About forty minutes later we entered the town. First off, we went to the sports store. Inside, my father asked the salesman about skates. What a great idea, I thought. Both of us tried on some skates. I particularly liked the Bauer pair and my father chose Reebok. Then we looked for some knee and elbow pads, and pucks. It was funny to pick up a puck that weighed so little compared to my power-pucks. Next, we found a hockey net. It was disassembled in the box, but might be a nice project to work on together.

"Dad," I said, "what do you think of this stick?" I held out a bluish composite stick that was far too short for me.

"I'm partial to the wooden ones. Always had a wooden stick. But I guess those composite ones are good. That one, however it's much too small. Remember, when you're on skates you're several inches taller. On skates, it should be up to your nose." With that, he pulled out another stick and put it up against me. It came to my forehead and he nodded. I was tempted to buy all the proper equipment, but settled for the minimum. My father did insist on us getting helmets. "We can't have you denting that delicate brain of yours," he said with a smile. "Mine's already mush, but your mother would kill me if she saw me skating without a helmet."

Next we dropped by the home furnishing store. They had decorated it for Christmas, but half-heartedly. We wandered around picking up Christmas lights, ornaments, and knick-knacks. We got some Christmas crackers, a plum pudding, a tablecloth, candles, and chocolates. Then it was off to the grocery store. We got a medium sized turkey, lots of vegetables, potatoes, broth, bread, butter, and beans. Well, that about covered the B-section. The cart was filling up.

After groceries, we stopped at a lot in front of the hardware store to pick out a Christmas tree. They all looked the same really, wrapped tightly in some kind of mesh. There were a couple of fellows leaning up against a big old Pontiac car, smoking cigarettes and waiting for a customer to come along. They looked like a couple of good old boys, one wearing an old checked heavy shirt and faded ball cap, despite the cold, and the other in a canvas work jacket with an old cowboy hat. They stayed there at the front of their car, watching us and waiting. I suspect they duck into their tiny trailer once in a while to warm up.

We found a tree that looked straight and tall. The checked shirt fellow came over and said, "Is that the one you want?" I nodded yes. "That'll be $20." I handed him a twenty. He hoisted it up on his shoulder and carried it over to the truck for us. "That sure is a nice truck you got there," he said, admiring it.

"Thanks. She's not brand new, but she looks it, eh? Got her in the fall," I said.

"I could use a truck like that. You see all those trees there?" He pointed at his lot. "I had to hire a flatbed to get them here. A few loads in a truck like this and I'd have done it myself."

"Where'd you bring them from?" I asked.

"One hundred and twenty-two kilometres south of here, on 97. I have 240 acres of bush and about 40 of that is tree farm," he replied, cigarette hanging out of the side of his mouth.

"Sounds like a nice property," I told him. I thanked him for the tree and left. We picked up some wine and beer and a bottle of rum at the liquor store and then drove back to the house.

"Mom!" I yelled, opening the back door. "Mom, we got a tree." Christmas was exciting, even for a twenty-one year old. There was so much to do today and I couldn't wait to get started.

"Well, let's see this tree." Mom called back. I stripped the netting off and shook the tree to open it up. A spattering of needles fell off. I picked it up and hoisted it into the house. With a grin, I held it for my mother to see. "Oh, that's a beauty!" she said.

My father carried in bags of ornaments and decorations. We pulled out the simple tree holder we bought and let the tree slide in. With a quick adjustment, the tree was snug in its base. I carried it over to the corner between the living room and dining area. It looked so plain. My mother had started opening bags and uncovering tree decorations. She pulled out a box of small white lights. "Let's wrap the lights on first," she said with a commanding voice. After that we all put hooks on the ornaments and placed them on the tree. A bit of tinsel and ribbon and it looked pretty good.

My mother opened another bag and retrieved a box of skates. "What in heaven's name were you two doing in town?"

"Well," I started to explain, "Dad said…," I smiled and looked at him, "we should start a hockey team. Ha ha ha, I'm joking. But we do have this great rink right out front. Why not use it. So we picked up some hockey equipment."

"You better make sure that ice is safe first," she said.

"We will," my father reassured her. "We better get all those groceries in." I forgot about that. "Some of those things might freeze out there," he added.

We brought everything in from the truck. "Anybody want eggnog?" I asked. A resounded yes came from the living room. "Anyone want a touch of rum in it?" A second resounding yes was heard. I poured three glasses of the white creamy drink and splashed a bit of rum in each. It was getting dark outside already. We then ran a set of the small white lights around the two front windows. I connected them all together with an extension cord. My parents sat in the living room with their drinks in hand. The radio played a quiet, soft Neil Young song, maybe called 'Bluebird' because he kept mentioning a Bluebird.

"Everyone ready?" I asked.

They looked at me, wondering what I meant. I knelt down and plugged the extension cord into the outlet. The tree and windows lit up, sparkling with the tiny white lights. The tree glistened with its tinsel and ornaments. It was a beautiful sight. Christmas had come to the farm.

My mother went into the kitchen and turned the radio dial until she found some Christmas music. Humming to the song, she opened the fridge and began putting food away, except for a few items. With that, she started dinner. It looked as though my parents were settled in and making themselves right at home. I loaded more split logs into the wood stove.

I saw my father heading for the door. I knew what he was up to. I picked up one of the bags I had brought in and kept out of the way, and took it up to my loft. I had bought a couple of gifts when my father was occupied. A little wrapping and they'd be ready for the tree. As I wrapped, I saw my father come in and place a few presents under the tree. When I finished, I went downstairs and placed mine there as well. We both laughed.

My Mother whipped up a nice dinner and we sat at the table long after the meal was done. This may have been the first time I'd ever had more than one drink, and I was on my third. We joked and laughed, more than we ever did in the past. Before going to bed, the three of us managed to assemble the hockey net and stand it up by the tree.

****

I had put all thoughts of my research aside, caring only about my parents visit and Christmas. In the morning, while having breakfast, we gave each other gifts. I got my mother a fine china teapot, and for my father a fur hat. My parents brought me a very nice Nikon camera with a regular lens and a second zoom lens. It came with a leather carry bag, tripod, memory card, and a flash. I suppose they knew I didn't have a camera.

They gave me a few other small gifts which were as nice as the big one. We lounged around the house all morning, enjoying the moment. That afternoon, I took the push shovel from the garage and a hand auger down to the river. I checked the ice, a little at a time. It was thick in this little bay, more than thick enough to walk on. I began to shovel when my father joined me, carrying down the hockey net.

"You want a hand?" he asked.

"Sure. I'll do a couple swaths, then you can take over for a bit," I said. We cleaned off a big rectangle. The ice was a pretty, light greyish blue colour, not unlike the water colour in the fall. My mother pulled all the hockey gear down to the river on a sled that I had left in front of the house. We suited up. I was a disaster. Thank God I had a helmet. I must have fallen a dozen times. I learned to use the stick for balance. Most of the time I stood to shoot the puck.

I last skated when I was about twelve, and I seldom skated back then. My father, on the other hand, was quite adept. He could skate fast, stop sharp, go forwards and backwards. He tried to give me tips, but what I needed was practice. I suppose it would come in time. After an hour or so, I was able to get around. We passed the puck to each other and I occasionally got a shot off that went in the net. My mother stood at the side and clapped to encourage me. The cold began to take its toll and my feet began to hurt, so we called it a day. Wow, I couldn't believe how much I enjoyed that. Back in the cabin, we sat with our feet up and Mom made us hot chocolate. This may have been the best Christmas ever.

I could smell roast turkey coming from the kitchen. I don't know when my mother started the bird, but it was already cooking.

"Mom, is there anything I can do to help with dinner?" I asked.

"No, just sit right there and relax," she replied. Oh thank God. I'm not sure I could stand up, let alone move around. Had I become stiff and sore that fast?

Maybe I just wasn't used to all that activity. Nonetheless, I sat right there, laid my head back and drifted off to sleep.

****

I awoke to the tinkling of dishes. My mother was tapping a glass with a fork in an attempt to signal dinner. "Come and enjoy, skater boy," she called, lyrically. I was hungry enough to haul myself out of the chair and into the kitchen where I plunked myself down in another chair like an old man. It was an early dinner.

Outside, through the back window, was a magnificent sunset. It looked like water colours of pink and violet leaking into each other in a broad semicircle on a blank canvas. It was almost unearthly. Mom had created a bounty of food: turkey, stuffing, carrots, roast potatoes and salad. Though not unlike my Thanksgiving dinner, far better. Dad must have already cut the turkey as it lay in slices on a plate. Dad brought a couple of beers over to the table, but my mother interjected. "What about the wine?"

"Oh, right you are," he replied. I think he secretly wanted the beer. He put the bottles back and retrieved a red wine we picked up in town, and my mother selected wine glasses. After decorking and pouring, we were all seated and dinner began. I had missed my mother's cooking. It was so complete. Mine was always ad hoc; just throw stuff together. Gravy was the element in this dinner that tied it all together, like a link between the meat, potatoes and stuffing. Cranberry sauce was like the salt on chips. I must learn these things.

An hour later, the bottle of wine was drained. Few scraps remained on our plates. The leftovers were packaged and the dishes washed. We spent the evening playing a board game and watching TV.

"I must say, Johnny, you get a lot of channels on that TV," Dad said.

"I know, eh? I don't know what most of them are. I hardly ever watch it. I like the news and some comedy shows," I told him. "I do keep it on a lot when I'm in the house though, but just for the noise. It's nice to hear talking and laughter. It can be very quiet here."

"Well you know you can call me anytime and I'll talk your ear off," Mother joked.

I laughed. "Yes Mom, I know you would."

Boxing Day came with overcast skies and a dampness in the air. Gloomy as it was, we were all cheery. I was happy my parents were here and they were happy that we were all together. I knew that I had to get back to work on my projects. At breakfast, I explained what had to be done. "Dad, Mom, I have to get back to work on my research. Do you want to help?" I suggestively asked.

"Sure," my mother spoke, without hesitation.

"Good. Either way, I want you to stay. You can just relax and be at home here, or you can give me a hand with some of the tests I'm going to run. It will be exciting and I really want you to see my progress."

"We had planned on staying until New Years. Your father has a contract but doesn't need to be back until the fourth," my mother exclaimed.

"You guys can stay as long as you want. You know you're welcome here. Dad can work from here if he wants." I would have been very happy to keep them here forever.

"Thanks Johnny," my father said. "But I do have to meet with the client. So we will have to go back on the first. But I want to see your research and it would be great to help out if we can."

"Great," I replied. "I'll need a couple days to get back up to speed, and then we can run some tests. I think you'll be surprised."

****

Two days passed. I occasionally asked my dad or mom to help with small tasks so they would be involved. I replaced that black and white camera in the nose of the old rocket with a colour camera. Though it was a wide angle lens, I mounted it on a small remote controlled arm that could point it up, down or side to side for better viewing. I was finally ready for a test drive. I summoned the folks to the living room and pointed to the new and improved spacecraft outside. It looked like a tiny simplified version of the Griffon jet fighter, sitting on a plywood pad out about 40 metres from the house.

"Is that it?" my father asked, peering out the window.

"That's the probe," I said. "I hope it lifts off, shoots into outer space and goes to the moon."

"When are you going to try it?" Mom asked.

"There is a little something I have to do first. Just waiting for a passenger to arrive." I left that out there for them to think about.

The folks looked at each other in confusion. "What do you mean, passenger?" Dad asked.

"I need an occupant, to see how a life form handles the flight. You guys want to volunteer?" I joked.

"Somehow I doubt either of us would fit inside that little plane." my mother answered.

"Yeah, OK, if you're afraid, I understand." We all laughed. "I had another volunteer in mind," I said. "I'll go check outside and see if he showed up."

"I'll come with you John," said my dad. His curiosity was showing.

We put our boots on and walked out to the barn. I went over to the side, near a corner and checked on a small cage trap. There inside sat a tiny, anxious mouse. I picked up the trap by a handle and looked at him. "There he is dad, volunteer number one. Thanks little buddy. You're a brave wee soul."

"You think he's going to like this trip he's destined for?" asked my dad.

"He doesn't really have a choice, does he," I replied. "He's a prisoner. If he makes it back home alive, I'll give him a block of cheese and freedom. If not, well then he died a hero in the name of science. Either way, he has no choice."

We took him over to the window outside the kitchen and tapped on it. My mother came close and looked at the mouse. We carried his little cage over to the drone and placed it inside. He would be kept comfortable for the flight. Back inside the house, we sat at the laptop and I tapped away at forms to set up a flight plan. I put the TV on the table and hooked it up to output the camera views, a split screen of the inside and outside. That way I could concentrate on the instruments.

"OK, we can see everything in the plane," I said. The laptop showed the temperature, twenty degrees Celsius, and oxygen level normal. "Mom, your job is to keep an eye on the mouse. We want to know if he panics, struggles, or, God forbid, dies. Dad, you be the eyes in the sky while I test how the plane maneuvers."

They both gave me their OKs. I had the laptop and the control panel in front of me. "Here goes," I said. I slowly turned the knob to activate the bottom jet. The plane popped a few feet off the ground and then slowly rose as I cranked the knob.

"She's up!" Dad said with excitement. "Still rising, 5 feet... 10 feet... 20 feet... 40 feet."

I held the plane there. "OK Dad, I'm going to move it around. You tell me what happens." I turned another knob to the right.

"The nose is going up. It's at about forty five degrees. It's going up again. Now it's straight up," he said.

This was trickier than it looked. I had to activate the main jet at the back to keep the plane afloat. I started a second maneuver.

"I see it slowly spinning now, clockwise. It's spinning the other way now. I see the nose coming back down. It's back to horizontal. No, wait, the tail is rising up. Coming back to horizontal again now." My father was good at letting me know what was happening.

My mother joined in. "The mouse is fine. He's been moving around in that cage as the plane moves, but he's not panicking or anything."

"Good," I said. All's going well." I had the plane turn left, then right. "So what do you think, is it ready for a trip?"

"I don't see any reason why not. I haven't seen any glitch so far," my father said, encouragingly.

"OK, so here's what I'm going to do. I'll tip the nose up eighty three degrees to the east. Then I'll fire the main jet at the back to push it ahead. I'll make it climb from one hundred to one thousand kilometres per hour until it reaches four hundred kilometres. Everyone ready?"

"All set," they both exclaimed.

I tipped the nose up until my instruments showed the right angle and direction, then slowly moved the main thruster knob. "There it goes," my father shouted. "It's rising well. I can see it speeding up."

My mother gasped. "The wee mouse is looking very concerned. His nose is wiggling and he's been pushed into the back of his cage."

"That's fine. He's moving very fast. He's almost going the same speed as the Concord but straight up. As long as he's breathing, he should be fine," I told her.

My dad spoke up. "I'm losing it. I think it has just gone too far to see."

"I expected that. Come on down here. You can watch the camera view on the screen." I told him.

The three of us sat there staring at screens on the table. There wasn't much to see out the front except blue and white. The poor mouse just appeared to be hanging on for dear life at the back of his cage. I'm sure he was hating his adventure.

"All we can do now is wait until we escape the atmosphere. I'll put some coffee on." I got up and went to the counter seemingly unconcerned, but in truth I kept my eye on the screen. Before and after pouring the coffee, I checked the instruments to make sure everything was OK. Twenty-four minutes later, coffee in hand, I sat down and exclaimed, "We are there."

"Where?" asked my dad. "I can't see anything. It's all dark."

"Almost four hundred kilometres up." I used the control panel to adjust the direction and speed. As I did, the Earth came into view on the camera.

"Johnny!" My dad yelled. "I can see the Earth!" He was excited, to say the least. "I can't believe it, there it is." Yes indeed, there it was, a blue mass with swirls of white and patches of brown. There it was, indeed.

"We're in orbit now," I said.

"And the mouse… he's frantically trying to swim," my mother announced with a laugh. "Look at him. He's scrambling his little legs."

"Good. He's alive. I hope he doesn't push off from the side of his cage or he'll fly into the bars. He might settle down when he realizes it's futile," I said. He did settle down. He did get his claws on a bar and clung to it, only to realize it was unnecessary. "Keep an eye on his eyes and nose. As long as they're working, he's alive. I still read twenty degrees and normal air."

"Look," Dad said as he pointed to the screen, "I can see Italy. There's the Mediterranean, North Africa, France and Spain. The plane is zipping along well." It was. Zipping along at a pace of sixteen thousand kilometres an hour or so.

The scenery passed by. When China was below, I changed the orientation of the plane to face the moon, or more correctly slightly off the moon. I fired the main jet to start us moving along that trajectory. "OK, now comes the dangerous part. This is the function I have never tested. This is where I need the mouse the most." I adjusted several fields in a form on screen. "When I hit this button," I pointed to it on the control panel, "I just don't know what we'll see." I entered two more values in the screen form, 1.3, and then 1.0, hit enter, and then placed my finger on the control button. "Here goes." I pressed it.

"Johnny, the screen went blank," Dad said. I did see that. Both the inside and outside screens were black. A moment later they flickered back on. I could see faint stars in the outside view and the mouse, clutching the bars with his feet inside the cage.

"How's the mouse, Mom?" I asked.

"He looks the same. Nose is still twitching."

"Good. That's good," I replied. I checked my instruments. I don't think they lied, but they were hard to believe.

"So what just happened, John? Why did we lose video?" Mom asked.

"Good question. I don't know why it all went black. But I do know what caused it. Bear with me for a sec and we'll check something." I fired a side jet to turn the plane. Nothing. I kept firing slowly, and then a glow illuminated the side of the screen.

"John." My dad called out. "I see light. I think a bit further and we'll see the edge of Earth again."

I smirked a little and turned the plane a bit more. "What do you see now, Dad?"

I think I heard a small gasp from both of them. It wasn't Earth. It was a light grey, crater strewn rugged surface. It was the moon.

"Good God, Johnny! How… how did it get to the moon?" my father nearly shouted.

"That's where I was hoping we'd go. And in ten minutes, I hope to land. We are two hundred and twenty kilometres off the surface. No atmosphere, so I can fly down fast."

They all sat and watched as the probe rocketed toward the surface. I can only imagine what the wee mouse must be thinking now, seeing this rocky ground zoom toward him. As the plane got close, I levelled it off, flying about two thousand feet above ground. I fired the front jets to slow it down until I was able to hover, and then gently drop it onto the surface. It was dusty, rocky and eerily desolate. There it sat. The mouse walked around on the cage floor, sniffing for something he could recognize. We could not see Earth, but could see the moon's horizon where it met black space.

"We did it!" I turned and shouted to the folks. "We're on the moon!"

"That's remarkable, Johnny," said my mom.

"Indeed it is Johnny," added my dad.

"I guess we better bring the first mouse on the moon home, eh?" I laughed.

Like an old pro at a video game, I lifted the plane and shot it off toward Earth, once again employing the rifter to move for 1.3 seconds ahead at the speed of light. Once close to Earth, it was just a matter of spotting the coast, dropping the plane down to near surface level, bringing it to the farm and landing.

"Come on, let's check on that mouse," I said. We raced out to the plane, now sitting on the plywood pad beyond the kitchen. I examined the hull. All seemed perfectly fine. No scrapes, dents, scratches, burns, etc. It seemed almost incredible that not a grain of space dust marred the shell. I opened the hatch on top and lifted out the cage. The mouse was visibly anxious, but that could have been because a human was staring at him. He settled down soon and stared out at us. I brought him into the kitchen, placed a dropper with water through the bars. He bit the end, and then tasting water, licked at it. I then put a piece of cheese on a stick and fed him. He eagerly ate that.

We took him out to the barn and I opened the cage door. He cautiously exited the cage and then scurried away with the modesty of a regular mouse, not one that had just flown to the moon at the speed of light. If only he was aware of the incredible journey and accomplishment he had just made. But I was aware for him. I understood now that rifting space was possible, and better yet, without any apparent side effects. There was much I didn't know about rifts, more than I did know. But I knew it worked. I was ready to move forward. I was ready to be the guinea pig, or mouse in this case. This was an ambition I would not reveal to my parents. The long winter was still ahead of me, and it would take months to assemble a plane scaled to fit a passenger. The technology was ready however. I was confident of that.

I looked up into a spruce tree beyond the barn, its arms spread out in all directions, covered in heaps of fluffy white snow against a deep blue backdrop. It was perfectly designed for this part of the world. It was adapted to life in the foothills at fifty eight degrees north latitude. It exists, survives and thrives and yet we have no understanding of its life. What does it think? How does it feel? What is its consciousness? If we didn't know any better, we might think it was as dead as a rock. So too is our understanding of space, that enigma we call a void.

****

Over the next few days, I poured over the data I collected from the flight. We all reviewed the video from takeoff to landing over and over, looking for anything that could help improve the technology. It was still a mystery what happened during the time in the rift. I catalogued all the materials needed for a real sized plane.

In between long sessions of research, my father and I would go to the river to skate. I was getting better. I think this was something worthwhile that should be continued all winter. When I lived in Vancouver, I often took walks. I would be distracted by the city, then later refocus on studying. I had a clearer vision this way. The same happened with hockey or anything I did that took my mind off work, like feeding the chickens, plowing the lane, or eating with the folks. I thoroughly enjoyed having them here. We were all so relaxed. No one seemed the least bit stressed.

I asked them to keep my research a secret. I was worried they'd brag about what their son could do, and then it would spread. Either people would disbelieve it and call my folks liars, or they would gossip and the news would reach someone I didn't want knowing about it. I told them they could tell people that their son was now a cowboy, or that I owned a chicken ranch. Somehow I knew they wouldn't say that. But we had a good laugh over it.

FIVE - The Winter

December 31st came to the chicken farm. An average day it was. Mom made a wonderful dinner. We all tried very hard to make the mood light, but truth was, we were all a bit somber. This was our last day together. Tomorrow morning Mom and Dad had to leave. I don't know who would be more upset, them or me. We had such a good time together, better than we had had in many years. We played games together, cooked together, shopped, skated, and even worked together. I was proud to show my parents how much I had changed and progressed. I was proud of my independence, even though I secretly wished my parents would stay here forever.

Now, I was faced with a long, cold winter of isolation. That may help focus my efforts, but mentally it would be hard. I suggested that the folks get to bed early so they wouldn't be tired in the morning, but they would have nothing to do with that. They were determined to see the New Year in. We watched them roll the New Year in with parties in Newfoundland, then Halifax. Next we saw a celebration in downtown Toronto, then a frosty sky with fireworks in Winnipeg and hoopla in Calgary. Vancouver would be next. We went outside and I lit a good bonfire. I suppose we lost interest in TV parties.

"Hey, anyone want a marshmallow?" I asked.

"Yes, bring the whole darn bag out here!" my mother replied.

My father wandered over to an alder bush and snapped a few twigs off. He came back to the fire and handed one to my mother and then one to me as I came out.

"Here." I handed out the marshmallows.

"I haven't roasted a marshmallow in years," my mother exclaimed. "I seem to remember it's best not to burn them." On that note she stuck it in the fire and a moment later it was engulfed in flames. "Ah! I guess it's hotter in there than I thought." She frantically blew on it, only serving to fan the flame and burn it more.

"Here, Mom. Take another one. Just scrape that charred goop off," I told her.

"What time is it?" asked my father.

"11:58," I answered. "Two minutes to a new year. Have any New Year's Resolutions?"

Dad perked up. "Yes. I want to work less. I think it's time I catalogued my collections."

"Collections? Of what?" I asked.

"Stamps and coins."

"I didn't know you collected stamps and coins. When did you start that?"

My mother chimed in. "He's been doing that since before I met him. I remember when we first got married he would ask friends for old envelopes so he could get the stamps. He still rips them off letters today. I don't know where he puts them all."

"I keep them in a big box in the basement. It's a shame really. Same as my coins. They're all in tins. I bet they're tarnished now. I haven't dragged those out in years. I'm an accountant you know. Money is my thing." Dad laughed. "I want to get them all out and sort them and then put them in albums."

"That sounds like fun. I'd like to help out. What's your oldest coin?" I asked.

"Well, I have a Chinese coin that's about two thousand years old. It's actually in great shape, but apparently pretty common. I have a Roman coin from England. It's in poor shape. If I didn't know better, I'd think it was just a new piece of bronze made to look old. It's worn right down." My father could probably talk all night about his hobbies.

"Oh my goodness!" My mother yelled. "What time is it?"

"Uh oh. It's 12:11," I said. "I guess we missed the New Year."

"Fuddle duddle," Mother answered. "Happy New Year!" She roared.

My Father and I yelled it too, as loud as we could. "Happy New Year!" It echoed off the mountain and down through the valley.

****

The next morning came too early. After a quick breakfast, my parent's luggage was packed and placed at the back door. I hugged them goodbye and helped tote the bags out to the car. I was happy they were leaving in good weather. I dreaded the idea of them travelling the long haul in snowstorms. They would be fine with this weather for a couple of days, then they'd be in dry land through the interior and finally warmer weather near the south and coast. I waved as they drove away down the lane. I made my mother promise to call me every morning, noon and night until they got home. I hoped she would not be as forgetful as I was.

I dreaded walking back into the house. I decided to go collect eggs and feed the chickens. This momentary distraction would only keep me busy for now. Finally, I dragged myself back to the house and in through the back door. The best thing would be to keep busy; clean up the kitchen, change the bedding and put the couch back together. I noticed there was still a puff of smoke from the fire pit outside. That reminded me to stoke the fire in the stove. The house was quiet. I had forgotten how quiet. I turned the TV on. Any channel was fine.

My mind drifted back to work. Everything I had invented, designed and built took time and effort. Now I had the biggest challenge. I had to put all of this together in a plane that would fit a passenger. Everything must be sized accordingly. That meant rebuilding radiant percussion jets, main thruster, fuselage, wings, cockpit, instrument panel, space suit, oxygen exchanger, water purifier, etc.

It was January first. I wanted to have everything fabricated and assembled by spring. Maybe that was a little ambitious, but with little else to do here, I could just focus on work. If it was delayed, then I might not be able to test it in the summer. Frankly I had hoped to be able to enjoy the farm and community in the summer instead of working on the plane. I grabbed a pad and pen and sat at the kitchen table. I had a list of items I would need already jotted down from the other night. I started adding to it. I needed more carbon fibre, aluminum, insulation, copper wire, titanium metal, silicon, solar cells, prefabbed buttons, dials and instruments. The list grew. There were in fact some things I wanted that I did not know how to get. I decided to send an email to Dr. Manning. I hadn't talked to him in quite a while.

Hello Dr. Manning,

How have you been? Did you enjoy your holidays? My folks came up to visit me over Christmas. I ran some tests and all were very successful. I attached a photo of my mini plane. I hesitate to call it that, but since it is aerodynamic, it does seem to fit. Of course it's more like a shuttle when beyond atmosphere. Thanks for your tips on orbital velocity. By the way, I need to get hold of very large neodymium magnets, and aerogel, or learn how to fabricate it. That is the one weakness I found in my prototype; insulation. I need something that will last more than a few hours. I would appreciate any help you could offer.

Thanks.

John.

I found it very hard writing to an aerospace engineer and not divulging all that I had done. Obviously sharing my results would garner a lot more credibility. Maybe when the time was right I would trust him and open up.

****

The month of January wore on. Days were cold and nights colder. Twice a week I ventured into town to check mail and get supplies. My father had sent me a couple of good finance books. I didn't spend time with people. I had too much to do.

Lots of materials arrived; thick aluminum sheets, rivets, high temperature lubricants and sealants, lithium, silicate, potassium, and so on. I made crimps and bends in the aluminum and riveted sheets together to start forming the fuselage. The body had to be wired front to back.

I received some data on aerosol insulation and adapted it to create a padding for the inside of the hull. On the outside I made a fibreglass cloth, soaked in a colloidal solution of Silicon and zirconium oxide, providing strength, heat resistance and insulation. Over this I glued on a carbon fibre cloth. The result was a very strong, insular body. On the bottom I added thin sheets of refractory brick covered with another sheet of carbon fibre. This would face the sun for the most part, shielding the cabin from heat, and add weight to the underside for stability.

The cockpit windshield was the entry point. It, like an elongated bubble on top of the plane, would open to the side. There would be no door. I had no time to make this fancy. The fuselage, from tail to nose measured 3.5 m, or 11.48 feet. After installing the wiring and insulation, accounting for jets, dashboard and equipment, I realized I had more room for cargo than needed. I decided to add a second seat so a passenger could fit. It would be tight. More so, it would be uncomfortable because of the height.

The fuselage would ride very low to the ground. There was no need for spring loaded wheels and I had no desire to add steps. I wanted this plane to be as compact as possible. So the top of the windshield was 1.4 m high. The plane would stand upon three feet, or more accurately pads. I would be able to exit the windshield by simply stepping down on the ground. As a result though, the chair would sit very low. My legs would have to extend forward, as though sitting on the floor, or knees jut up. The passenger could raise his legs up and round the seat in front, or have knees up as well.

January rolled into February and everything was progressing well. I still needed to fabricate the windshield with some form of super strong glass. I looked up Corning, a company known for their glass strength, and found what was necessary. It would be especially difficult because I had to combine strength with UV protection.

The days were getting noticeably longer and the sun slightly stronger. Cold days persisted however. I spent countless hours on the jets, especially the main thruster. They had to be perfectly balanced or they would push the plane to one side. I had 4 smaller jets and one main thruster, exactly like the small probe, but requiring far more power and stability. Precision was key here.

I needed seats. I decided to take a trip down to Fort St John, about a five hour drive, where there was a large junkyard. It was staggering how many old cars were stacked and strewn in this enormous field. It was a difficult task looking through all the junked cars plastered by wind driven snow. I came across an old Austin Mini. I had no idea the age, but apart from rust and missing engine parts, the interior was OK. I unbolted the two seats, removed the track that held them to the chassis and dragged them, one at a time to the office.

"Hi," I said to the guy that sent me off into the field to rummage around. "I found a couple of old seats. How much do you want for them?"

"What did they come out of?" He asked.

"It was an Austin Mini," I answered

"Oh yeah, I know that one. I think they cleaned out most of the good engine parts before it even got here. You can have them for $300.00 each," he said, matter-of-factly.

"$300.00? Oh, I don't know. That's a bit steep. I don't need them that bad." I turned to leave. I knew that was an absurd price.

"Well, how much were you thinking of paying?" He countered.

"I'll give you $40.00 a piece." I knew that was cheap.

"Make it $150.00 for the pair and you got a deal," he said, firmly.

I was in no great position to bargain further. "Alright." I pulled out cash and paid the man. No doubt someday that little car will be stripped of every last part by people restoring their own Minis. In fact, that just might be my hobby someday. I could come pick up an old car and restore it. God knows I have enough tools and equipment to do it. I loaded the two seats in the back of my truck and went into town. I hadn't realized how little shopping there was in Fort Nelson. Here they had big stores like Canadian Tire and Wal-Mart. I had intended to return right away but changed my mind. I did some shopping at Canadian Tire and asked a clerk what the best hotel in town was. She said the Pomeroy along the highway and so I drove there hoping to get a room.

It was nice on the outside, a basic light beige building with several stories. I went inside to register. That store clerk was not kidding, this was a nice place.

"May I have a room for the night, please?" I asked the desk clerk.

""Do you have a reservation?" she asked.

"No, I don't"

"That's OK. Let me see what we have available." She tapped her keyboard. "Will two queen beds do?"

"Yes, that will be fine." I'm not sure why it wouldn't be fine. She asked for my credit card and ID, then processed my form and handed me a key card.

"Have you stayed with us before?" she asked.

"No, this is my first time," I replied.

"Great. We have a free breakfast in the lounge from 6 AM until 10 AM. There is a pool on the first floor with a water slide. The bar is next to the pool and has a casino attached to it. The restaurant opens for dinner in two hours, the Wi-Fi password is on the envelope I gave you and check out is 11:00 AM," she explained clearly.

"Thanks." I nodded and left for my room. I had not come prepared. I had no clothes or toiletries. After inspecting my room, which was very nice. I decided to go find the Wal-Mart and get some clothes. Along the way I spotted a Marks Work Warehouse and dropped in. There were a lot of things I could use here. I picked up some jeans, a fur hat, gloves, underwear, shoes, and a nice pair of work boots. Then I wandered over to the Wal-Mart, which was practically next door, and got a new bathing suit, toothbrush, a bathrobe, and an assortment of items that would be handy at home, things that were unavailable in Fort Nelson.

Back at the hotel it was nearing five O'clock and I hadn't even had lunch. I went down to the bar and ordered a beer and a plate of wings. There were only a couple of other people in the casino, which was open to the bar. I suppose most people gamble at night. I had never tried.

"Do you ever try the slot machines?" I asked the bartender.

"No. I played them a bit before I started working here. I came with some friends and we made a night of it. But I'd be fired, or broke, or both if I was over there playing them at work," he replied.

"What do they take, loonies?" I asked, like a true casino virgin.

"There's all different sorts, from nickels to twonies. My advice... stick with quarters or less. You can lose a lot of money playing with bigger coins." Sounded like good advice he was giving me.

After I finished my wings, I fumbled through my pockets and found three nickels and two quarters. "Do you have change for a ten?" I asked. He handed me a roll of quarters. I wandered over to the slots with a beer in my left hand and the quarters in my right, looking for the 25¢ mark on the coin slot. I sat down at a Dragon Ball Zed machine, dropped in a quarter and pulled the lever. The symbols rolled around, one after the other stopping until they were all locked in place. Nothing happened. There was no noise. I guess I lost. I don't know how you win.

So I got up and went to a machine with fruit symbols. I tried a couple of quarters in it to no avail. On the third attempt, the machine played a ringing sound and out came four quarters. I won. "Hey", I called to the bartender, "I won! Four quarters." He smiled. I could see how this might be addictive. It's a thrill winning money. I drank my beer and played a few more times, losing the four quarters. I decided I'd play the rest later when hopefully more people were in the casino. I dropped the beer glass off at the bar, thanked the bartender and told him I'd be back later.

I went for a quick dip in the pool before it was overrun with kids. I even tried the slide. It was quite fun. The slide twisted around several times before terminating about four feet above the water. I went feet first, then head first. I can't be the only adult that enjoys this. I let out a "woo" every time I left the slide, anticipating the splash of water. Too bad there wasn't a ramp at the end that would launch you out over the pool. Come on, do I have to invent everything!?

Back in the room, I showered, changed and tried on the new shoes. I felt a bit more comfortable walking around the hotel in nice canvas shoes, rather than my big old work boots. However I now felt out of place without my cowboy boots. As much as I dreaded sitting alone in the restaurant, I wanted a good meal. I dropped by the front desk and picked up a Vancouver newspaper, then navigated the halls to the restaurant. I spotted a booth and asked if I could sit there.

"Certainly, sir," I was answered, and shown the way.

There was lots of room on this table. I opened the newspaper to the left of me and the menu to the right. Not sure which to look at first until I spied the photo of a plate heaped high with ribs, mashed potatoes and beans. Could I really just order the first thing I saw? Why not. I bet I'd look at everything else there and then come right back to the ribs. I turned my attention to the newspaper. Front article: political scandal in the mayoral race. Why do these guys always think they can over spend and then hide it? Idiots, I thought.

What else was going on, besides foolish politicians and their power trips? Lots of construction around the airport. A snowstorm crippling Toronto. The Flames looking to trade for a rookie. The stock market down. Geez, you know, I should have talked to my dad about investments when he was here. I'd like to do something with the cash I had in the bank. I wasn't making any money from it. I browsed the markets, checked commodities, foreign exchange, bonds and lending rates. I wonder if there's a way to predict changes. I bet that's something people have been trying to figure out for ages. I pulled out my phone and called my dad.

"Dad, It's Johnny."

"Everything OK?" he asked.

"Yeah, everything's fine. I was just looking at the markets and was wondering how I could learn a bit more about investing."

"I could send you some stuff if you want. I should have mentioned it to you before. It's a waste sitting on all that cash," he advised.

"I know. I was just thinking that. Send me some info on how to understand the markets, trends, that sort of thing. OK? I'll call you when I get back home."

"Back home? Where are you?" he asked.

"Oh, I just took a trip down to Fort St. John. I was looking for car seats. Little ones. I found some in a wee Austin Mini."

"I'm not sure I want to know what they're for," he added.

"Ha ha ha. No you probably don't. Neither would Mom. Thanks Dad. I'll talk to you later."

I hung up the phone. You know, I could learn a lot about investing, and I could probably write an app. I could even do this with my dad. Might be a nice project and we could make some money. The waitress came and I ordered the ribs along with a beer. I saw some ads in the paper for investment guides, so I used the phone and ordered research material from the Wall Street Journal, Financial Post, Bloomberg's and a couple others. That would be money well spent. The ribs and my beer came. They were as pretty as the picture and smelled awesome. I dug in, cleaning off one bone after another like some prehistoric caveman. You know what I should have got at Wal-Mart was a slow cooker. I'll have to make a quick stop there tomorrow before heading home.

****

Later that evening I strolled back down to the casino with my roll of quarters. The place was hopping. I waved at the bartender and he waved back.

"Give me a Bass Ale, would ya?" I asked.

"Coming up," he replied and poured a glass full. I walked over to the slots and found a vacant one. I was now on my third beer, a record for me. Without question this was the only way to gamble, as long as you only had a roll of quarters and no more to play with.

"Hi," a lady beside me said as she looked over. She was in her early thirties or so, short brown hair, attractive rosy lipstick and faded tight jeans.

"Hi. You winning tonight?" I asked.

"Not so far. Perseverance is the key. Play long enough and you'll win," she spoke authoritatively. I'm sure she was right, but how much would you win? Half the amount you lost? Unless you were one of the lucky few that comes out ahead. It's a fact; the machines are stacked against you.

"Well I've got twenty quarters and a beer. If I finish the beer first, I win. If I finish the coins first, I lose." I laughed.

"You live in town?" she asked.

"No, up near Fort Nelson. I'm just here to shop, and gamble, obviously."

"I can see that, big spender." She smirked.

Another lady carrying a martini glass came over and stood behind her. "Winning?" She asked her friend, watching the images roll around in the machine.

"No. Nothing. I think... what's your name?" she turned and asked me.

"Johnny." I replied. "And yours?"

"Tammy. This is Fiona." She pointed at the martini lady, who greeted me with a "hi". "I think Johnny here is a jinx. You'd think a handsome man like that would be good luck, wouldn't ya?" Fiona nodded and smiled. "OK, I'm changing machines," she said and the ladies both walked a few steps away. I watched as they left, admiring them. I noticed Fiona gave a quick look back. I wondered if they wanted me to chase after them.

Well this is awkward. I am not experienced in casino dating. They were out of my league anyway. I'm sure anything they had in mind would scare the willies out of me. I continued playing quarters as quickly as I could, hoping the roll would be done soon and I could exit without facing any more unexpected encounters. Once again, I lay my empty glass down on the bar and retreated to my room. TV, that was more my pace. But the evening had been an adventure, and a few new experiences to add to my list.

****

A night's sleep and a stopover in Wal-Mart to get a crock pot was all I needed to set me on the road back home again. I thoroughly enjoyed the trip. The hotel was nice, the bar and pool were fun, and I got what I needed. Now the work to fit the two seats into the fuselage. I knew they would fit because I measured them.

The plane was really coming together. The entire body was now fabricated, including the wings and tail. Much of the instrument panel was installed. I made sure there was a manual control for every function. I wanted this override in case there was a software glitch. I had not intended to put maneuvering artifacts in the plane, rather rely solely on jets, but changed my mind and added a simple flap on each wing and the tail so I could fly it without jets while in the atmosphere. That would come in handy when gliding.

February had passed and March brought with it warmer temperatures. Today was plus three Celsius. The sun felt warm and snow was just starting to slowly dissipate. March is a fickle month. One day can be spring-like and the next blizzardy. The last piece of the puzzle was finished. I mounted the windshield on top of the plane. It had to be hinged to open, but also had to be secured to the body to prevent loss of pressure. My plane was an engineering feat, especially for a theoretical physicist. I had not concerned myself with space suits. I was not at that stage yet. Eventually I would have to figure out how to make them. I doubt you could just buy one online, as convenient as that might be, and I certainly didn't see any at Wal-Mart.

It was March 17, a nice, sunny, semi-warm day. I decided to test a few controls. I put my hockey helmet on, wheeled the plane out and slipped into the cockpit. It was indeed a tight fit. Those old Mini seats were small. I started up the lift jets and slowly raised the power. The plane lifted straight up. I rose to around thirty feet. I had hoped for forty. I may have to adjust the power to the jets. I made a turn right. I made a turn left. I tried to go through all the steps I did with the probe. I tested the software controls and the manual controls. I lifted the nose, then the tail, and then the nose again. I leveled off, pointed northwest toward the lowlands along the mountains and activated the rear propulsion jet to slowly move forward. I lowered the flaps, cranked the jet higher and raced up to one thousand feet where I leveled off and tried some maneuvers. I brought it down again to one hundred feet and swept above the trees back to the farm where I gently landed. Everything worked, however I noted some minor flaws I could adjust. I pushed it back into the barn and covered it with a large tarp.

On April 1, I drove to town with an agenda in mind. I didn't know if I could accomplish this, but I had to try. I wanted to find a seamstress. I asked around and got the name of Mildred Waterton on Spruce Avenue. I went to meet her. It was a small white bungalow with fake green shutters on the windows. I rolled into the driveway, walked up to the front door and knocked. An older lady answered. "Yes?"

"Hello, are you Mildred?" I asked, knowing it probably was. Apparently Mildred had worked most of her life for a garment factory in Calgary, but moved to Fort Nelson with her husband in the early eighties when tariffs were removed and cheap clothing started to arrive from Asia.

"Yes, I am." She looked puzzled.

"I understand you used to work in garments. I'm looking for someone that can do some sewing for me."

"Oh," she said. "I can sew, yes. What do you need?"

"I have a special order. This is a bit unusual. I want you to make me an astronaut suit," I replied.

She looked at me with a curious face, not sure if she should take me seriously. "Is this an April fool's joke?" she asked.

I laughed. "No. I need an astronaut suit."

"So you mean like a costume for a party?" she continued.

"Nope, a real astronaut suit. I have the plans and the material. That's why I need you. I need someone who can understand what I want and ensure it's done right. I need someone with lots of experience. The material is not usual. It's very strong and rigid. I have a lot of intricate specifications on it."

"I don't know. I've never done anything like that before," she said.

"I can show you the material, and the plans. I will take care of the helmet myself, at least until I need an expert to complete the sewing, if need be," I explained.

"OK. I can look at it if you want," she replied, cautiously.

I ran back to the truck and retrieved a large box. Inside her house I opened it and showed her the plans and the material. It was difficult. Essentially, each suit required an inner suit, wiring, insulation, and an outer suit. After completion, I could apply some bonding to the seams and special aerosols to the surface. I had to talk her into it, but eventually she accepted the job. I wanted two full suits made. She estimated three weeks, but I gave her my phone number and told her to call me if there was a delay or problem. I assured her there was no rush. I preferred she took her time and did a good job.

My task would be far more difficult. I had to fabricate the glass face plates and helmet. The glass had to be hard, UV blocking, and sealed to the helmet. I would have to affix a nozzle under the face plate for an oxygen hose to attach. I had designs off the web, but it was still a tedious task. I set my mind to it and diligently worked to make the helmets and face glass. Day in and day out I molded them, occasionally making mistakes and starting over. I wanted them done quickly so I could be ready when the suits were finished.

****

To my surprise, I got a call back from Mildred on April 12. She said she had completed the suits and asked me to come see if they were acceptable. I was due to get groceries anyway and promptly drove to town. I checked her work and the suits were excellent. We went through all the buttons and attachments to see if they were secure. I wrote Mildred a cheque and added one hundred dollars as a bonus for doing it so quickly. She was thrilled. She said she would be available if I needed alterations. We sat and had tea in her living room and talked about her past and the people in town, upcoming events and me. I asked her to keep the suits a secret. It was part of my research and I did not want the town abuzz with chatter of astronauts and spaceships.

"John, what are you going to do with those suits?" Mildred asked.

I was concerned about telling her, but I did. "I'm planning to fly in space. But you have to keep this a secret. No one else knows. I would probably get in trouble with some air transport government department if they knew what I was doing."

"You mean you're going to do it on your own? Wouldn't you need a rocket or shuttle or something?" she persisted.

"I'm working on that. Someday I'll get there." That was my equivocal answer.

"I think I know who you are," Mildred said carefully. "Somebody mentioned a fellow in town has been getting a lot of odd packages in the post office."

"That could be anyone. I wouldn't say my packages are all that odd. But now I'm a bit concerned what people might be saying or thinking. Heard anything else?" I asked.

"No. There's plenty of gossip in this town. No one escapes scrutiny." She laughed.

I nodded. I guess I should have guessed my deliveries and purchases would draw some attention, but didn't think anyone would care. That was naive of me I suppose.

"Have you ever been in space before? I mean did you used to work for a space agency before?" she asked.

"No. I did lots of research in this field, but all theory really," I responded. "So tell me about you. What do you like to do in town?" My turn to ask questions, and change the subject.

"Me? Oh not much anymore. I play bingo on Wednesday nights at the church. I gave up curling a couple of years ago. My back was too stiff bending over with that heavy stone. I suppose I mostly do volunteer work. My husband is the active one. He's out fishing, ski doing, curling, and helping out at the rink. He drives the Zamboni between games for some of the teams. He's still only seventy-three. I'm eighty-one."

"Well, Mildred, you do not look eighty-one. You seem pretty young to me." I smiled.

My tea was gone and I was ready to get back to work. I needed to finish my helmets, coat the suits and put it all together. I said goodbye.

"You be careful. I don't want to read about a daredevil smashed into the side of a mountain," she quipped.

"I'll be careful. I don't want you to read about that either." We laughed and I departed. That thought though had crossed my mind a time or two in the recent past. The closer I got to finishing, the closer I came to taking huge risks. A man can be completely sure of himself and still be wrong. That's part of the human experience; perception. Have you ever looked out and seen what you thought was a big animal in the distance, only to learn it was a small animal up close? The brain is a complex braid of knowledge and interpretation. Sometimes we are fooled by assumptions.

****

April 29 broke with a chattering of songs from all the birds returning home to the north. I had completed the helmets and outfitted the suits with all electronics, air nozzles, oxygen tanks, etc. They were, in effect, done. I had added a rifter to the plane's nose. It was the same power level as the one in the probe. It could only go one light year. I just hadn't had time to improve it. That would have to wait.

I stood in front of the chickens and stared at the plane. That seemed like such an inaccurate name for it, plane. It wasn't a plane, a shuttle, a rocket, nor a ship. It was a space plane I suppose. Maybe I should have called it a 'spane'. Well, whatever it was, it was ready to fly. But was I ready? All the work I had done in UBC and all the work from September till now culminated here at this point in time. I could procrastinate and test components until I was blue in the face and still not be ready.

I covered the plane up again. It was early. I wanted to take a walk on this fine spring day. I wanted to smell the air, listen to the birds and feel the breeze on my face. I had waited all winter for the warmth and now I could just spend a few hours enjoying it before risking my neck. I guess there was more to life than research, and I felt it now.

I fixed a sandwich and packed it with a can of pop water. I put that and my camera in a small backpack, put on my work boots, collected my fishing rod and walked down toward the river. I followed the bank for a little while to a small pool. A small spinner was already on the rod from the last fishing trip.

With the backpack by my side, I cast out into the pool. The spinner made a small splash and disappeared beneath the surface. The rod tip tugged ever so slightly as the spinner twirled through the water. Right below me, the spinner hopped out of the water and snapped against the rod tip. I had to let a little line out to loosen it. The hooks dangled below the spinning shield which shimmered in the sunlight. A few drops of water dripped back into the river. A flick of the wrist and the spinner was flying through the air, destined to splash down in a slightly different spot this time, hopefully in front of a nice fish. Drag and cast, drag and cast. The dance repeated itself over and over from one end of the pool to another. Maybe the fish just weren't hungry tonight. You can lead them through water, but you can't make them bite.

I decided to give up. I followed a direct path across the field to the barn and put the rod away. From there I went down the laneway and then climbed the hill. The poplar trees were still bare. Not sure when the leaves come out. But most of the trees were spruce anyway. The ground cover had begun to green up. Grass and small plants were growing. I climbed higher until I reached a wide open slope and found a good spot to sit down. A few flies buzzed around me but thankfully no mosquitoes or blackflies. I leaned back against a tree and viewed the property.

The garden was obvious with furrows plowed into it. What would be good crops for there, I thought. I suppose it's whatever I wanted to plant. I liked corn, tomatoes, potatoes, beans, onions, and herbs. I wonder if that's enough to fill an acre. It'll be fun. The field looked quite natural. I didn't want to change it. You could see the farm from a bird's eye view. This was the perfect place to spot damage to the buildings, but none was apparent.

I opened the pack and started eating lunch. There was something so natural and primeval about eating in the forest. After lunch I closed my eyes and questioned whether I was really destined to be an astronaut. Not sure where this anxiety was coming from. I never feared testing my research. I test flew the jet just a few weeks ago. That was brave. Maybe I was just starting to appreciate the gift of life.

What I had, laid out before me, was beauty, safety, comfort, and peace. The land and water, forest and farm was my refuge. It was also my base for research and possibly the source of inspiration that got me so far. This paradox only served to confuse me. I had to regain confidence in my abilities. I needed to test the plane, to its maximum. On that resolve, I swung the pack over my back and headed down the hill.

Inside the barn sat the plane, covered and still. I whipped the tarp off and stared for a moment, then pushed the plane's pad out in front of the doors. The space suit took some time to squirm into and the helmet fit snugly on top. I climbed into the plane, closed the cap and fitted the oxygen hose into the helmet. The power-puck levels were full. All systems seemed ready to go. With the flick of a switch and a few twists of knobs, the plane rose as it had done before. I was up about forty feet this time, better than the last time. I moved forward about two hundred feet into the field. It was now or never.

The nose tipped up at an angle of fifty-five degrees. Turning the main thruster on, the plane sped ahead from slow to 1000 Km/hour. This was the fastest I had ever flown. It was thrilling, and frightening. Flying upward at these speeds created significant gravitational pull. I was pressed back into the Mini seat, staring intently forward, watching a few tufts of cloud sweep by.

It was blue sky after that, lots of blue sky ahead of me. Wouldn't it be wonderful if my parents saw me do this? Well, they may not think it was wonderful. Some things just have to be shielded from parents, and this was one of them. In what seemed like minutes, though I'm sure it was longer, the blue changed to black with a twinkling of a million stars. I checked my gauges. I was nearing 300 Km. I started to change trajectory, slanting more to my left. Out the window I could see the bluish haze that defined the planet's edge. With the main thruster on full, I accelerated to such a speed I entered orbit and instantly felt weightless. It's a humbling experience to peer down at the ball of land that sustains all known life.

I felt completely alone, separated from all that life. It was almost like being dead. I was in a place where life cannot exist, yet I was alive and aware. This was in fact spiritual. I was a singular soul. Down below were seven billion people, and not one of them knew I was up here. Imagine all the activities going on below me; parties and fights, laughter and tears, celebrations and wars. And where was the creator? Was Earth between Heaven and Hell, or was Earth Heaven and Hell? Even with this unique perspective, answers to such questions evaded me.

From the other side of the plane, I saw the moon. It shone brightly. I turned the plane toward it and fired the thruster to move out of orbit. Entering coordinates into the computer screen, I hesitated for a moment with my finger ready to hit enter. I felt myself brace for the unknown. My finger tapped the screen. All went black. I mean pitch black. There was no light from the moon or the dashboard. I felt immobilized. Was I breathing? Was my heart beating? I don't know. It was only a 1.3 second rift in space, but I couldn't tell if this was a shortcut through time or if I lost consciousness. All I remember is seeing black as though my eyes were shut tight for a brief moment and then open again. I saw stars ahead of me and all the lights in the cockpit.

Off to my side was the moon, half lit as I was now in a different location. It was, as you can imagine, enormous. I was only 326 Km off the surface. No picture can compare to actually seeing the surface. How alien and desolate it looked with craters pockmarking the surface. The crust was various shades of grey, almost as if looking at it through a black and white TV screen. I twisted the plane around and blasted my way downward. I could come in fast as there was no atmosphere to fear. As I approached, I levelled the plane off to whiz over the surface. Firing the side jets, the plane began to slow. There was a wide, flat, illuminated surface ahead which I guided the plane down onto. Descent was very slow. Feeling like a feather, I sat in the plane gazing at the rugged dusty ground, and the Earth in the distance.

The oxygen hose was removed from the intake on the plane and plugged into the tank on my back. I had fifteen minutes of oxygen out there. The suit was stable at one atmosphere to maintain nitrogen levels in the blood. I decompressed the fuselage and opened the cap. It felt odd moving around in such low gravity. I stepped out beyond the front wing and then down onto the moon's surface. My foot found a firm place and dust rose up around it. I took a few steps away from the plane, turned, and snapped a few pictures of the plane with the Earth behind it, floating in space, and then a couple selfies. There was no reason to loiter, so I bent down, collected a fist-sized rock and retreated to the plane. I was tempted to jump up and down but thought that might tempt fate.

Back in the plane I reconnected my oxygen, pressurized the cabin and placed the rock beneath my seat, which is what a good stewardess would tell me to do on a long flight from someplace on Earth to someplace else on Earth. That thought made me laugh out loud. Maybe I was a bit giddy from taking a walk on the surface of the moon. In any case, I was ready to depart this enormous, scarred, space boulder.

Secured in my seat with my harness, the plane lifted off easily and I sped away into space. Following the same procedure that got me to the moon, I activated the rifter, curious to relive the odd experience of rifting. All went black and then all reappeared. I knew what I had done, just not what happened while doing it.

Sure enough, the big blue sphere hung in space beside me. With skill, I found my drop zone and sped toward earth. This time however I had to slow the plane down. Atmospheric entry was around 120 Km above surface. I would begin using forward jets at 180 Km, gradually slowing the plane to 1000 Km/hour and then reduce the speed more as the plane neared the surface.

My goal was to come straight down, then gently level it off and sneak home just above the ground. I would have to do this past the mountains. I had radar in my plane so I could watch for planes, but I had made my plane almost undetectable by radar, partly due to size, but also by sending out simple, weak electromagnetic waves in a small array around the plane. I had no desire to be spotted by aircraft or by aircraft control centres, especially military. There was no easy route, but I chose to come down over Great Slave Lake and then follow the Liard River south, branching off near Fort Nelson. This bypassed the mountains and the likelihood of commercial and military planes.

SIX - The Tribe

I landed on the plywood pad that remained in front of the barn. The flight was a great success. The plane handled well, all systems functioned OK and the suit withstood the cold, airless void of space. I wanted to go to town and tell Mildred what a fine job she did, but that would have to wait. I raised the cap and pulled my helmet off. All systems were shut down and I exited the plane feeling the full force of gravity under my feet. I was hot and sweaty in the suit and had to squirm out. It was not an easy task. The suits were not designed for quick or easy removal. I turned the suit inside out and hung it up in the barn to dry, then pushed the plane back into the barn.

"Hey chicks, I'm back!" I called out to the squawking hens. "You oughta see what I just saw," I said, leaning over the rail. "But you know what? I'm happy to be home again." I think my soothing voice calmed them down. "You gals want to go for a walk? Come on…" I opened the gate and they fluttered out. I led them out the barn doors and into the laneway. We walked around together like a flock.

The images of Earth and Moon played over and over in my head. I felt empowered. I could go to the moon anytime I wanted, just for a joy ride. I could fly up and drop down in any remote area around the globe, if I was willing to risk it. Once the hens were contentedly pecking in the yard, I went into the house. Sitting in the kitchen, I brewed a pot of coffee. The full realization that I had just walked on the moon was only now starting to sink in. I actually trembled. Then I remembered my rock and ran out to the barn to get it. Reaching under the plane's seat, I groped around until my fingers touched the rough, dirty edges of the rock. Pulling it out, I looked at it.

I stepped outside and gazed up into the sky. I had just picked this up off the surface of the moon. Back in the kitchen, I placed the rock on the table and stared at it. This rock was the symbol of a truly great accomplishment, not a little patent, not a theory, but the embodiment of practical application. I sipped my hot black coffee and then picked up the rock again, rolling it around in my hands slowly. Dust crumbled off the edges, coating my hands and falling to the table. This was a rock that had never touched water or air. How long had it been exposed to the sun and the battering of meteoric grains? I almost felt like I rescued it, but somehow it seemed out of place in my kitchen.

The coffee did not serve to waken me up. I felt more tired than ever. The trip had been stressful. It required a great deal of focus. I decided to go sit on the chesterfield and relax for a few minutes. Those minutes turned into a deep sleep that lasted for hours. I rose only long enough to go to the washroom and crawl into bed. I slept until the next morning.

****

I finally woke up at 7:00 AM. Sitting up in bed, my mind wandered. Perhaps it was time to take a break from the plane and enjoy the spring. I remembered seeing the farm from the hill. I decided today would be a good time to plan the garden. Downstairs at the dining table I drew a rectangle on a sheet of paper and then charted out the different plant locations.

With coffee in hand, I went to the barn and tried to start up the tractor. It grumbled and choked. I lifted the front hood and placed the slender steel arm to hold it in place. Looking at the motor was a glimpse into the past, the rudimentary function of sparse cylinders, wiring and hoses. In the day, this would have been a state of the art combustion engine. Some farmer back then would have proudly taken this home, marvelled at the evolution in man's technology and kept it well oiled. Actually, that it's still in use after all these decades is a testament to the quality of work that went into it.

Well, it was not in use right now, but I was sure it was a simple task to fix it. The motor was cranking, so the starter was OK. Perhaps it wasn't getting fuel. I checked the fuel lines. I pulled them off and put them back on. They seemed OK. I checked the oil level. It was OK. I had this thing working months ago when I plowed the lane. I pulled the spark plugs and looked at them closely. Maybe they were shot. I checked the cabinet and found spares. It was easy enough to replace them. I went around to the seat and cranked the engine again. It started up. It still didn't sound like a purring kitten, but it worked. I was sure I could do a lot more to enhance the performance, but for now, I just wanted to get the job done.

There was an attachment called a tiller for the back that would dig into the earth and turn over the soil. I backed the tractor up to it and hooked it on, then drove over to the garden plot. It was a very bumpy ride. After parking at the southwest corner of the plot, I used a lever to drop the tiller blades. I drove slowly along the edge of the garden looking back occasionally to check my progress. The blades rotated and cut into the brown earth, heaving it up into ridges. It felt very warm, almost hot. I guessed it was twenty degrees Celsius, though in spring it can feel warmer than it really is. That relative contrast can play tricks on you.

The tractor jerked and bumped along. The tiller thumped as it struck rocks here and there. At one point, a big rock stuck in the tiller. After turning the tractor off I jumped down and tried to dislodge the rock with my foot. It took quite an effort and I was sweating. I took my plaid shirt off and flung it over the back of my seat before resuming the job. As I turned at the end of the garden, I noticed my path was not so straight. I continued crosswise and then down the other side of the garden. The further I got, the better my lines were. Occasionally, I stopped to throw rocks out of the garden so I wouldn't hit them again.

It dawned on me that I had just flown to the moon and back in a highly advanced plane and now I was digging up soil on Earth with a 1962 Massey Ferguson diesel tractor. That thought made me chuckle. Somehow, sitting on an old tractor, wearing my cowboy hat and boots gave me a virtuous feeling.

What could be more Earthly than growing your own food? My singing however lacked the purity of nature. Thankfully, my voice was drowned out by the tractor engine. I was growing closer and closer to the land, and to the local people.

When the plot was finally plowed, I put the tractor away in the barn and detached the tiller. That was a good job and done in good time. I left the barn and stood outside under the sun. I felt strong. All the wood chopping, shovelling, hockey, mechanical labour and chores had really strengthened my body and hardened my skin. I was almost an outdoorsman, or so I felt.

I needed to get the seeds. I put my shirt back on, hopped in the truck and drove to town. I wanted to get lots of chores done while I was there. I dropped by the post office and checked my mail. There was quite a pile, mostly investment newspapers and research material I had ordered. I went to the liquor store and bought a case of beer. On the way to the grocery store I saw Mildred walking along the street. Should I say hello? I guess so.

"Hey Mildred!" I called out to her.

She waved and hobbled over to the truck. "Well, hello John. How have you been?"

"Not too bad, and you?" I replied.

"Much better now that this spring weather is here," she laughed. "How are you making out with that science project of yours?"

I tried to resist, I really did, but I felt the weight of the cell phone hanging in my shirt pocket, tugging at me. I lifted my hand instinctively and touched it with my fingers. "It's coming along fine, thanks. Can you keep a secret?" I asked.

"What? This sounds intriguing. Yes, of course." She said with a smile.

I took the cell phone out, fumbled with it until a set of images displayed on the screen. I selected the selfie of me with the plane and Earth in the background. The illuminated, light grey moon surface was clearly visible. I turned the phone around to show her. Mildred's eyes widened. She looked up at me and then back at the picture.

"That's not really where I think it is, is it?" She almost demanded the truth.

I nodded. "That's the moon. And your suit worked perfectly. But please, don't tell anyone about this. It'll be our secret."

"Mum's the word." Mildred touched her finger to her lips. "But you can't fool an old bird like me. You're pulling my leg. Nice work on the photo though." She winked at me.

I smiled, half relieved she didn't believe it, and half wishing she had. "Can I give you a lift somewhere?" I asked.

"Sure, if I can get up into this truck. I'm used to a small car," she said. I leaned over and opened the passenger door while she went around the front and stepped up on the running board. "I'm going to the United Church."

I drove her there, about two blocks away and then went around to the passenger side to help her down. "Thanks for the ride. You'll have to tell me more about your adventures next time you're in town," she said.

"I will. And I'll show you the rock I brought back with me."

"You're quite the joker, John. Oh, by the way, do you like beer? Because my husband's next door at the community centre. He's demonstrating how to make your own beer. Why don't you drop by and say hello. His name is Frank."

"You had me at beer," I said. "I will. Talk to you later."

We said goodbye and I immediately worried that I had made a terrible mistake in divulging my trip. But then again, if you can't trust a little old lady in a small town on her way to church, who could you trust? She didn't believe me anyway. I drove less than a block away to the community centre, or Rec Centre as some call it here, the same place where the arena was, and parked the truck. I recalled the last time I entered this building I was a homeless wanderer. Inside, I saw a sign posted that read 'Brew Your Own Beer' and an arrow facing left toward a door. I went in. There were about fifteen men in a semi-circle watching another man describe cleaning chemicals.

"Hello," the man said. "Come on in. We've just gotten started."

"Johnny!" Came a familiar voice from the group. It was Charlie, and there was Bob next to him. He waved me over, and I gave them a smile and a nod.

"Hello everyone," I announced. "You're Frank, correct?"

"That's right," he said.

"I know your wife, Mildred. She told me to stop by. I'm Johnny Biskit."

"Oh yes, she told me she was mending some clothes for you. Well we've just been talking about sterilization and how important it is to keep all your utensils clean." Frank carried on. "After you clean your pail, carboy, stir stick, etc., then the fun starts."

Frank went on about barley, grain mash, yeasts, and corn sugar. The whole process seemed relatively easy. "What's this?" I asked, pointing to a gadget that looked like a big thermometer.

"That tests the specific gravity of the liquid. It tells you how much sugar there is relative to alcohol. You can see there are guides on it for beer and wine. This tells you where the sugar content is before fermentation and when the beer is ready to bottle." Frank gave a good description.

He poured a brown liquid that he had already prepared into the bucket, showed us the specific gravity, then dumped in a solution of yeast, stirred it vigorously, placed the lid on and plugged a central hole with a small plastic vent. "So, we let it sit at room temperature for about five days, then check the sugar content. If it's at the ready stage, and it should be, then you siphon it out and into bottles. First though, mix the corn sugar with clean water and add it to the beer. Remember to clean the bottles properly. Once all the bottles are filled, then cap them." At this point he demonstrated the bottling process. "Put the bottles away in your basement or closet, and wait two weeks. Then invite me over to your house." We all laughed.

"Hey, maybe we should start our own little beer company," Bob joked.

"Maybe we oughta brew a batch first and make sure it's drinkable, you know, by drinking it all," I replied. "So where can we get all this stuff?" I asked Frank.

"Go to the hardware store. They have a full kit, like what you see here. Save your empties. You can get a tin of ready-made malt at the grocery store any time if you want, or go to the feed store and get a sack of barley. It's a whole lot more difficult to make the malt yourself, but your beer will be better. I printed up some guides for ya. This one is for malting grain. Only takes a few days, but it's lots of work. The other guides are for the mashing and fermenting steps." Frank handed out some sheets.

"Thanks Frank. I'll give it a try this week." I told him. "I think this was very helpful, especially for Bob. Let's keep him drinking at home so he doesn't embarrass me playing darts at the bar."

"Me, embarrass you? You're your own worst enemy." He turned to Frank. "I was afraid he was gonna plunk a dart in the waitress's ass, he was so far off." Then he turned back to me. "You just need to practice more, preferably out in a field, without livestock present. Even drunk I was beating you." Bob and Charlie laughed.

"Alright, that sounds like a challenge. I'll see YOU in the bar next time I come to town. If you're not there, I'll just assume you're chicken," I said.

"How will I know when you're in town?" Bob asked.

"Does it matter? I thought you were always in the bar?" I quipped.

"OK, you're on. Might want to bring a steady arm." Bob could chat all day.

I said goodbye to everyone and left the building. I had to pick up that sack of barley and a beer kit before heading home. First stop was the feed store.

"Hey." I greeted the lady at the counter. I doubt she remembered me. I was rarely in here.

"Hi, can I help you?" she offered.

"Yeah, I'm looking for seeds. I have about one acre and I want to grow these." I handed her a paper with my sketch and list of seeds.

"OK, let's see what we've got. Come on back here." She led me into the storage bays. "The problem is you need way more than the little packets and not as much as the farm sacks. I do have some loose seeds. We charge by weight, so you can get just the right amount you need, but we don't have everything." She grabbed a few brown paper bags and started filling them. "OK, we got corn." She wrote the seed names on each bag as she filled them. "Here's the seed potatoes, the beans, and the onions. You'll have to buy small packets of tomatoes, carrots and herbs." I decided to buy a few other packs, like hot peppers, lettuce, and beets. I asked for a sack of barley too. It was surprisingly cheap. I also picked up a sack of chicken feed while I was there. "How are the chickens doing?" she asked.

I was surprised she remembered. "They're doing good. I get more than my fill of eggs from them."

"Yeah, treat them right, feed them well and they'll keep popping those eggs out." She smiled.

A quick stop at the grocery store and the hardware store to get food and the beer kit. Forty minutes later and I was pulling into my laneway. I was busting to get the seeds in the ground but had to wait a bit longer. Frost could still be a problem til late May, and I didn't want to waste my time with dead plants. So I put the seeds away in the barn, collected eggs and unloaded the truck. Inside the beer kit was a can of premixed malt. I would start with that and see how it goes.

As I learned from Frank, I cleaned all the tools and the bucket with a chlorine solution. Then I boiled some water and added the malt. I stirred and stirred for an hour and then added a pouch of hops. Next, I was supposed to cool it down fast, so I took it outside and laid it in a hole I quickly dug and filled the hole with cold water. I had to keep filling the hole as it drained away slowly.

After twenty minutes or so I cleaned off the pot, brought it inside and mixed the syrup with more water in the bucket. Finally I added the packet of yeast and stirred madly, trying to make lots of bubbles to oxygenate the yeast. On went the lid and then the small bung with a plastic vent inserted. It didn't look so great at this stage. Hope it tastes better than it looks. I carried it over to the side of the house and left it there to ferment. Thankfully, I had accumulated a few empty two-fours that I could use when ready to bottle.

****

I decided to take the fishing rod down to the river. I hadn't caught anything since my trip in the fall, though hadn't tried much. I put my big rubber boots on, collected my rod from the garage and walked down the slope to the river's edge. Not sure if it was the time of day or some other reason, but the black flies started coming out. They were bad. I could imagine if I was in the woods I'd go mad. I'm sure the poor animals suffered this time of year, especially in the evening and at night. I swatted and waved as they swarmed around me.

A few minutes passed and it was not looking favourable. I casted several times into the calm pool with no luck. I then flung the lure out toward the rapids and immediately hooked something. It pulled and I played. There was to and there was fro, but I kept the line taught. I worked it all the way in and dragged it up on the sandy shore. Well it wasn't a Pike, nor a Grayling, nor a Catfish. This must have been a Pickerel.

It was long, yellowish green, and had a dangerous looking fin on its back. Oh, and it had teeth. I slipped my fingers into its gill and lifted it up.

From the corner of my eye I spotted something on the river. It was far upstream. It looked like a boat; a canoe. Then another and another. I rushed up the bank and counted five canoes in all. These were not ordinary canoes either. They were a dull, brownish in colour, curved up at the ends. They looked like they were made of canvas patches or something, with seams. As they drew closer, it was apparent these were natives. They looked quite traditional, in big canoes filled to the top with sacks. Some carried spruce poles. I saw adults and kids. Who were they? Where were they coming from and where were they going. I felt a bit anxious and hid behind a tree just beyond the sand spit, still holding my twitching fish. I really wanted to meet them and yet my heart raced at the thought.

The first canoe slid up on the sandy bank that jutted out into the river and an older man with long greying hair wearing clothes of skins stepped out. He pulled the canoe further up on the bank and the second passenger, possibly a teenager stepped out. He looked my way. "Hello." He called over. I stepped out from the trees and came over to meet them.

"Hello," I replied. "My name is Johnny."

"My name is Benjamin," the older man said, reaching his rugged hand out.

"Where did you come from?" I asked.

"Up river, about six hours by canoe. Where is the old man that lives here?" he asked.

"He died last year. I bought the house in the fall."

"Oh. I see. Do you mind if we camp here tonight?" he asked.

"Of course you can." Somehow I felt like they belonged here.

"Thank you," he said with a nod of his head. He turned to the others and waved them in. "That's a nice fish you have there." He pointed at the fish I was still holding.

"Oh." I chuckled. "Thanks. I just caught it. First one I ever caught in the river here."

The other canoes started landing. Men, women and children in traditional clothes heaved their canoes up on the bank and began unloading. I just stood and watched for several minutes before putting my rod and fish down on the path to the house. I came back to the canoes and asked the same man if he needed help.

"No, we are OK, unless you want to help. We need to unload everything," he said. I walked over to another canoe and touched its side. It was so real, so rugged. The inner gunwales were made of bent branches. Thicker branches were strapped crosswise to the sides of the canoe. The sides were made of patches of bark and skins, sewn together and tarred with what smelled like pine or spruce.

I reached in and lifted a bundle of skins. It was much heavier than I expected. I was clearly not as strong as I thought I was. They moved sacks and packs with ease. After the canoes were emptied, people began opening bundles and spreading out large stitched skins or canvas. Others assembled spruce poles in a radial shape, tied in the middle at the top of the poles. These were then lifted to form frames for small teepees. Everybody worked at it. After the frames were half up, patched skins were draped around to form the tents. The poles were then heaved higher. This was all done fast and effortlessly. In no time, the camp looked like it had been there all along. Someone began collecting rocks to form a fire pit in the centre.

Benjamin came over to me and shook my hand. "Thank you for your help."

"It was my pleasure," I replied. It really was a pleasure to meet them and help out a little. I felt like I had just travelled back in time hundreds of years.

"I better clean my fish," I said. "Have a good night."

"You too. Enjoy your dinner." He nodded at the fish and we both smiled.

I walked back up the hill to the house. Although I started cleaning the fish in the sink, I couldn't stop running to the window and peeking out at the tribe of natives on the beach. I never knew anyone lived such a traditional life now. I wondered where they were going and why. I gutted the fish, skinned it and sliced nice fillets from the sides. I pulled down a couple of pans, one for the fish and one for an assortment of vegetables. I dipped the fillets in flour and then lay them in a bubbling froth of hot butter seasoned with salt, pepper and oregano. I chopped up a bunch of carrots, broccoli and mushrooms and threw them in hot oil. It didn't take long. I sat, alone, at my table, peering out into the dusk, wondering what they were having for dinner.

* * * * * * * * *

Later that evening, I strode outside to a tree up high on the hill above their camp. I leaned against the tree and watched flames and sparks rise from the fire. People moved about from tent to tent or sat around the fire. It looked like a nice little community. Down below I could see a young man bending down and talking to an old woman. Then he looked up. Did he see me? How embarrassing! I stepped back a bit behind the tree. He looked back down and talked to the old lady again. Maybe I was imagining things. Then a girl said something to the old lady. She looked up too. A moment later, I saw her coming my way. She climbed the hill. Then she was close, a few feet in front of me and just under the hill's sharp bank. "Hi," I said. I reached out my hand to help her up that last sharp edge. She reached out and took my hand and stepped up. I don't know what made me think she needed my help up the hill. She could probably navigate the river banks far better than I could.

"Hi. I saw you helping us when we landed. My name is Ashenee," she said.

"My name is Johnny," I replied. I remembered seeing her at the boats too. She was very pretty. She had long silky black hair in two pigtails, tied by bands halfway down. Her neck was adorned by several tight fitting necklaces of white and black. Her top was animal skin with a few ornate designs, and she wore a long skirt. I was still holding her hand. I didn't really want to let go, not yet, and she didn't object.

"Do you want to come down with us for a while?" she asked. "My grandmother wants you to join us."

"Yes, that would be nice," I said.

She led me down the hill by the hand and brought me to the fire where she addressed the old lady,

"Nohkom ekwawa wihisow Johnny". I assume she was introducing me to the old lady. That must have been her grandmother.

"Ah, Johnny," she looked up at me and smiled, "Tansi," she said. I smiled back at her and nodded.

"This is my Grandmother," Ashenee said. "She says hi. You can call her Nohkom."

Ashenee led me around and introduced me to everyone, and I mean everyone, from old to young. We sat down by the fire and someone passed around a platter of food. Not sure what it was, but I ate some. I think it was dried or smoked meat. Ashenee's cousin brought an old, somewhat broken down guitar out of a tent to the fire and began to play. Everyone sang. The fire crackled and spit sparks high up into the air where they looked like little orange stars.

"Ashenee, where do you live?" I asked.

"We live up the river, before the town," she said. "You can't get there by car, only by boat."

"Where are you going?"

"We go down river to find fish. We camp there for a few weeks and then come home when we have enough. We smoke them and put them away for the winter. What do you do out here?" she asked.

"I'm doing some science, and I'm planting a garden." I tried to sound interesting, though felt completely dull compared to her and her family.

"Science? What are you studying?" asked Benjamin who sat on the other side of Ashenee.

"I'm studying the stars, and flying. I like to fly," I answered.

"Did you go to school to learn that?" Ashenee asked.

"Yes, down south in Vancouver."

"Have you ever flown a plane by yourself?" she asked.

"Yes, sort of. Maybe someday I could take you." I smiled at her. Ashenee giggled.

Benjamin said, "You can fly, and you're smart. You're like kahkākow, the crow. We should call you Johnny Crow." He turned to the old lady and told her my new name. She laughed and nodded her head. Here I sat with Ashenee, her father Benjamin and her grandmother. It was very comfortable. These people were relaxed and generous. I enjoyed their company.

"That's a good name. I like it," I announced.

"Do you live here alone?" Ashenee asked.

"Yes. I haven't lived here long though, just the winter."

"You're very brave. I would not like to live alone," she said.

"Yeah, it was hard. I never lived alone before. I was lucky I had so much to do. That kept me from feeling lonely. Not always though. Sometimes I had to go to town because I wanted to talk to someone. I went to Fort St. John just a few weeks ago. I had a good time and stayed in a hotel. Tell me about you and your family," I asked.

"We are Cree. A long time ago our tribe lived in Alberta. When the oil wells came, the tribe was pushed out. They left and travelled west looking for a good place to live. They came to British Columbia and settled near Fort Nelson. The story is better told by my father," Ashenee laughed. "We live away from roads and towns. We try to keep some of the old ways and stay the way we were. It's good. We're all happy."

People started disappearing into tents until there were just a few of us left at the fire. "I should let you sleep. I'm sure you have a long trip tomorrow. Thanks for inviting me. I had a good time," I told them.

"We will come back in a few weeks. Can we camp here again?" Benjamin asked.

"Of course. You can stay here anytime, as long as you want. Think of this place as your place. You're always welcome here. You don't need to ask." I wanted them to come back here.

Benjamin nodded and Ashenee smiled. I said goodnight and walked back up to the house. I wasn't happy going back to an empty house when they were all right here, together. I had a shower, went to bed and read a book until I finally fell asleep.

****

Morning came and I got up early. I looked out the front and saw the tribe breaking camp. My goodness they get up early. I ran down to help them. They were quick and methodical, bundling everything up neatly and loading the boats. I found Ashenee. "Do you want to come up and see my house before you leave?" I asked.

"OK," she answered. She went to her father and said something, and then we walked up the hill together. I brought her in through the front door. She looked around.

"This is nice. Show me everything," she said. I took her on a tour through the living room, the washroom, my little sitting room and the kitchen. I pointed up the ladder and told her that was the bedroom.

"Would you like to sit down? I can make you a drink. Do you like coffee?" I asked her.

"I have never had coffee. I like tea," she said, and sat down at the table.

I put the kettle on and scrounged through the cupboard for tea. I knew I had some because my mother liked to drink it. I found the tin and took out a tea bag and placed it in the pot. I put out two cups on the table. When the water boiled, I poured it in the pot. "Do you like sugar and milk?"

"Yes, I like sugar," she replied.

I brought out a small bowl of sugar and a spoon.

"I like the house," she said. "The old man who lived here was nice, but never invited us to the house. I always wondered what it was like inside. We have cabins too, but no electricity. I like your high ceiling. It makes the house seem bigger and brighter."

"Yeah. My two favourite places are the little den where the wood stove is. It's so cozy, especially in the winter. And I like the loft up there." I pointed up. "It's nice to be up high and be able to look down over the house and out the windows. It feels safe being up there."

We drank our tea. "I'm glad you're here," I said. "You're my first visitor. Well I guess my parents were my first. They came for Christmas and stayed a week. But apart from them, you're the first."

A voice called from the river. "Ashenee! Ashenee!"

"I have to go," Ashenee stated. "Thank you for the tea."

"I'll come down with you." I opened the door for her and then followed her to the awaiting boats. Some people were boarded and some just boarding. Ashenee stepped into a canoe and I walked over to her side. "Take care. I hope I see you on your way back."

I got a sweet smile from her. "Bye, Johnny Crow," she said in her quiet voice.

I pushed her canoe out into the river and waved goodbye. I stood there a long time, watching their canoes silently drift down the river toward the mountains. I felt a profound sense of sadness seeing them all go, especially Ashenee. As they disappeared into the distance, I kicked around some sand and twigs. They had erased all evidence of their presence except the marks the tent poles made in the sand. I was alone again.

SEVEN - The Engineer

Over the next few days my mind was absent. I didn't think about my plane at all. I thought about my visitors, the beer I would soon bottle, the garden I should start planting, the tractor's faults, investments and fishing. I had never gone more than a day without thoughts of work. Now it was far from my mind. I remembered my father talking so enthusiastically about his stamps and coins. There was absolutely nothing productive about a hobby, yet it could bring such pleasure and fulfilment to someone. It would appear my hobbies, or pastimes were becoming important to me. I did enjoy all the things I did that were not part of my work, and I was learning more things all the time. I was beginning to think I might even lose interest in my research one day. Naw, that was crazy. I was just in a slump. Strange time to lose interest, just after taking the maiden voyage to space. But I couldn't focus for some reason.

I walked the house in my underwear. I ate simple meals, like cereal. I slept in. I often sat outside on the hill staring at the river. I thought about my new name, Johnny Crow. I couldn't have picked a better name than that. Crows might be smart, but they are also social, often flying around in groups, calling to each other. I wondered if crows ever got depressed. Maybe not. They probably spent all their time looking for food. Maybe I was a crow, but not because I could fly high above the rest of the world, but because I liked to be with others.

I had read the finance books my father had sent me back in the winter. I had a pretty clear understanding of the markets, how they worked, and financial analysis. I also started reading the news, looking at graphs and charts of individual companies, indexes, bonds, commodities and currencies. The relationships between these segments were apparent and undeniable.

Since I had little motivation to do anything else, I started writing a computer app. If someone entered a stock, commodity or currency, the app would source all possible information and give a recommendation. In order to make money, the app would cost $5.99 and would display a simple ad. I assumed the appeal of having someone else make a recommendation for people would easily lure investors in. That was basic human nature. With seven billion people on the planet, if only one billion had access to apps and only 1% were greedy, lazy and stupid, then I had a potential market of ten million people. At six dollars each that could be a pile of money. The ads would be very simple and add to the profit. I just had to make it look professional and enticing. I was sitting in my easy chair writing code for the investment app when an email came in from Dr. Manning.

Hello John,

I haven't heard from you in a while. I wondered how you were doing. I think the last time we talked you asked me about astronaut suits. I hope the plans I sent you were helpful. I saw a suit on a recent trip to Cape Canaveral. They are quite intricate. I'm a bit curious why you would need it though. It's a safe assumption that you only need a suit if you plan to go into space. I can't emphasize enough how dangerous it is to try and launch a rocket, never mind ride one. I hope you aren't planning anything like that. If you are, please let me know so I can try and talk you out of it or at least examine your setup and advise TSB. Send me some specs on what you have. Perhaps you can tell me a little more about yourself and your qualifications.

Regards,

Dr. Manning.

Well, that was an interesting communication. It sounded like maybe he was taking me seriously, albeit without much faith in me. Who could blame him? He was concerned. If anyone else told me they were planning what I was doing, I'd doubt them. I think a return email was in order.

Hello Dr. Manning.

I'm fine thanks. Hope you are well. I'd love to hear about your trip to Cape Canaveral. Did you get to witness a launch? The specs you sent me on the space suit were very useful, thanks. At the moment, I'm taking a little hiatus from my research, but all is going well. As you know, my name is John. I have a PhD in theoretical physics from UBC. I left the school last year to pursue my own research. I appreciate your offer to review my work. If you'd like to visit me, I will be happy to explain my work on the condition you promise to keep my name and all my technology confidential. I think you can understand how this technology could be used by people or governments for the wrong purposes. Just let me know your decision. I would suggest late in May. That will give me time to finish some odds and ends.

All the best,

John.

It was a bold move, but he seemed like a trustworthy man. I'd look for any hesitation in his reply or concern about secrecy. But it would be great to share my accomplishments with someone that would truly appreciate it. The email helped snap me out of my funk. I had to get back on my feet. I had beer to bottle, a garden to sow and a rifter that could only go one times the speed of light.

****

I put the app on hold, got dressed and began rethinking the design of the rifter. Why was it limited to one light year? I had used a mineral called Apatite to derive the rare earth element Yttrium. It was the easiest element to extract and it worked. I decided to test other rare earth elements. What I found was the properties of a combination of Europium and Promethium far exceeded Yttrium, to an extent of one thousand times.

I decided to extract enough material and recalibrate the rifter. To be on the safe side, I simply varied the input from what I knew was one light year to one hundred light years. In other words, my top 'speed' would be one light year in just 3.65 days. That was too slow to explore other solar systems, but it was just the next level in development. I would have to see how it worked before aiming for one thousand times or higher speeds. Altering the rifter would be much easier than extracting the rare earth elements. This would be a slow process. I had to crush some ore material and setup an acid bath, then bake the solution and finally leach out the elements. I wanted to do this soon in case Dr. Manning came up. I hated showing a project that was just in progress.

That evening, I bottled my beer. I put all the bottles, a few at a time, in a bleach solution and then rinsed them off. I covered the table in towels and laid all the bottles out in rows. After lifting the beer bucket up on the table, adding the corn sugar to the bucket and letting it settle for an hour, I started siphoning the beer into the bottles. Steadily, the bottles were filled up, one after another. I made a rather sticky mess of the towels, but wasn't worried about that.

After they were all filled, I cleaned the rims and started capping the bottles. It was an art, that's for sure. I worried the first few bottle would break as I had to exert a fair bit of pressure to crimp the cap on. But once I got into the rhythm, then it became easy. All the bottles were put in boxes and tucked in the corner. That was a hard job. My back ached. Now I had to wait two weeks to test the beer. I was hoping that, after all this work, the beer was good. In any case, it was a fun exercise. I was glad I did it in the evening. I could lie down and rest now. I slumped into my easy chair, flung my feet up and turned on the TV. I don't think I watched more than twenty minutes of the news when I dozed off. After an hour, I simply went up to bed.

The next day I checked how my solution of rare earths was coming along. All seemed good. It would need a lot more time. I put the rubber boots on and went to the barn to collect eggs. It was a nice spring day. The leaves had come out on the few poplar trees and bushes. I noticed the seeds and figured this was as good a day as any to plant them. I put the eggs away and then dragged all the seeds out to the garden along with a hoe. If I thought making beer was hard work, I would soon learn there were harder tasks.

With my map in the back pocket, I started dropping seeds down the rows. After finishing each row I worked backwards, pushing the dirt from the ridge over the seeds to cover them. The corn was easy; drop a seed every six inches or so. The potatoes were much more difficult. I had to cut them into pieces and make sure the eyes faced up. The onions were hard too, as they were bulbs and needed to be placed properly. Other seeds were tiny, so I mixed them in some sand and dispersed the sand down the row.

I stopped half way to have some lunch. I couldn't really imagine being a farmer full time. I liked being outside and I didn't mind getting my hands dirty, but it was back breaking work. Maybe I was doing things the hard way. I'm sure most farmers use the tractor to do all this. But still, I bet they work hard. Finally, I finished the garden eight hours later. I went inside and took a well-deserved shower. I could see another deep sleep in my near future. Before retiring though, I checked my email. Dr. Manning had written back, confirming he would like to visit at whatever time fit my schedule. I replied to him.

Hello Dr. Manning.

I'm ready anytime you are. Can you make it June 3? If you can get to Fort Nelson, I can come pick you up at the airport and bring you out to my farm. Let me know if that is acceptable and when you will arrive. You are welcome to stay with me or you can stay in Fort Nelson if you are more comfortable in a hotel. I would suggest you allocate at least two days here.

John.

It didn't take long for a reply. June 3 would be fine. That was two weeks away. I could easily finish refitting the rifter in the plane. Peter later sent me his itinerary and we exchanged phone numbers, in case of any problems.

****

The days of May continued with nice weather, warming more every day. I continued working on the rifter, rebuilding and tweaking until I was satisfied with it. June 3 rolled around and I had fitted the new rifter on the plane. I also added some safety features, like if any solid body was detected between the plane and its destination, the plane would exit speed of light, or fail to employ, before hitting it. This seemed hardly necessary, but was easy enough to do.

I decided to add a name to the plane; kahkākow. I wrote it on one side of the tail and did my best to paint a crow on the other side. It wasn't so hard to do, considering I had pictures to copy from the internet.

I spent the morning cleaning the house. After lunch, I drove into town to meet Dr. Manning. His plane was due in at 2:00 PM. The airport, about three kilometres north of town, was quite nice, despite its small size. I waited inside anxiously. A plane came in from Edmonton. There were eight passengers; two kids and their parents and four men who undoubtedly worked for the lumber company. I went to the vending machine and selected coffee. It was 1:54 PM and I was becoming more nervous, or excited, I couldn't tell yet. "Hey," I said to the clerk, "how are you?"

"Fine thanks," she replied.

"I'm waiting for a flight that's due in at 2:00 PM. I don't know where it's coming from though. The origin is Montreal."

"At two we have a flight coming from Calgary. Any flight booked from Montreal would probably come through Calgary," she continued. "I see it's been delayed ten minutes. Should be here by 2:10. It'll be the next plane in."

"Thanks. No executive lounge around here, eh?" I joked.

She laughed. "It's a good thing. I'd be slipping in there between arrivals and departures. Are you going to the social on Saturday?"

"Social? I hadn't heard about it. Where is it?" I asked.

"At the community centre. No special occasion. I think they put it on then because everyone's away the May two-four weekend. Last year no one showed up when they planned it then," she explained.

"Oh yeah? Do lots of people go, usually?" I was intrigued.

"Seems like everyone in town drops by, except maybe old people and kids. Have to be nineteen to go," she answered.

"I see. I'll have to think about it. Can't say I have any reason not to go." I felt like I was flirting with her or she was flirting with me. I heard the buzz of propellers outside. "I think I can hear the plane now."

The clerk turned and looked out her window. "Yup, that's them," she replied.

A man in an orange vest, shorts, and ear protectors went outside to wave the plane into a holding spot. Two other men met him outside and waited. They opened the door and shifted a staircase to let the passengers out. Another man opened a small hatch on the plane and dragged out several small bags. I watched as the passengers descended.

A middle aged woman, a husky man with a big moustache and boots, another husky man, another husky man, a middle aged man in a sweater with slightly greying hair and slacks - that must be him. Next another husky man. Let's see if I called it right.

They collected their bags and entered the building. I stood there, the only fellow waiting inside. The husky men walked right on through. The women went straight to the washroom. The man I chose came in and looked around aimlessly.

"Dr. Manning, I presume?" I smiled. That was an overused line, I'm sure.

"Yes. Are you John?" he asked.

"I am, John Biskit. Welcome."

"I didn't expect you to look quite like this," he said in surprise. I think I'd be surprised too if I expected a physicist and I encountered a man in cowboy boots and hat. "Is everyone in the west a cowboy?" He laughed.

"You're either a cowboy or a lumberjack out here," I joked back. "Is this your only bag?"

"Yes. I can't stay long," he answered. "Is it a long drive to your place?"

"About forty minutes."

"I haven't had any lunch. Do you think we could stop in town for a bite?" He had no idea how much joy it would bring me to sit and eat in a restaurant with someone. After countless uncomfortable, lonely dining experiences, I finally had company.

"Of course. I know just the place," I said. We rolled into the parking lot of my favourite pub and went inside. "Mac," I bellowed. "How are ya?"

"Can't complain, Johnny. How's it going?" he countered.

"Not too bad."

"Who's your friend?" he asked.

"This is Dr. Peter Manning from the Canadian Space Agency in Montreal."

"Hello Peter. It's about time we had some class in this joint." Mac laughed. Go grab a table. I'll bring you a beer. What are ya drinking?"

Peter asked for a Bass Ale, a good choice I thought. "I'll just have a coffee," I said.

We found a table in the middle of the room. The beer and coffee came. Seems I can't drink coffee like I used to... in moderation. Some people have a drinking problem with alcohol, but I was wondering if I had a coffee addiction. Here I was on my third of the day. I ordered a smoked meat sandwich and Peter ordered a burger. There was no doubt this was packaged smoked meat, but it still tasted fantastic, all smothered in mustard.

"John, I checked you out before I came. I looked for a John who left UBC recently. Wasn't hard to figure out who you were. You blew up a lab at UBC and subsequently left. You've published many papers, and you're only twenty one years old. Tell me, what on Earth are you doing way up north in a small logging town? I checked the map and you are fifteen hundred kilometres from home."

"All true," I replied. "I was working on a sophisticated battery. One slight miscalculation and you're branded a shocking liability for life." This said with a smile, of course. "Anyhow, I needed a place to continue my research and I wanted isolation. I needed a testing ground. I mean you can't very well fire rockets off over the city, can ya? Actually, this isn't as far as I intended to go. I was heading for the Territories."

"Why did you stop here?" he asked. He almost seemed like he wished I was in the Territories. Maybe he would have preferred a trip up there.

"I guess I was a bit road weary, and worried about what it would really be like way up there. I took a day to rest here and just happened to find an interesting farm for sale. I figured this was isolated enough. Turns out the farm was perfect. It's right at the foot of the mountains and on the river. Do you like fishing?"

"Are you kidding? I sure do," he perked up.

"Well then, you've come to the right place. We'll have to throw a line in while you're here. I've caught some very nice fish," I told him. "You might as well have a bit of fun here."

"How did you afford a farm and all this research? I only ask because I happen to know you're quite young. Just curious," he stated.

"Fair question. I leased a patent out to a manufacturing company. I'm burning through that cash quickly though. I'm hoping to develop an app with my dad for investments. I have no idea what will come of that. In any case, come next year the manufacturing company will likely lease the patent again and I'll have more cash. Frankly, if it wasn't for the research, I wouldn't care if I was rich or poor. I'm pretty happy living on my farm, though sometimes wish it was a lot closer to town. Without my research project, I'd probably go stir crazy." I rambled on. "Tell me about you? I read through your research online, but know nothing of the details. What specifically are you trying to achieve at the CSA?"

"Well, I'm a bit more of a manager now than a scientist," he said. "But my group is working on the robotics for a new grip. NASA has contracted us for the work and hopefully it will be ready in eight to ten months from now. I am an engineer, actually; a mechanical and aerospace engineer. I worked at NASA for several years, but decided to move back home and join the CSA."

"Have you ever been asked to go up in space with the shuttle, or whatever they're using now?" I asked

"Oh no," he answered, emphatically. "As thrilling as that would be, only a very select few even get the chance to take training for it. I doubt they would ever consider me because of my age."

"That's too bad. Never give up hope though." I hoped he might take the opportunity if given to him. We finished lunch. Mac came back and asked if we wanted another drink. "No, I think we better get going," I said. "Here," I gave Mac my credit card.

"That's OK," said Peter, "I'll pay."

"Sorry. Mac has orders. You're money's no good here," I joked.

"Well thanks," Peter replied.

Back in the truck, we started our drive to the farm. As expected, there were very few drivers on the road. Forty minutes later we pulled into my laneway. He agreed that the scenery was beautiful and understood my attraction to the place. He left his bag in the truck and stretched when he got out.

"Come on, I'll show you the garage slash workshop slash lab." I waved him over. Inside was a cluttered array of instruments and apparatus. I pointed each one out and explained how or why I used it. We went upstairs where more lab equipment and materials were selectively placed. He had a few questions about the reason for some oddball minerals, elements, metals and glass cut-outs.

"I'm impressed," he said, "but I'm confused about the use of some of these things. Like the glass sheets."

"Those are not ordinary glass sheets. That's hockey rink glass, intended to withstand shock. I had to cut pieces and then heat mold them."

"I see," he went on. "I understand refractory minerals, but why are you using rare earths?"

"Perhaps I can explain all that in the house. Come on, I'll give you a tour." I led Peter out of the garage and into the house. This time he picked up his luggage and brought it with him.

Inside the back door, Peter stopped and looked around. "Very nice. Quite a cozy place you have here, and all log. I've always dreamed of having a log house. There's just something solid and comfortable about it."

"Yeah. Believe it or not I made it through the winter mainly on firewood. The propane heater just kicked in on cold mornings when the fire died down. But otherwise the logs really kept the heat in. And the shutters all work." I took him around in my normal loop and ended up back at the couch in the living room. "This is a full pull out couch." I moved the cushions and demonstrated. "You are more than welcome to stay here. The hotels are no better. And you can stay as long as you want."

"Yes, this will be fine," he said.

"Good, because I have some homemade beer I haven't even tried yet and we can hoist a few tonight," I suggested.

"Ha ha ha, that sounds great," he countered. He put his bag on the floor beside the couch. "I have not tried making beer, but I've made plenty of wine in my time. Actually I can't take credit. I go to one of those brew shops and pretty much everything is done for me. By the way, it smells great in here. What is that?"

"I have ribs slow cooking. I may have to try wine someday. Problem is I hardly drink it. I think I've had one bottle in the last year." I said. "And by the way, fridge is stocked, here is the kettle, the coffee percolator, and the dishes are up here. Make yourself at home." Peter nodded back.

I took some paper and pencils out of a drawer and placed them on the table. "Have a seat. Let me describe a few things to you." I started drawing some diagrams. "I had three goals. My first was a battery. I call it a power pack, or in my case the power-puck, because it looks like a puck."

I pulled a puck out from the drawer and showed it to him. I went on to describe the theory and general construction. For the most part, I think he understood the concepts, but was lost on the implementation. I then began describing the thrusters and how rare earth elements along with hyper electricity and noble gases could in fact move an object. It was like describing relativity to a grade nine class. I know he couldn't grasp the concepts. I boiled it down to a comparison with springs attached to one's feet; springs of radiant waves. I could tell he was impressed with my understanding of physics, but all these ideas were not even conceptualized by anyone else. I had invented a locomotive in the Stone Age. Finally I got to the rifter.

"Whoa!" he said. "Are you really telling me you can go faster than the speed of light? Because I know that's not possible. Even Einstein said it wasn't possible."

"Well, Einstein was not God. He didn't know everything. But I'm not talking about travelling faster than the speed of light. I'm talking about getting somewhere faster than it would take light to get there. I call it a shortcut, like taking a piece of paper, pinching the ends together. Space is a medium. It is not really a void, only a void of the substance we measure. Einstein even said space can be bent. It can be ripped, wrapped, and rolled too. It has substance. The rifter cuts a slice and you travel between the void of space. If there was a wall of stone in front of you, it would take a long time to muscle through it, because it's a hard, dense medium to pass through. Basically you'd have to scratch your way through. But if you could just step around it, or use a method to separate the dense elements in the middle by flowing it apart, creating a hole temporarily, then you could pass right through. That's rifting." I boiled it down to a simple explanation because the theory and math did not make sense to him.

The time dragged on. Eventually he looked exhausted and it was late. "How about we make dinner?" I suggested.

"Yes. I'm afraid you have befuddled my brain. I will have to digest this," he replied.

He continued looking at my notes and calculations while I went to the counter to check on the ribs. They were done and they looked incredible. I grabbed some vegetables from the fridge and threw them into a pan. I liked to sear them on high heat quickly so they were just a bit scorched but still crispy. I made the mashed potatoes with cream, cheese and chives yesterday and they just needed warming. So within ten minutes I had everything prepared. I pulled out the plates, cutlery and two beer glasses. Peter was standing at the front window gazing out over the river. "What river is this?" he asked.

"That's the Tetsa. It branches off from the Muskwa not far from here." I answered.

I had all the food out on the table and retrieved two oversized Grolsch bottles from the fridge with my homemade ale in them. "Alright, this is the moment of truth," I said. I opened the lid with a pop and a hiss, then slowly poured the liquid gold into a glass, careful not to drain the sediment at the bottom. It had a nice head. I placed that down in front of Peter and then poured one for me.

"That looks like a well-made beer," he announced.

"Cheers. To Science, eh?" I smiled and we clinked glasses.

"It's excellent!" Peter proclaimed. I'm sure he was just being nice, though I liked it too. It was almost like an IPA; hoppy but not overwhelming.

"Thanks. I'm glad it turned out OK. It was a lot of back breaking work to make this stuff," I said, feeling justified in accepting acclamation.

"I'll consider this an early birthday party. It's my birthday next week. I'll be 58 years old. I can hardly believe it. Time has just flown by, so to speak."

"Congratulations! And happy early birthday," I said.

"I just hope nobody throws me a surprise party back home. At my age, that could be fatal," Peter said with a laugh.

We ate and drank and talked about life. You can learn a lot about a man over a beer. After dinner we moved to the living room and drank more beer. Talk turned to laughter as we told stories and jokes. I think I had more memories of the past six months than my first twenty years of life. Peter picked up a rock I had set on a pedestal on the small side table. "What's this?"

"What do you know about geology?" I asked

He looked at the rock closely. "Looks like a basalt."

"That was my thought," I said. Little did he know he was holding a piece of the moon.

"What's on our agenda for tomorrow?" Peter asked. I wonder if he was privately thinking about fishing, or hiking up in the hills.

"Well, I'll show you my drones and how I made them fly. Then I'll share a surprise that I've been holding off on. And then we can top that off with some free time for fishing, hiking or anything else you'd like."

"A surprise, eh? That's sounds interesting. I'm sure you do have more surprises." He laughed. "Can I take a shower tonight?"

"Of course. I put fresh towels in the washroom and a new bar of soap for you. Help yourself," I replied.

"Good heavens, I am staying at a hotel." We both had a laugh. I said goodnight and I went up to the loft, pulling the drapes shut. I wondered what was going through his head. Did he believe all these theories would work? Did he think I made all this up? Maybe he thought I was a dreamer. I kept my light on and browsed the web for a while. I really was kind of wired from all this excitement. I knew if I put my head down I'd lay awake for a while. I sent an email to my parents describing Peter and my day. I asked my dad for some input on the app and then fumbled with the code a bit more before finally closing the lid and falling asleep.

****

The next morning I got up, went out to the barn to collect eggs, and then had a shower. After I emerged from the washroom, Peter had gotten up. "Good morning," he said.

"Good morning. How'd you sleep?" I asked.

"Fantastic! I don't know if it was the beer, the travel, the fresh air, or the mind boggling equations you bombarded me with last night, but I slept like a baby," he replied.

"Good. And now I hope you're ready for a hearty breakfast," I stated.

"I am. I think we have a big day ahead of us today," Peter acknowledged.

I went into the kitchen, followed by Peter, and took eggs and bacon out of the fridge. Peter wanted to help, so I got him to slice some bread and then watch the bacon while I fried the eggs. "By the way, these are the freshest eggs you'll ever have. I just brought them in from the coup twenty minutes ago. I bet they're still warm," I joked.

"Wow, this is a hotel and a real farm. I'll have to see the chickens later," Peter said.

"Yes, and the garden plot. Everything's just starting to sprout. I can't wait to harvest fresh vegetables," I said. "How do you like your coffee?"

"A bit of cream, or milk. Whichever is fine," he replied.

We sat down and ate rather quickly. I'm not sure if it was because of hunger or excitement. Afterwards, I led Peter out to the barn. Inside, I walked Peter around the big obstruction just inside the door and over to the chickens. They squawked a bit and then clucked quietly. They were used to me by now, but seldom saw a visitor. Peter marveled that just a few chickens could supply me with eggs. Then I turned him toward the wall and showed him my first drone, the one that was difficult to fly because I made it like a rocket. He did not laugh at it as I thought he might, but carefully inspected it.

"I think it's remarkable that this thing flew and came back home," I said. "It was a ridiculous design to start with. I'm a physicist, not an engineer by training. There was lots of learning as I went along."

"Well, as a rocket it looks fine. I still don't get the propulsion." Peter said.

"The main thruster is always at the back. These other small jets," I pointed to them, "are for balance and turning. But disregard this thing. It was flawed." I picked up the small jet fighter model. "This was drone number two. I went with a Gripen model because I liked the aerodynamics and wanted to add a passenger." I opened the hatch on top and showed him inside. "This is where I put a mouse in a small cage. I moderated the temperature, kept it oxygenated and maintained pressure. The mouse was fine. He made it up and back and is now running around in the barn here somewhere."

"What do you mean 'made it up'? Where did he go?" Peter asked.

"Space, up in space." Do you know if this is the first mouse in space?" I asked.

"No, I think there have been several mice launched into space, however not sure any went into orbit and not sure if any came back alive."

"Well mine did, on both accounts," I said. "I was happy with this one. It was all radio and satellite controlled. I could send it signals and make it do whatever I wanted. That's how I got it home."

I put it down and walked over to the big tarp. With an easy tug, the tarp slid off the plane, the larger scale Gripen model. "This is the real deal," I said. I opened the barn doors wider, then pulled the pad it sat on outside in front of the barn. Peter examined it with excitement.

"Tell me about it," he demanded.

"Well it's just like the small drone. Aluminum body; carbon fibre wrapping, UV ultra-hard windshield, four small jets and a main thruster at the back. The rifter is on the nose." I pointed it all out.

"What are these pins?" He pointed little nibs out.

"Those are the radar interference EM transmitters. I don't want anyone knowing about this." I opened the cockpit cap and Peter looked in. "I plucked those seats out of a junked Mini. They fit well, eh?" Peter nodded. "Here is the oxygen and air refresher. Here is the puck for the main thruster, another for the other jets and life support, and I keep two spare here." I kept pointing all the features out.

Peter noticed the word on the tail. "What does this mean: kahkākow?" he asked.

"That means 'the crow'. Look over here." I showed him the image on the other side.

"Why a crow?" he asked.

"A while back, a group of Indians came down the river and stopped right here. They were really nice. They named me 'kahkākow' and called me 'the crow' or Johnny Crow, like the bird." I recounted the story.

"Why a crow?" Peter asked.

"They said I was smart like a crow," I answered.

"That's great. When I was a kid, I always wanted an Indian name. I still want one. What would you call me?" He laughed. I guess we never lose some childhood dreams.

"Hmm, let me think about it. Maybe I can come up with one."

Turning back to the plane's interior, Peter continued to ask questions. "I see this is the suit you made." Peter picked up the spare suit from the back seat.

"Yes, that's one. I have another over here." I went around the corner in the barn and plucked the other suit off a hanger. Peter examined it closely.

"When are you planning to test it?" Peter asked.

"I already have. How about we take it for a spin?" I asked with a smile.

"Are you joking?" Peter was not asking. He fully expected I was joking.

"No joke. This is your chance. A chance to see the Earth from space. A chance to float. You brought a camera with you, didn't you? Take pictures. I'm not taking it for a flight if you don't come along."

"We could get into a lot of trouble flying without clearance," Peter said, worrying.

"I'm the pilot, not you. Just relax and enjoy," I said.

"I cannot see anyway to relax going up in a tiny, unusual, handmade aircraft. Even as a plane, I'd be worried. But hold on... I'm nervous but excited at the thought just the same. You say you've flown it, right?"

"Uh-huh."

"In space?"

"Uh-huh," I kept saying with a nod.

"No glitches?" he asked for reassurance.

"None worth worrying about." I said. "Go ahead and put the suit on. See how it feels. Then I'll run through all the safety procedures."

Peter reluctantly squeezed into the suit. I checked it over for any flaws. I helped him place the helmet on and then showed him how to hook up the oxygen and power inside the cockpit. I patted the seat and he climbed in. It was a tight fit for sure. "What do you say? We'll be back by noon. I wouldn't want you to miss lunch." He just sat there thinking. I removed his helmet and started describing how the flight would go.

"Alright. If you say it's safe, I'll go," he said.

"Good. Let me get my suit on." I began squeezing into the suit before he could change his mind. I put the helmet on, turned on the microphone and spoke to Peter. "Can you hear me?"

"Yes."

"There's a knob by your arm to adjust volume. Is you oxygen OK?" I asked.

"Yes. Breathing fine."

"Good. Don't worry, I pressurize the cabin as well."

I checked all systems. Everything was on and normal. "OK, Dr. Manning, when we are ready to ascend, we will pop upward with a small lurch and then tip up and accelerate fairly fast to about 1000 KM/hour. We will remain that way until we reach space, at which point I will put us into orbit. Understood?"

"OK, understood." Peter's voice was undeniably nervous.

"Alright then. I will float us up to forty feet or so. Hang on." I turned a knob and we popped up a few feet and then slowly rose to forty feet. "I'm raising the nose now." The nose went up and we leaned back into the seats. "I will count down so you know when to expect launch."

"I admit, I am very nervous right now," Peter announced.

I laughed a little and said, "It'll be fun, like a roller coaster. You like roller coasters don't you?"

"No! I hate them." Peter laughed, nervously. I would almost say hysterically.

"Five, four, three, two, one, GO!" I pushed the button for the main thruster and slowly increased power. We went up, faster and faster. I could hear a groan in the headset, like someone scared out of their mind. "Doin' good Dr. Manning." Not sure my encouragement helped at all. It takes nerves of steel to withstand a steep climb at nearly 1000 Km/hour in a tiny tin can. It wasn't easy the first time I did it and it's not easy this time. Sometimes a scientist must take that leap of faith. We whipped through a few wisps of clouds, but mostly just blue sky, which became a pale shade the higher we rose. Finally we struck black sky with the clear dazzling of stars; millions of stars. I kept firing to bring our speed up and then turned the plane into orbit. "Are you still with me, Dr. Manning?"

"I'm here. Where is here?" he asked.

I tilted the wing slowly and the edge of the Earth came into view. It was dead silent. Then Peter said, "Wow," in a whisper.

"Dr. Manning, raise your arm and let it fall," I told him.

"It's not falling. It's NOT falling! We're in orbit!" He was so excited.

"What do you see on Earth?" I asked.

"I see Hudson's Bay, and Quebec. I see weather and lakes and forests. I see Earth," he replied.

"It's a nice sight, eh?" I suggested.

"Yes. Yes it is."

We coasted for several minutes, circling the globe. Looking down, I could appreciate the relative stability of the world. An endless rotation keeps everything firmly planted on a world that spins to a beat we cannot perfectly time. "I want to take a wee detour. We'll come back. I want to try this rifter."

"OK," Peter answered, but I don't think he was listening. He was too consumed in looking at the planet. Anyways, I don't think he believed the rifter could work.

I turned the plane and pointed to new coordinates. I selected a power level and set the rift for seven seconds. I didn't want to run the rifter at full tilt, I just wanted to test it at a moderate level. "OK, Dr. Manning. This is gonna get a bit weird," I said.

"What do you mean, weird?" Peter asked, hesitantly.

When I hit the rifter button, everything will go black. All lights will disappear. All stars will go black. You won't see or hear anything. Your mind will go blank. It will only seem like a moment and you may be confused about what happened. Just want to advise you, OK?"

"Is there any way I can talk you into going back now?" he asked.

"Ha ha ha. In for a penny, in for a pound. We gotta do this. Countdown commencing... five, four, three, two, one, GO!" All went blank. No sound, no sight, no thought. A moment later the lights flickered on, the stars re-appeared, the intercom crackled. "Dr. Manning? Are you with me?"

"That was strange. I take it we survived?" Peter asked.

"It would appear so. All systems look good. But only one way to determine success. Have a look out your left side," I said.

"I don't see anything but stars." Peter stated.

I dropped the wing, tilting the plane gradually. A glowing red crust slowly edged up in the window until we were staring down at a rusty, rugged terrain. "No. That cannot be. That just isn't possible! Is that..." Peter paused.

"Yes, Dr. Manning, that is Mars," I answered.

"But there is no way we just flew here in seconds. No way!" he almost shouted.

"Sight is a trait of life, Peter. Observation is a trait of intelligence. Study it closely," I said. The mouse may have seen space, but he made no conclusions about it. Understanding the impacts makes us human.

"Let's go have a closer look," I said.

I not only wanted a closer look, I wanted to feel it. I nosed the plane downward. The atmosphere is very thin on mars, so I could come in faster than on Earth, but decided to be cautious anyways. I brought it to 2000 Km/hour, and then 1000 Km/hour and finally slowing to 200 Km/hour at a height of about one thousand feet. We flew with the faint sound of wind washing over us.

I looked for a flattened area that was near the equator so we would have moderate temperatures. Up ahead, I saw a flat desert area and aimed for a small outcropping toward the centre. I slowed the plane to a hover and descended gently until I saw the foot pads sitting on solid ground beneath us. We sat there for a moment completely silent looking out over the landscape. "OK, I'm going to depressurize the cabin in a minute. I would like you to remove your oxygen hose and plug it into the nozzle on the side of your suit, just like I showed you at the farm. Go Ahead. As soon as it fits in tight, oxygen will start to flow. Tell me when you're done."

A moment later I heard the crackle of the intercom. "It's done. I have air."

"OK, good," I replied. "I placed a puck in your suit to power everything. It's on at all times. I'm going to open the cap and get out, then I want you to release the harness. You have twenty minutes of oxygen. We will only spend a few minutes out there though. The temperature is a comfortable twelve degrees Celsius."

I undid the snaps holding the windshield down and then pushed it up out of the way. I stepped up on the seat, over the side and down on the Martian ground.

"Unplug your power cord. The communication system will work on battery," I said, helping him. Then I stepped back so he could dismount. We turned and looked outward. "We are the first humans, maybe the first ever organic life forms on Mars. How does that feel, Dr. Manning?"

"Unbelievable. Absolutely unbelievable. And please, call me Peter." His reply couldn't have been more humble and respectful.

The landscape around us was hilly with towering hoodoos. The ground was sandy with rubble and outcrops jutting up here and there. The sun was high above and notably smaller than from Earth. A haze lay across the valley in front of us and strangely, there were white, wispy clouds high in the sky. It looked barren, yet not alien.

"Let's find a sample to take home," I told him. We both looked around for a chunk of stone and each found a sample. "Peter, make sure you leave footsteps for future generations to find. Let them wonder who was here." We put the rocks under our seats in the plane.

"We should have brought a branch or log to leave behind," Peter joked.

"Ha ha ha, that would cause quite a stir, eh?" I said. "I brought a little flag. Where do you think we can put this?" I asked. We rigged a rock to lean against the top of the outcrop and then we tied the little flag around it. I thought it looked quite natural. "You should get a picture," I said.

"I would, if I had remembered to bring my camera. I can't believe I forgot it. I suppose I didn't really believe we were going into space," Peter said. "Sorry, I shouldn't have doubted you."

"I brought my phone," I told him. "I'll take a selfie of us." I snapped a photo. "OK, let's get back into the plane."

We went back to the plane, climbed in and placed our rock samples underneath the seats. I closed the cap and tightened down the fasteners and then repressurized the cabin.

"Peter, unhook your oxygen and fit it back into the plane's nozzle. Connect the power now. Let me know if everything is working," I told him. "Then make sure your harness is on and secure."

"Yes, it's all connected. I can breathe fine," he replied.

"OK, we are going to do it all in reverse. Rising up in five, four, three, two, one, GO!" I said sharply.

We popped up to about ten feet abruptly. I hadn't taken into account the lower gravity and lack of atmosphere. From there we cruised up to forty feet. I raised the nose, counted down from five again and thrust ahead. We shot up quickly, breaking into space in no time. No grunts from the rear this time around. Maybe Peter was getting used to it, or maybe the lower gravitational pull dulled the rush.

Once up in space I did a roll so we could see the planet down below. It was a sight to behold. Once again I warned Peter about the rift and once again we descended into an oblivious blackness that defied logic. I wondered if I would ever understand where I went in the rift. If our consciousness could be in a space separate from our body, perhaps we could travel in time. That would be a question only answered when the blackness between space is understood.

We broke back out about four hundred kilometres above Earth staring down at India. I oriented the craft to the north east and started the descent. As I reached three hundred kilometres, I powered the forward thrusters to slow us down. "Hey Peter, should we stop over in Hawaii on the way home?" I asked.

"If it was January I'd highly recommend somewhere in the south Pacific. But I'm rather anxious to throw a line in the river and catch a big fish. As much as I loved walking on Mars, I'll be happy to see your farm again." Peter said jovially.

I kept the plane above atmosphere until reaching the coast, then dove for the mountains like a skydiver. Once I saw the foothills I looked for the rivers and navigated home, like a canoe winding around bends atop the water. I expertly lowered the plane onto the pad. With a few flips of the snaps, the lid was open and we were back home, walking on our biological soil. Peter removed his helmet. His hair was damp and wayward. His expression of overwhelming euphoria was muted by his stress. I believe he was exhausted.

"Let's hang our suits up in the barn to dry out," I told him. Then I pulled the plane back into the barn. I would cover it later, after checking it over and disconnecting the power-pucks. I took Peter into the house and he sat in the living room. "Peter, you look like you could use a cold beer."

"You read my mind," he said. "I feel like I just ran a marathon."

"The longest marathon ever," I said.

Peter reached out to the rock on the side table. "This rock; it's from the moon, isn't it?" he asked.

"Yes. I landed there in a test flight," I replied.

"Very nice. I can see it now, but would never have guessed it before flying to Mars."

He should have guessed it. There are telltale signs that it was lunar. But I can forgive him. Who would ever think someone had a moon rock.

"OK, that is the best beer I have EVER tasted," Peter said as he swigged and sighed. He looked at me with intensity. "We just walked on Mars. Hey, my rock!"

Just as I had done with the lunar rock, he ran out to the barn to retrieve it from the plane. He dashed back in like a little kid with a new toy. He looked it over intently. It was sharp and angular, the size of a baseball and brownish in colour.

"It's a sandstone," Peter stated. "The grains are spherical, from wind erosion. Probably cemented together by groundwater."

The man knows his geology. I let him admire his rock while I sipped my beer.

"Listen, that may have been a lot to digest in one morning. Relax. Put your head back and snooze a bit. I'm going to whip up some lunch for us, then we can go down by the river and see what fish are swimming by today."

"Oh, that would be great. Much appreciated," he said.

****

I did indeed put lunch together; a cold cut sandwich with tomato, lettuce, mustard, and roast beef on white bread. Yeah, I know whole wheat's better for you, but sometimes I just like the old fashioned, fluffy white stuff. I heard some snoring from the living room, so I put the sandwiches out on the table, covered them and went out the back.

I wandered around the garden, admiring the plants that were pushing higher under the sun. They could probably use some water. I pulled the hose over and sprayed them for ten minutes or so. I went into the barn, collected my rock and then checked over the plane, pulling all the pucks out to re-energize them. I covered up the plane with the tarp. I wasted time until about 2:00 PM and then went back inside and clanked around a bit to roust Peter.

"Hey," I said, "how ya feeling?"

"Good. What time is it?" he asked.

"A few minutes past two. You had a good nap," I replied.

"Good heavens, really? Sorry about that," he said.

"No problem. I took care of some chores around the place. There's a sandwich here for ya, and a fresh beer."

"Ah, you are too kind." He came over to the table. "I feel invigorated now."

"Good, you'll need your strength to haul in the big ones." I laughed. I really hoped there were a few fish lingering out there. If not, I'd take him to the Muskwa where Bob and Charlie took me. We sat at the table and ate. After lunch we went on down to the river and I showed Peter a good place to cast.

"See where the rapids meet the pool? Aim for that. Just get it into the rapids and drag it back toward the pool. Do it in a few places along that line," I told Peter.

As he cast, he talked about fishing with his dad as a kid. "I remember this trip my dad and I went on up near Wawa. We picked this small lake and dropped the boat in. We trolled around for most of the day and caught nothing. Then, around six in the evening I had a strike. It felt like a log. In fact, I thought I was stuck at first. But it was coming in slowly. When it got close to the boat, it just ran so hard my reel went 'zzzzzzzzz' and I had to fight it in all over again. I swear it took thirty minutes to get it in. It was a thirty three pound pike. I was so proud of that. Best fishing trip of my life. We stayed on that lake for three days."

"Wow. I've never caught anything that big. Last fish I caught was right here. I'd guess it was a six pound pickerel. Weird thing is, just as I pulled it in, that's when the Indians came down the river and I met them. They landed right here and camped, birch bark canoes and teepees and all. I'd never seen anything like that before.

"We're not having much luck here, eh?" he stated.

"Yeah, it's too bad. I thought this would be a good spot. Let's go further along. I know they like the fast water." I led him along the river a ways. "Do you have any kids?" I asked.

"Yes, a son and a daughter," Peter said. "He is twelve and she is fourteen. I'm sure they would both love to be out here. My daughter would like the hills and forest, and my son the fishing. My wife on the other hand is far more suited to the city. Hey, I think I got something!" Peter shouted. "I do!"

"Awesome. How big?" I asked.

"He's not heavy, but a good fighter," he replied. Sure enough I could see the rod tip shake up and down. Then a fish splashed the surface and jumped clean out. "Woo! Did you see that?"

"That's a beauty," I told him.

"Do you know what it is?" he asked.

"That's a grayling. They are great fighters," I answered.

The fish twisted and turned. Once it came in close and I reached toward it but the wily thing darted side to side. "Come on, ya burken guy!" I yelled. As the fish came close, I quickly slid my fingers in his gill and lifted him up high on the bank and handed him to Peter.

"Great job!" I commended him. "Hey, that's your new name: The grayling; Peter Grayling. Now you have an Indian name," I said with a smile. He laughed and said he liked it.

"What's with the 'burken guy' thing? What's that mean?" Peter asked.

"Oh, just a little saying we have around here for someone, or I guess something, that annoys you. I guess it's the same as 'jerk'. Came from a guy not well liked in town," I answered.

"That's funny," he said. "I'd never heard that one before."

"Next time someone cuts you off in traffic, you can call him a burken guy," I said.

We continued fishing for a while and he brought in another grayling and a pickerel. I snapped a picture of him holding up his catch along the river. He grinned widely.

Up at the house, I put the biggest grayling in the freezer, then filleted the other two fish for dinner. We baked the pickerel with onions and herbs, and fried the grayling in butter. Along with rice and tomatoes, it was a very nice dinner.

****

The next morning, I took Peter to the airport. He had to be there at 8:30 AM for his 9:30 flight. He would change planes in Calgary, as he did on his way here, and arrive in Montreal around 5:30 PM. All in all, a long day just to cross the country. We joked about it on the way to the airport; it took us less time to fly to Mars than it did to go from B.C. to Quebec. Of course that was the fault of the airlines, not just present day technology. The Concord was a marvel of technology, and that technology should have become standard on every flight today.

"Well, Johnny Crow," Peter laughed, "I doubted all your claims before arriving. You slowly won me over with your impressive, albeit confusing knowledge. I can't pretend to understand the theories you explained to me. I still don't know what possessed me to take a leap of faith and ride in that homemade craft of yours, but I am so glad I did. You are not an ordinary man. You are extraordinary, in so many ways. I hope you will keep in touch. I would love to hear all about your new inventions and adventures to… wherever. The sky is not the limit for you."

"I'm very glad you decided to come for a visit. I have not had anyone to talk to about my research in a long time. It was a pleasure sharing the adventure, and my home made beer with you." I smiled.

We shook hands and he was off. As he walked away I called out to him. "Hey Peter, it's all about the journey, not the destination… unless, of course, you're just going to the washroom." I grinned at him. He gave me one last wave as he boarded the small, twin prop plane out front. I, once again, was on my own.

EIGHT - The Girl

I had a lot to think about. Should I dare expand the rifter to its full potential? Should I expand the life support capabilities in the plane? All in good time, I thought. Right now, I had a quick mission to accomplish in town. I drove to 3227 McKenzie Road where I found a brick house sporting a sign out front that read, 'Ted's Taxidermy'. I rang the bell and a man answered the door.

"Hello, are you Ted?" I asked.

"Yes, can I help you?" he replied.

"I have a fish I'd like to get taxidermied." I held the package under my arm.

"Oh, OK, come on in." He held the door for me. I walked inside and he led me to an office room. It was plastered with fish and animals of all kinds. "So, what do you have?"

I showed him the fish. "It's a grayling."

"OK, that should be easy enough to do. Do you need it done by a certain date?" he asked.

"No, but I would like it done as quickly as you can. It's a gift," I said.

"No problem. I can have it ready within two months. Here are the mounting board styles. Pick the one you want and fill in the name to put on the plaque," he said.

I filled in the form like this: Peter "Grayling" Manning. I thought he'd like that. I asked him to add a date and Tetsa River to the plaque as well. Then I gave him a card and asked him to mail the package to

Peter's address along with the card. I paid him in advance, reasonably sure he'd do a good job. That chore done, I did some shopping and headed back out to the farm.

****

The days of June were pleasant and warm. I made a new batch of beer, this time with barley grain. I spent countless hours weeding the garden. I often let the hens out and would wander around with them. They always went back into the barn at night, safe from the wily predators. I had no desire to lose my great egg producers.

The grasses grew tall, dandelions flourished and bugs multiplied. These were all fair attributes of a northern B.C. summer. I occasionally tinkered with the rifter to amplify its power. With modifications already made and new materials, I was confident I could attain ten thousand times the speed of light. Theoretically I could go fifty thousand times the speed of light. Unfortunately, at that level a power puck would be completely drained within three hours. That meant it would take about ten minutes to move one light year and my limit would be 18 light years on a single power puck.

I would need extras if I ever wanted to travel around the stars. I suppose I could use solar panels on the plane to charge a puck, but that would be slow and require being close to a star. If I was ever out in space and lost power, I'd have no way to get back. All things to seriously consider in the future. But would be worth my while to add solar panels to the wings just in case.

I got back to work on the app again. The house was warm. The sun streamed through the big window lulling me into a comfortably relaxed state. Arranging formulas to compute earnings per share, price to earnings, price to sales, debt to equity, price to book, etc. was straight forward, but boy was it boring. Such a struggle forging through the day working on investment analysis. I did learn a lot though, which I could put to use in my own finances. I wondered how my father could stand to work finance his whole life.

Whether I saw my coffee cup half full or half empty, It was only noon. So there was an upside and downside. I took plenty of breaks, strolling outside to smell the sweet pollen filled air. I kept refilling my cup until I finished writing the code. I thought about the user interface. How could I make this fun for the average person? I recalled the casino. People loved the slots. There was something exciting about pulling the handle and waiting to win.

So I designed something similar. Put a stock symbol in, swipe the graphic handle and watch the indicators revolve. I started testing it with a few stock symbols. Actually it was kind of fun. It was almost addictive. You could play it like a game and 'gamble' a starting amount. The app would reward you for selecting good stocks, commodities, bonds or currencies. That way you could amass a good portfolio by keeping the good ones and selling the bad. Then you could export the list to email. Even non investors would use it just for fun. I'd have to charge less to attract them though. Maybe a free version with limitations, and a paid version for real investors. I still had lots of work to do to get it ready for market.

****

A white BMW drove over the Francis Case Memorial Bridge in Washington, DC. The driver, Mr. Roger Enright, a middle aged man in a tweed jacket, reached for his cell phone which chimed a tinkling bell. "Hello?"

"Hi, is that you Roger? It's Peter Manning."

"Hey, Peter. How are you? Haven't heard from you in a while."

"I'm fine thanks. How are you?" Peter asked.

"I'm good, just heading over to the office. I was running an errand in Arlington."

"I wanted to discuss something with you. Remember I told you about a fellow that contacted me? I thought he was a crank, pulling my leg?"

"Yeah, I remember," Roger recalled.

"Can you keep a secret?"

"Sure."

"Well he isn't a crank. He has technology that you just wouldn't believe."

"So who is this guy?" Roger asked.

"I can't say. He wanted me to keep him and his technology secret. But I can tell you he's the real deal. Listen to this… I flew into space with him."

"What? Like up to the edge of space?"

"No. Like full orbit. I was weightless."

"What's his craft like?" Roger asked.

"It's this tiny little jet, barely big enough for the two of us to squeeze into," Peter said.

"Peter, I have to park the car underground. I'm going to lose you. Let me call you as soon as I get up to my office."

"OK. I'll wait," Peter said.

Roger parked his car by a pillar next to a blue SUV and raced over to the stairs and up to the lobby. Once there, he badged in and took the elevator up to the third floor. He dropped his leather case by his desk, sat down and looked up Peter's number. A moment later they were back on the phone together.

"Hi, Peter. It's me, Roger. So what happened?"

"OK, so we were in orbit and then he activated some weird function and seconds later we were beside Mars."

"Get out of here. Now I know you're pulling my leg," Roger snorted.

"Gets better… We LANDED on Mars. I even got out and walked around." Peter was so excited to tell his friend about this that he almost ran out of breath. "I have a picture."

"Send it to me," Roger said.

Peter had the picture that John snapped on Mars and emailed it to Roger.

Roger
Here it is, a photo of me on Mars. I'm the one on the right.
Peter.

"Did you get it yet?" Peter asked.

"I see it, but you can't expect me to believe you walked on Mars. Are you sure he didn't just trick you somehow? You do know it's physically impossible to get to Mars in less than eight months, right?"

"Apparently not. I can just tell you this guy is like a new and improved Einstein. He has theories on space that are far ahead of anything we've understood so far. He explained to me that space is a medium and to go faster than the speed of light you have to cut the medium to make a shortcut. And he has done it. Here, I'll send you another picture," Peter frantically said. "Did you get it?" Peter sent a snapshot of the rock he picked up from Mars.

"Yes, it's a rock," Roger noted.

"It's a Martian rock," said Peter.

"Can I come up and see the rock sometime. I would like to examine it," Roger asked.

"Of course. Anytime you want," Peter proudly replied.

"So tell me, what did it feel like, up in space and on Mars?" Roger asked.

"Well the takeoff is scary. You're pointing up and rocketing at breakneck speed. Not as fast as with a conventional launch, but then again it's a tiny craft. Once you're in orbit you feel this complete calm. There is no noise. I was always strapped in, but could none the less feel my arms drift and when we rolled the plane, there was no sense of up or down. Quite freaky. When we landed on Mars and I got out, I did not feel like we were on another planet, apart from the lower gravity. Seriously, apart from the lack of any plants and water, there was sky and clouds and fog and hills just like Earth."

"Maybe you were still on Earth, somewhere up in that northern wasteland where only polar bears can live," Roger laughed.

"No, there was a slight reddish orange hue everywhere, probably cast from the ground which was this rocky, sandy terrain. Well, just look at that photo I sent. We only stayed a few minutes and then returned."

"So how did you not burn up on re-entry? It's not an easy thing shielding a craft from that kind of heat," Roger asked.

"That's the thing, we never came in that fast. He slowed the plane down before re-entry and we simply fell, or glided back down," Peter explained. "So there was no need for heat shields."

"So, he didn't burn any fuel?"

"No, it was completely electric. I know that," Peter noted.

"Fascinating. Even with electricity, I don't understand how he could propel himself into space and through space."

"He explained it all to me, but it was way over my head. He has a great little lab set up full of equipment." Peter said.

"Peter, I have to ask, what convinced you it was OK to get into this craft of his and risk your neck? I don't know if anything could have persuaded me to do that!" Roger said.

"Good question. I guess I was just in the moment. I had listened to all his technical explanations, seen his craft, and he offered me the chance of a lifetime. He never said we were going to Mars, just space. That alone was enticing. You can't tell me you haven't dreamed of going into space." Peter explained himself. "Looking back, it was the biggest risk of my life, and the greatest thrill of my life. He and I were the first people to walk on another planet. Maybe no one else will ever know that, but I will, till the day I die."

"Well, you're lucky that day didn't just pass with the space flight." Roger admonished Peter for taking such a risk.

"You are right. Listen, I better go. I haven't told anyone else, not even my wife. Good God, especially not my wife!" Peter laughed. "But I just had to tell you. We've been friends a long time. I thought you'd like to hear about it."

"Thanks, Peter. I'll come up and we can chat more about it. I would love to figure out how his setup worked. Take care."

"OK, see you soon. Cheers." Peter hung up the phone. A weight had been lifted. He shared his experiences with a friend, someone he trusted. That felt good.

****

A week had passed since I finished the app and uploaded it to the Android and Apple marketplace stores. I hadn't looked to see what was happening. It was now July first. I had to go into town to see what was going on. Hopefully they'd have some fireworks in the evening and maybe a party at the community centre. I locked the place up and drove through town to the pub.

"Hello Mac, How are you?" I asked, as I walked through the door.

"Johnny, what brings you into town?" Mac asked.

"Well I was hoping there'd be some kind of party tonight. Today seemed like an appropriate day to drink cold beer," I replied.

"Yes, there's a celebration at the Rec. Centre and fireworks at ten in the field out back. I'm closing up at nine so I can go too," Mac said. "How did your visitor make out? Did he have a good time?"

"He had a great time. I took him fishing and showed him around the farm. He only stayed a couple of days, but it was good," I replied. I decided to sit at the bar and eat. I ordered fish and chips and a Kilkenny. Lots of people came and left while I sat there.

I wondered what people who came in thought of me, sitting at the bar in my hat and boots. They were well worn in now and felt natural on me. I might even feel awkward without them. I was quite happy with my life as it was. Still a bit lonely out on the farm.

Maybe I should come into town more often. Lots of nice people around, I just didn't really have anything to do in town.

I could take a course at the college, like a trade's course on how to build a shed. Or maybe I could teach a class there. I'd have to look into it. I can't say I was ever a good teacher. I was pretty impatient. But if it was just for fun, like Frank and the beer class, I could enjoy it. There seemed to be this lacking in my life. I could create something so advanced it would forever change the world, but that did not fill a small void in me, a hole that could only be healed by the knowledge I helped someone; I needed a connection.

In all my deep thoughts and travels, I often wondered what the meaning of life was. My final answer was always the same: To live; just to live. There is nothing more to it. Why does a mosquito risk death to drain my blood? To live. Why does a wounded animal continue to fight for survival? Because he does it to live. Do we struggle to achieve something? No, we struggle just to live, because it is our job to live, just as a tree does, or a virus, or the most awkward animal on the planet. Where would we be today if all the predecessors questioned the meaning of life? I asked myself again, what's the meaning of life? It's to live; just to live. Our atoms, bonded in molecules and collected in tissues that have been organized over billions of years serve just one purpose... to live. Life is organized collections. No, there is no more meaning to life than just to live. Whatever our fate, we live. The human mind complicates this fact. What we strive for in our lives is a different matter.

Here I sat in this warm and comfortable oasis, an animal on a stool consuming another animal in the struggle of life. OK, it had become less of a struggle for most of us in the twenty-first century. The struggle for life has been replaced by the struggle within our minds; depression, fear, stress, and hate have driven many good and healthy people to end their lives. The great error in thinking there is a special meaning to life has left many feeling disappointed with their achievements. But if we live as best we can, as long as we can, until we cease to live, then we have achieved the meaning of life. No one should ever be disappointed with that. Some may regret past decisions, but the future is theirs to change. Lamenting the past will not forge the future. Questioning the future will not alter the past. We just live on. We all go through moments of self-loathing and doubt. That's the dark side of our human ego.

I stared up at the TV on the wall, completely oblivious to the news, simply deep in my thoughts. Dan Mangan sang about road regrets over the speakers. Maybe that put me into this reflective mental state. I don't know. Maybe I need a religion, one with answers, not studies; one that brings peace and solves mysteries. Maybe that's not a religion at all.

I ate up and paid the bill. "Thanks Mac. I'll see you over at the community centre later."

"I'll be there. Bring a coffee cup. I'll smuggle some booze in with me." Mac winked and smiled.

"You think of everything, Mac. Nod nod, wink wink, eh?" I said.

It was only 7:00 PM and everything in town was closed for the holiday. I drove over to the community centre and went in to see what was going on. The party was supposed to start at 8:00 PM but several people were there setting the place up. I walked up to an older lady.

"Hi, anything I can do to help?" I asked

"Sure. We need to put all the tables and chairs out." She pointed towards the wall where they were stacked.

"No problem," I replied and started to get to work.

****

Josh Harris popped his head into a small lab. "Roger, the director wants to see you right away."

Roger looked puzzled. "Alright," he said. He removed his lab coat and goggles, hung them up and left down the hall and up a floor to the director's office. The door was slightly askew. Roger opened it discreetly. "You wanted to see me, sir?" He asked, noticing two other men in black suits standing on either side of the director.

"Yes, come in. Close the door. These gentlemen are from the CIA. They want to talk to you," the director said, formally.

The taller of the two men said, "You are Roger Enright?"

"Yes," Roger replied.

The CIA agent asked the director, "Is there a room we can talk to Mr. Enright in private?"

"Sure. Right across the hall is an empty office. Help yourself," the director replied.

The three men crossed the hall into a dingy old room. The lighting was cold, almost bluish white fluorescent bulbs in the ceiling. An old style metal desk sat in the middle of the room with an old wooden chair, probably from the nineteen sixties. It looked as if this room was only used for storage and files. "Have a seat, Mr. Enright. Do you have a cell phone?" They asked.

"Yes." Roger touched his jacket pocket.

"May we see it?" Asked the agent.

"I guess so." Roger slipped the phone out and gave it to the agent who handed it to the second agent. He began searching through it. "What's this about?" he asked.

"You have a friend in the Canadian Space Agency by the name of Peter Manning. Is this correct?" the agent asked.

Roger felt a lump in his throat. The CIA must have intercepted his conversations or emails with Peter. They must know about Peter's claim of flying to Mars. But what could they want, he thought. "Yes, this is correct. Is he in trouble?"

"Peter manning claims to have flown in a spacecraft, to space, and to Mars. Since you and Dr. Manning are noted scientists, I see no reason to consider this a hoax. We want answers," the agent spoke, seriously.

"Well, yes, he claimed that. But that was a private conversation. How do you know about it?" Roger asked.

"We will ask the questions. This is serious. This may be a matter of national security. Do you understand?" The agent sat on the edge of the desk as he talked.

"No, not really. How is this related to national security?" Roger probed.

"If a foreign government gets their hands on technology that we do not have, they could threaten the United States."

"But a foreign government does not have the technology." Roger pushed back.

"We want to know what this technology is. We want to find the man responsible for creating it. We want to secure the technology so our enemies don't get it. Now, tell us everything you know. Who is the scientist? Where is he?"

"I don't know. Dr. Manning kept that secret. He only told me he flew. Nothing else." Roger was steadfast.

"Listen, we can solve this now, or we can take you to Langley and draw it out of you. We have every resource at our disposal to acquire the information. It can take a little time, or a long time. That's up to you." The agent was ready to play hardball.

"Apparently you have all my emails and phone conversations. You know as much as I do. The only ones who know more than me are the unknown scientist and Dr. Manning!" Roger shouted.

"So then we need to speak to Dr. Manning. We want you to call him and invite him down here. It will be a lot easier than having to go up there and do things the hard way," the agent demanded. They handed Roger back his phone and said, "Call him, now. Get him down here ASAP. Make up a reason. We want that rock, too."

"I think I had better speak with my director first." Roger started to stand up.

The agent put his hand on Roger's shoulder and pushed him back down. "No, this is not his business. This is between you and us. Make the call or we take you with us. Put him on speakerphone."

Roger picked up the phone from the desk with trembling hands. He tapped the screen and rang Peter.

"Ahem, hello Peter?"

"Yes. Who's this?" Peter answered.

"It's Roger. Remember I said I'd like to come up and see you?"

"Yes. When are you coming?" Peter asked.

"Well, I was wondering if you wouldn't mind coming down here."

"I can do that, if you'd like. When's a good time?"

Roger looked up at the Agent who nodded to him. "Why not tomorrow. Do you have time?"

"I'll see what I can do. I'll send you an email when I have my flight booked." Peter unwittingly accepted.

"Great. Bring that rock too, OK?"

"No chance. That rock stays in my safe deposit box. "I'll bring some crumbling dust for you." Peter laughed. "See ya."

They hung up. Roger felt terrible, betraying his friend, leading him into a trap like this. What choice did he have? He knew the power the CIA wielded. There are many departments you do not want to mess with, but the CIA was the worst.

"Good work, Mr. Enright. You'll see, this is the best thing for the country. You are a patriot. We want his schedule. As soon as you get it, forward it to me." The agent handed him a card with contact information on it. "Now, if Dr. Manning has a change of heart and decides not to come, I will assume you tipped him off. That will land you in a great deal of trouble. Treason is a serious matter. Are we clear?"

"Oh, we're clear." Roger stared at the agent with great contempt.

The agent smiled. "Let's just keep this conversation private, shall we?" They left the room. Roger sat at the desk a while, absorbing what just happened. He had been drawn into a dirty international incident with no villains. How did this become so evil? Roger could not understand the entire situation; flying at the speed of light, space travel without fuel, walking on Mars. All this trouble because of a little conversation with an old friend. Was any of this real; the space flight, the espionage, the threats?

There was a knock on the door, and the director looked in. "Roger, what's going on? Are you in trouble?"

"No, I'm not in trouble, but trouble is brewing."

****

I sat in the grass out back of the community centre. What a night, still twenty degrees Celsius, a clear sky with the sun just about to set at 9:20 PM. I was surrounded by Mac, Charlie, Bob, Frank, Mildred and everyone else in town. We chatted and drank. Kids played. A few dogs even ran around and barked. I saw some people setting up fireworks in the field. This was an event I never would have attended in Vancouver. Now I craved it. A lady with a basket came around handing out bags of chips and juice boxes. I had my coffee, a la rye whiskey, thanks to Mac.

The sky slowly darkened. Sunsets are slow in the north. There would still be a wisp of light on the horizon at 11:00 PM. At 9:55 sharp the fireworks started. The crowd gasped and cheered. The sky, though not entirely dark was splashed with blue and pink and green flashes. Sparkling coloured stars spread out in all directions, raining back down to earth. Pops and bangs vibrated in the body and some kids covered their ears.

By 10:00 PM, it was all over, and everyone was hyper with excitement, chatting exuberantly about the show. I had been lying back in the grass, partly watching the fiery show and partly searching the sky for stars. I was comfortable enough to just stay there a while, but everyone began to roust and leave. I followed along, walking out to the parking lot and chit chatting with people, people I didn't even know. Forty five minutes later I was home. Another thirty minutes and I was showered, changed and snug in my bed, fondly remembering my evening. I felt safe and happy.

The next day was just an average routine day. I made slight modifications to the rifter. I weeded the garden; the plants were growing well. I logged into Google and Apple to check on my app. So far it had been downloaded 7,085 times and purchased 296 times. That wasn't bad at all. I made a simple dinner and ate in a hurry. I was just finishing up the dishes when I heard noises come from out front. I went to the window to see my friendly tribe back on shore. I ran outside and down the hill. I was greeted by a wide smile from Ashenee. Benjamin yelled over from the back of a canoe, "Hello, Johnny Crow!"

"Hi Benjamin. It's good to see you again." I looked around. "Good to see all of you."

I grabbed a canoe and pulled it forward. People started disembarking and pulling their boats ashore. As I had done before, I began unloading bundles. It was all like clockwork. This time I helped bundle poles and wrap tents. In no time the camp was built and this small spit of sand came to life once more. Grandma came up to me and said, "Tansi kahkākow". She remembered my name.

"Tansi Nohkom". I remembered her name too. She looked happy about that. I walked around saying hello to everyone. Ashenee was sitting by a canoe, fixing the binding along its side. I went and sat down beside her. She smiled at me and said, "I missed you." It was a sentiment I had not expected to hear, and it startled me. This girl missed me. I wonder what she really meant by that. How did she miss me?

"I missed you too. I'm glad you're back. Did you have a good trip?" I asked.

"Yes. We caught lots of fish and dried them," she answered.

"Can you stay longer this time?" I asked.

"I can ask my father. Or you can ask him. He likes you, Johnny Crow."

"I wish you didn't live so far away." I told her

"You should get a boat. Then you could come visit me."

"I have a canoe, but I've never used it. I don't know how," I explained.

"My cousin can teach you. He'd enjoy that." Her cousin, Ahanu, was only about fourteen but built like a football player. He was very enthusiastic, about everything. He would make a great teacher.

I admired her clothing. "Did you make this yourself?" I asked, touching her sleeve.

"No, my grandmother made it for me. I made some of the kid's clothes," she pointed at kids playing nearby, "and my Father's clothes. Do you like them?"

"Yes. They're beautiful, and strong," I answered.

"I learn a lot from my grandmother. How is your garden doing?" she asked.

"Great. Do you want to come see?"

"OK," she replied.

We jumped up and ran up the hill like kids. I took her around the side of the house to the garden.

"Wow," she exclaimed, "the garden is doing very good. We have a garden too. Some old people stay behind when we go fishing and they look after everything. You must spend a lot of time working on it."

"I do. Sometimes it's a distraction. It takes my mind off other things. But I like that. It's nice to look at what you've done and know you made it. I get pleasure being close to the land." I said. We walked down some of the rows, admiring the health of the plants. Some things were close to ready for picking. "Do you want to see my chickens?"

"OK. We have some chickens too," she said.

We went into the barn. I handed her a bowl and we collected eggs. "Let's take these down to the beach later and give them to your grandmother. Maybe she will like that."

"Yes, she hasn't had any eggs in a long time now. What is this?" Ashenee pointed to the tarp.

I pulled the tarp off and Ashenee's eyes lit up. "You have a plane! It's beautiful. Does it fly?"

"Oh yes. I have flown it. I went to the moon and to Mars in it," I said.

"Really? It's so small." She looked through the windshield.

I opened it up and helped her inside. She sat, gazing out like she was flying, a big smile on her face. "That's exciting," she said. "How did you make it? No one can just make a plane."

"Well, I have been designing the parts for many years now. So I had a good start. I learned a lot at school."

"My aunt is our teacher. She went to school and then came back. She taught me. I don't learn from her anymore. I'm too old now. But I help teach the other kids. I learned math, science, history, geography, and language. Go ahead, test me?" she teased.

"Uh-huh, I see. OK, what is ten times ten?" I asked.

"One hundred. That's too easy, silly." she answered.

"OH, well then… what is the area of a circle?"

"Pi - R - squared!" she shouted in a playful tone.

"WOW! I'm impressed. Beautiful and smart," I said with a wink.

Ashenee covered her face and giggled. "No! Just smart," she said, and then giggled some more. I helped her out of the plane. I picked up the eggs.

"Do you want a cup of tea?" I asked.

"Yes, that would be nice," she replied.

We went inside the house and I put the kettle on. Ashenee took cups down from the cupboard for me and we made tea. "Oh, I made some cookies yesterday, would you like to try?" I asked.

"Of course. I love cookies," she replied.

I took some out of a cookie jar and put them on a plate on the table. "Hey, I have an idea. Why don't we bake some more cookies and take them down to the camp for everyone." I just wanted to find things to do with Ashenee. I thought this would be fun.

"That's a nice idea. They will all like that. What type do you want to make?" she asked.

"I have lots of oatmeal and raisins," I replied. And so that was what we chose to make. It was a fun experience. We mixed the flour and water and other ingredients in a big bowl, then we heated the oven and spooned dough onto pans. Ashenee put a small dollop of dough on my nose and laughed. I held up my finger with some dough, threatening her, but she was too quick for me. She snagged my hand and licked the dough right off my finger. We giggled at our own playful antics. Oh my goodness she could make me laugh.

In time, we baked dozens and dozens of cookies. Apart from a few burnt ones, they all looked great. We cleaned up the kitchen together and then took the eggs and cookies down to the camp where everyone was working on a project or playing along the beach. The kids came running over, eager to have a cookie. Then the older folks joined in. I gave the eggs to grandma and she smiled and nodded her thanks.

I asked Benjamin if they could stay an extra day and continue the next. He said sure. As before, we sat around the fire and talked. Some people told stories. I'm sure they had all heard the stories countless times, but enjoyed watching me hear them for the first time. It got late and people went to bed. Only Benjamin, Ashenee and I were left at the fire.

"Johnny, do you want to stay with us tonight?" Benjamin asked.

"Sure, if you have enough room for me."

"Of course. We always have room," he replied. We went into a tent where grandma was already sleeping. I found a spot on a thick fur and pulled a big Hudson

Bay blanket over me. "Good night Johnny," came whispering voices. I replied, "good night," and fell asleep.

****

Peter Manning shuffled in his seat as the Boeing 777 touched down at Dulles International Airport. He was excited. Peter recounted in his mind all the time he spent in Washington with visits to museums, tours of buildings, and great times with his colleagues. The seat belt sign soon switched off and everyone collected their belongings, exiting the airliner. Peter only brought a small attaché case with him, so he needn't worry about picking up luggage. He would only stay a couple of days. He walked with enthusiasm through the tunnel. When he reached the gate, two men in black suits stepped up to him. "Dr. Peter Manning?" they asked.

"Yes," Peter answered.

They flashed a badge. "Come with us, please."

As soon as he heard this, Peter had a sinking feeling. He knew his secret was out. But who would do this to him? Was it NASA, hungry for the technology I described? Was it the military, angling for powerful jets? Was it the CIA or NSA, or whatever agency is responsible for espionage? Peter did not know the inner workings of the U.S. Government, but he knew he'd been outed. The only one who knew about the secret was Roger. Peter couldn't believe Roger would betray him. The agents led Peter right past U.S. Customs to a car waiting at the front of the airport.

"Where are we going?" Peter asked, with no reply. "What's going on?"

One agent turned to him and said, "We just want to have a talk with you, that's all."

Peter sat in the car. He recognized the scenery. After all, he had lived in Washington for several years. He was on his way to Langley, the CIA headquarters. They pulled in at a building and the agents took him inside to a small boardroom. They left him alone for five minutes.

"Dr. Manning, how are you?" an agent asked.

"Confused. I did not expect to be abducted by the CIA today," he answered, curtly.

"You have not been abducted, sir. We merely wish to ask you some questions. This is a matter of homeland security. You can appreciate that, can't you? I mean, you are familiar with the importance of security in today's world. We've been speaking with a colleague of yours at NASA and it turns out you have some secrets that perhaps you shouldn't have. This is where you can help. May we have your cell phone please?"

"My cell phone is private," Peter stated.

"Dr., we are not the police. You are not in trouble with the law. There is no need to worry. But we are the CIA and we have a mandate to extract important information. If you do not give us your cell phone, we have the power to take it. So please, as a gentleman, give me your cell phone."

Peter knew he could not fight them. He was locked in a room with no view. He was surrounded by agents of espionage. Refusing their so-called request could not end well. Peter removed his phone and handed it to the agent. The agent then handed it to the second agent who left the room. Peter felt helpless.

"Would you like a coffee, Dr.?" the agent asked.

"No," Peter replied.

"Please tell me about your friend, the scientist who took you for a ride in space?"

"A ride in space? Where did you hear this nonsense?" Peter mumbled.

"Dr. Manning, we have conversations and emails of you with a NASA scientist. I find it hard to believe you were just joking around with him. The communications are quite clear. You stated that you flew into space. You stated you went to, and walked on, Mars. Are you telling me these are all lies?"

"You know, you remind me of someone. A guy named Burken. Do you really believe I went into space with some 'unknown' person and then we landed on Mars? If you really believe that, then you certainly have no sense of humour, whatsoever. I mean that is absolutely laughable!" Peter played the game.

"We know you took a trip recently. We know about the rock. We just need the name and location of the scientist you visited. Whether we believe your adventurous stories or not is immaterial," the agent stated.

The second agent came back with Peter's phone and handed a piece of paper to the first agent. "Uh-hum. You went to Fort Nelson in British Columbia.

You have been in contact with a John Biskit. You have no address in your phone for him."

"He has no address. He lives in a cabin just north of town along the river, about ten kilometres from the airport. He took me there. That's all I know." Peter lied about the location.

"I think we're making progress. Let's talk about his technology." The agent went on. Peter sat back in his seat and sighed.

****

I sat in the back of the Canoe, holding a paddle up in the air. Ahanu stepped into the front of the boat and pushed off. "OK," he said, "first, let's get used to the balance." Ahanu was actually standing in the canoe. He sat down and told me to gently rock the boat. I did, feeling it sway back and forth. It seemed safe enough, though I wasn't trying to sink us. "Good," he said. "Do you feel comfortable?" he asked.

"Yes." I was on my knees, as instructed.

"OK, hold your paddle like I showed you, out to the left side. You will find one side is stronger than the other. I like the left better." Ahanu faced me to watch and demonstrate. "Now, do a simple stroke, like this." Ahanu dipped his paddle in and stroked the water back. We moved with a steady, strong force. I tried to copy him. "Don't splash," he said. "Let the paddle dip in gently, then give a strong stroke." I practiced a few times, bumping my knuckles on the sides. It was awkward, but I started to get the hang of it.

"We're turning right," I called out, fully understanding the principle involved.

"Yes, that's good," Ahanu replied. "Now we will learn to compensate for that. First, we use a rudder. When you put your paddle in one side, we move that way. It slows that side of the canoe down. So stroke, then leave the paddle there and slowly back stroke." I did, and sure enough we moved slightly right, and then slightly left. But it seemed counterproductive. We moved ahead and then back.

"Now this time, don't backstroke, just use the paddle to steer, like a rudder. See? It is slow moving, but it works. Next we do a 'J' stroke to keep us straight. This will move us ahead and keep us straight. Do a regular stroke, then twist and move your paddle out from the canoe, like the shape of a 'J'." I did it, poorly, then better and soon I was paddling us along down the river in a straight line. "If you want to turn back, just put your paddle in the water and use it as a rudder to turn us around," he said. I did as I was instructed and, with a little extra paddling, had us facing the other way. I paddled us all the way back to shore.

"That was great!" I proudly yelled.

"You're a fast learner. You should practice a little every day and you will be an expert," he said.

"Yes. Thanks Ahanu. You're a very good teacher."

"It's my pleasure, kahkākow. You will be flying in a canoe soon," he laughed.

We dragged the canoe up on land. "Ashenee, did you see me out there?" I asked.

"Yes. I am very impressed. Now you have no reason not to come visit me," she joked. I think it was a joke. Maybe not. Maybe she was serious.

"You know I will," I answered. "Have you seen your father?" I asked.

"He is over there," Ashenee said, pointing to him. I looked around and saw him standing by the fire holding a bow.

"Benjamin. What are you doing?" I went over and asked.

"I'm stringing this bow," he replied. I admired it. "Do you want to learn how to make a bow?"

"Sure." I had admired the bow earlier, when I saw it in the tent.

Benjamin picked up an axe and we went to the trees along the shore. He selected a young poplar and with one slice, severed it at the base. He handed it to me and took out a solid looking knife from a sheath at his waist. He told me to cut off all the branches and remove all the bark. I sat down near the fire pit and methodically stripped the stem. My hands were not used to this work and they began to ache, but I continued. When it was smooth and skinless, I showed Benjamin.

"Good work," he praised me. "Now take the axe and slice here and here until these parts are half the thickness, like this one." He held up his bow to show me. "But be careful. Do not hurt yourself and don't take off too much or break it. This is a delicate job."

I set about slashing threads of wood off the slim trunk until it was much thinner. I then used the knife to fashion the pole similar to Benjamin's bow. It took a while, and no one bothered me. When I was done, I showed it to Benjamin.

"Hmm, very good," he stated. Then he used the knife to make notches in the ends. He retrieved a long strand of leather or such from a pouch and showed me how to tie it. After one end was done, we bent the stick and tied off the other end. "OK, that must be soaked." I took it to a secluded pool and weighed it down under water with rocks. Benjamin showed me how to make arrows, but we never got around to making any.

In the evening, we all sat around the fire pit. Grandma came and sat in front of me with a bundle in her arms. She opened it and first laid out a shirt in front of me. "Papakiwayan," she said. Then it was a pair of pants, "mitas." Then a set of moccasins, "pahkikinwiskisin." Finally a colourful sash, "pakwahtihon."

I picked up each beautifully made article, hand stitched with beads and tassels. "They are beautiful. Thank you," I said and nodded in appreciation. Grandma just smiled and then pointed to the tent and called out to Ashenee, who took me inside and dressed me. I came out looking like a different man.

"kahkākow," Grandma said and smiled. Johnny Crow was I. People jumped up and patted my shoulder and told me how good the clothes looked. I wondered how long it must have taken Grandma to make all those clothes. That was so kind. I proudly sat by the fire like a member of the family, enjoying all the talk and laughter around me.

People constantly moved around. Ashenee and I wandered up to the hill and sat looking down over the fire. It was dark now and the moon was full, up high and out over the river. "What are these clothes made of?" I asked Ashenee.

"Mostly moose. The beads are made from porcupine quills and shells. Are they comfortable?" she asked

"The porcupine quills?" I joked.

"No, the clothes," Ashenee said, giving me a little shove with her shoulder.

"Yes, they're very comfortable. Did you see the bow I made with your father?" I asked.

"I saw you making it with him. Does it work?" she asked.

"I don't know. I don't have any arrows. Is that important?" I laughed.

"You kind of need arrows. It's like having a car without wheels," she said.

"Hmm, I guess I better work on that," I agreed. "You know you can come here anytime you want."

"I know. Thanks." She reached over and held my hand. I smiled at her. "The moon is big tonight. I wonder what's happening up there right now. We have lots of legends about the moon. I know they aren't true, but they make nice stories."

"I have been there. Nothing happens on the moon. It is the quietest place in the universe. And maybe the coldest. I could have used these nice warm clothes from Grandma when I was there. Mars is better. There are clouds, wind, colours, and sounds. But it's just a rocky desert. If there were plants, you would think it was here." It was nice to sit close to Ashenee and hold her hand. Life is full of surprises.

"When we first came here, you were hiding in the trees," she said.

"I was kind of afraid when I first saw you," I said.

"I'm not scary, am I?" Ashenee teased me.

"No, you're not scary." I leaned in to nuzzle her cheek, but she turned to face me and we kissed. A few minutes later, I asked her a question. "Hey, I picked up a rock from the moon. Do you want to see it?"

"Yes," she replied.

I stood up and led her by the hand into the house.

NINE - The Spies

The phone rang in a room on the eighth floor of a nineteen sixties office building in Ottawa. "Hello. Understood." A man in a grey suit turned to his computer and waited. An encoded message came through which he proceeded to print out. He retrieved the message, slipped it into an envelope, sealed it and took it down to an office on the second floor. "Sir, this just came in from Dimitry Yanovitch. It is marked urgent." He handed the envelope over to the man sitting at his desk.

Derek Patterson, a director at the Canadian Security and Intelligence Service, also known as CSIS, opened the envelope and read the message. He picked up the phone and made a call to the office of Mr. Donald Williams, the Minister of Foreign Affairs. "Hello, this is Derek Patterson, Director of Communications at CSIS. I need to speak with Mr. Williams. It's urgent."

"Yes, Mr. Patterson. I can connect you. Just a moment," said a receptionist.

"Hello?" answered Donald Williams.

"Minister, this is the director of communications at CSIS. I need to meet with you. We just received some urgent intelligence," the director said.

"What's this about?" prodded the minister.

"I can't discuss this over the phone, sir, but it appears one of our scientists is being held by the CIA," replied the director.

"OK. Come to my office."

The director hung up the phone. He then reread the communication. Dimitry was a double agent, a mole for CSIS in the Russian secret service working out of the United States. The Russian secret service had a mole in the CIA. The mole in the CIA shared information about Dr. Manning with the Canadian mole, Dimitry, in the Russian secret service, who in turn relayed the information back to CSIS headquarters.

It was an intricate web of intelligence and counterintelligence that only occasionally resulted in useful information. Seldom did the Canadian mole in the Russian secret service get information about a Canadian from the CIA. Usually it was information that implicated the Russians or Chinese. This was a unique and delicate situation. CSIS certainly wouldn't want to expose their own spies or admit that they had a mole who could intercept such information.

The director called a specialist, a woman named Diana Lepage who had an office on the fourth floor. "Diana, can you get me information on a Dr. Peter Manning of the Canadian Space Agency and bring it to me." A few minutes later Diana was at the director's door with a folder. "Come in," the director told her, "sit down. What do you have for me?"

"I pulled a file we have on Peter Manning and then printed out any intel we have on him. He is a manager, so has top secret clearance, however his group is not really working on anything that we would consider sensitive. He develops robotics for a new mechanical arm that NASA contracted to the CSA," Diana said.

"I want to know if we have anything specific on a trip he made recently to B.C., or any contacts he's made in the past few months," the director asked.

"I have nothing on that. We're not actively watching him. I can check on his expenses and talk with his director," she said. "I'm sure he must have made a note of who he was meeting. I can talk to his wife and colleagues."

"Yes, please do that. Thank you."

Diana left the room. Director Patterson got up, put the documents into a case and left to meet the minister.

****

I once again found myself helping to pack up the camp. It was a sad occasion for me. I hated to see this tiny peninsula revert back to a quiet, vacant site. I said goodbye to everyone, pushed out Ashenee's canoe and waved. They paddled away, silently. I sat down on the sand and watched until the last canoe disappeared from sight. They say the most generous people are the poorest people, but they're wrong. Those people aren't poor, they just don't have a lot of possessions.

I was inspired to put my canoe in the water. I ran up to the barn where the canoe rested along the south side and I hauled it over the grass, down the hill and across the sand to the water's edge. It was a heavy boat but very nice looking. It was all wood ribs inside and a dark green canvas on the outside. There were 2 paddles in it. I picked one up and pushed out from the shore.

I rode around in circles for a while and then down along the shore, exploring the other side of the river slowly. It was immensely relaxing. I could hear the birds sing and occasional noises from the bush. I hoped a moose would step out, but it didn't happen. I paddled back to shore. I landed at the quiet pool where I had placed the bow I made. It was still soaking in the river. After sliding the canoe up high on the bank and tying it to a tree, I pulled the bow out and followed the directions Benjamin gave me to bend it more and tighten the drawstring.

There was no point in moping about. I had to get busy. I had to take my mind off this silence by working. I walked back up to the house and put my bow in the corner of the dining area. I had one goal: maximize efficiency of the rifter. I had to run tests on it now and ensure that ten thousand times the speed of light was safe. I had to push the limit based on the materials. If twenty or thirty or forty times the speed of light was possible with a power puck, then that should be explored. Since the nearest star system was 4 light years away, and so many more were much further, the rifter would only be useful if it could reach these extents.

I pulled out my research, opened the laptop and began running scenarios. I worked hard for many days. I attached the telescope to the underside of the plane and connected it to the console in the plane. I could search the sky from the console. I puttered with the rifter, altering it slightly and experimenting more with rare earths and gases. No explosions, thankfully. I was so wrapped up in this goal, I had forgotten all about the garden.

I took off my lab coat and walked out to check the plants. They were huge. The corn was taller than I was. I noticed the ears were full and when I ripped the leaves off of one, it was golden yellow. I decided it was time to harvest some. I got a big bucket from the barn and began at one end of the garden and walked down the row, snapping ears off each plant. Some stalks had two ears. I quickly filled the bucket. I emptied it into the back of the truck and resumed my harvest. I couldn't believe how much corn I was getting.

It was hard work and after a couple of hours I had stripped half the corn and partly filled the back of the truck. I ripped some onions out too. They looked good. I put them in the house for later. There was no way I could eat all that corn. I still had bushels of corn left on the remaining plants. I wished I could give it to Benjamin, but couldn't get there except by canoe, and that would take a whole day. I decided to drive into town and give it to people I knew. So I did. I went first to Mildred's.

"Hello," I greeted Mildred at her door.

"Why hello John. Come in," she said. I stepped inside for a moment. What brings you to town?" she asked.

"I have a delivery for you. Would you like some corn?" I asked her.

"Corn? Sure. Where did you get corn from?"

"I grew it myself," I replied with pride. "I have way too much for just me alone. I wanted to spread it around a bit."

"Well isn't that kind of you."

"I'll be right back," I told her. I went out to the truck and retrieved a few bags filled with corn. I don't know how many, maybe a couple dozen ears.

"This is a very nice surprise. I didn't know you were a farmer too. Is there anything you don't do?" Mildred asked.

I laughed. "I don't dance. Never tried, never will try."

"I'll bet you could if you wanted," Mildred said.

"My goodness, Mildred. Stop flirting with me. You're a married woman!" I smiled at her.

Mildred laughed. "Maybe you should find yourself a girlfriend, John."

"You're right," I acted surprised. "I'll do that right after I deliver my corn. On that note, I better keep moving. Nice to see you again, Mrs. Waterton." I emphasized 'Mrs.' and smiled.

"Thank you again John. Have a nice day," Mildred said as she closed the door.

Next, I was off to see Mac. I pulled into the parking lot, grabbed a couple bags of corn out of the truck and went inside. I plunked the bags on the counter. "Mac, how's it going, eh?" I asked.

"Fine. What's all this?" he asked.

"I stripped some corn at the farm, more than I could eat. Thought I'd bring some into town, you know, for select friends."

Mac looked into a bag and inspected the corn. "Nice stuff. Seems you know what you're doing. Thanks, I love corn. Staying for a beer?"

"Better not. I got a pile of this stuff to deliver," I replied. "I'll stop by another time." I gave Mac a wave and left the bar.

I dropped by Charlie's place and Bob's place, then donated the rest to the First Nation Family Centre to distribute to anyone they felt was in need. It felt good to share my bounty.

****

Director Patterson exited his car on the hill and walked over to the East Block where Minister Williams had an office. He flashed his credentials just inside the doors and was free to walk down the hall and up the stairs to the top floor. He paused for a moment at the minister's office and then knocked on the door. A receptionist opened the door and invited him in. The receptionist knocked on an inner door.

"Come," a man yelled. The receptionist opened the door and announced Mr. Patterson.

"Director Patterson, how are you?" the minister asked, half standing with his hand outstretched.

"Fine, thanks. How are you, Minister?" asked the director.

"I'm well. Please, have a seat." He motioned for the director to sit down. "So tell me what this intel is about," the minister asked, looking serious.

"We have information that a Canadian scientist from the Space Agency is being held and questioned by the CIA in Washington," began the director.

"What is he doing in Washington?"

"We don't know, exactly. But we have learned a number of things that may explain it. Apparently our scientist, a Dr. Peter Manning, met with an unknown scientist out west, in B.C. This unknown scientist has developed some very advanced technology capable of extreme spaceflight. They, as the intel documents it, have made a flight to Mars. They also kept it private until Dr. Manning confided in a friend at NASA and the CIA intercepted their conversations. It's my guess they either lured our Dr. Manning to Washington, or simply invited him innocently and then the CIA apprehended him en route. We don't know how Dr. Manning ended up in the hands of the CIA. But this is extremely problematic as the CIA seems to be mining a Canadian for data, the unknown scientist and his technology. It would be extremely embarrassing and dangerous if this technology is real and was extracted by a foreign country. Seems the Americans and the Russians know it exists. Maybe there are others now. We need to get to this scientist first." The director professionally outlined the scenario.

"I see," said the minister. "Are you telling me that someone, in this country, not affiliated with any legitimate organization, is operating flights from Earth to Mars, and we don't know who it is? How credible do you think this intel is? I only ask because, as you can appreciate, this sounds rather far-fetched."

"I did check on Dr. Manning. He is credible and he is missing. He went to Washington and has disappeared. Regardless of the actual validity of this technology, Dr. Manning appears to have been abducted and it appears the CIA have him. I don't think they would seize a scientist unless they believed the narrative. I do understand this sounds outlandish, but can we take the risk? What if we dismiss claims of advanced technology and they are true? That would be a big mistake," the director reasoned. "Remember, this is Canadian technology."

"Uh-huh," muttered the minister. Though he would never admit it, this was way over his head. The minister was a figure head. He was an elected member who had been given the foreign affairs portfolio to oversee in Parliament. "Can you leave the intel with me? I will discuss it with the appropriate people."

"Yes, of course Minister," the director said. The director's job is to gather, analyse, and report the information. That's all. "I will pass on any new information to you. As you can imagine, this information is very sensitive."

"Indeed," replied the minister. "Thanks for bringing this to my attention."

The director left with an uneasy feeling that this was going nowhere, but he followed the correct procedure. He would get more information on Dr. Manning and his recent adventures and would ensure the minister would get it with further appeals for urgency. He would also assign this commission to his most trusted agent for follow-up.

As soon as the director had left, the minister picked up the phone and called the PM. "Prime Minister, I have just been informed of a very difficult situation."

****

It was a warm, late afternoon and I was starting to think about dinner. I had picked some corn, pulled some onions, beets and beans. I had no cuts of meat, no fish, and no burger. I went out to the barn to collect some eggs. I could make some kind of stir fry with eggs and rice. I was picking up a few eggs and putting them in a bowl when I heard a car driving down the lane. That sounded like more than a car. I opened the barn door and closed it behind me. There, pulling up beside me was a big, black SUV, followed by another, and another, and then an RCMP SUV. What on earth was happening? Did some department of transport find out about unscheduled flights in the area and tracked it to this spot? This looked like some serious violations were performed. A man in a suit emerged from the first truck. He walked around to me. "Are you John Biskit?" he asked.

I swallowed hard, my nerves on edge. "Yes, I am," I said. "Is something wrong?"

"Are you alone? Anyone else in the house?" he asked.

"I'm alone." I probably wouldn't have admitted that if I hadn't seen the RCMP vehicle.

The man signaled other men to get out of the truck and check the buildings. They did. Then the man nodded to the second SUV. From the back seat a man emerged sporting jeans and a T-shirt that simply said 'Stanley's Cup'. The face was familiar. I had to think for a moment, then it came to me. It was the Prime Minister. Really? How is that possible? He would never come out here. But that face was unmistakable. This was a view of him that I, nor most people have ever seen. I didn't even think he existed this way. You come to believe some people live and sleep in a suit. I felt quite ridiculous standing there holding a bowl of chicken eggs in front of the Prime Minister. He walked over to me.

"John Biskit?" he inquired.

"Yes, and you are..." I paused for a moment, in disbelief.

"The Prime Minister. Listen, it was hard to track you down. We need to talk. Can we go inside?" he asked.

"Sure," I said, a little mesmerized. We walked into the house, me, the PM and the man in a suit. "Do you want a coffee?" I asked.

"I would, thanks," he replied.

The man in a suit, I assume he was a bodyguard, asked me, "Are there any weapons in the house?"

"No," I said, "though I have a deadly bow over there in the corner, but it doesn't shoot straight. And I have no arrows" No facial expression whatsoever. A man of no humour. I turned to the PM. "I made it myself," I said with a smile. The PM smirked. I walked over and picked it up and brought it to the PM. He examined it closely.

"Very nice," he said, putting it down on the table.

I dumped the coffee in the percolator, filled it with water and turned it on. I brought down two cups, then thought of the suit and picked out a third cup. "Please, have a seat." I motioned to the table. What do you take in your coffee?" I asked.

"I like cream and sugar," he said.

So I took some milk out of the fridge and grabbed a bowl of sugar from the counter and placed them on the table. I fidgeted with dishes for a few minutes and made some comments about the weather until the coffee perked, then I poured three cups of coffee, placed one before the PM, one for me and a third at the end of the table. I motioned to the suit to take it. He nodded, but never accepted. I suppose that would have been a breach of protocol.

"So, how can I help you?" I asked.

"We have a problem, and the problem surrounds you," answered the PM.

"Oh, really? I didn't realize I was notable," I said. "I'm sure the Prime Minister would not visit me unless this was serious."

"We have come to learn that your friend, Dr. Manning, was interrogated by the CIA. They came across information that indicates you have developed some advanced technology and they believe you can travel at the speed of light. Is any of this true?" he asked, point blank.

I looked up at the suit and he quickly looked away. I looked back at the PM. "Yes, It's true. I got up and walked over to the coffee table and retrieved the reddish rock. I came back and handed it to the PM. "That's from Mars," I said.

"Impressive," he mused. He turned the rock around in his hand, examining it, "So this is our problem. The Americans and the Russians both know you have this technology. They will want it. I think they will try to attain it, one way or another. You're probably also in danger. You understand the technology. Apparently, Dr. Manning couldn't understand it, or so he has said. So you may be in danger. You are not free to travel. You may not even be safe here. I want you to do something for me. I want you to hide your research. I want to be able to get access to it if, somehow, it's stolen by another country. We will be at a serious disadvantage in the world if others have this and we do not. You know it will be used by one country to oppress and threaten other countries, wield power and wage wars."

"Yes, I would be naive if I thought my inventions would never be abused." Peace is that fortunate disruption of interminable war and I had no desire to break the relative calm in the world today. "How do you propose I hide my research?" I asked.

"Let's pick a spot. We'll dig a hole and bury it. It will always be there. You can access it, we can access it, but no one else will know about it. I brought a specialist with me to apply encryption to your computer systems. Without your access, no one will have your data."

We stepped outside. I took the PM to the barn to collect some wood, tools and shovels. We hauled it all outside. A few men from the trucks came over and started building a wooden crate about six by four by four feet. I took the PM back into the barn and pulled the tarp off the plane.

"So this is it," he said. He admired the plane, running his hands over it. "How did you manage to get it to travel faster than anyone dreamed possible? Never mind, I wouldn't understand, would I?"

I chuckled. "No sir, I'm afraid you wouldn't understand. Let's just say the current understanding of physics and our universe is miniscule, and not very accurate. Maybe someday, when we get over the cultural differences and political scuffles, the world will be ready to know more. Unfortunately, I can't stop thinking and exploring. I may look like a chicken farmer, but there's a hunger in me that I can't subdue. I have seen things, in my mind and with my eyes that have set me on a path that can only lead forward, beyond our horizons."

A shout from outside brought us to find a completed crate. "We're done sir," said one man. Not a bad job for men in suits, I thought. "Where should we put it?"

The PM looked to me. I looked around. Not down at the river. Not up in the hills; too rocky. Not in my garden. Out in the field? Seemed far away. "What about directly behind the barn. The ground is sandy and it's accessible."

"That sounds logical," the PM said.

He handed a shovel to a suit, took one himself and went around behind the barn to begin digging. The PM was digging a hole. Really? I felt awkward just standing there watching them dig. So I went into the house and started bagging boxes of papers. I wanted them bagged so they would not get damp and moldy. I brought out one box after another. I brought out backup hard drives, the two drones I built, and some parts that may be indicative of my research. I was OK with this. I needed none of it. I knew everything. I had software specs. And I had the puzzle all pieced together in the plane. I had finished the puzzle as I had set out to do in the beginning. I could achieve so much more if I wanted to, but perhaps this was a good time to digest what I had done. The world was not ready for what I already had, how could it be ready for what I could yet do?

When the hole was dug and the crate lowered in, I filled it with all the boxes and items I had brought out. The lid was secured and the hole filled back in. After they were done, excess soil was taken away to the garden and the top surface gently replaced. Surprisingly, it looked like it had never been touched. Hopefully it would be safe for a long time. Hopefully the PM would keep his promise to never access it as long as it was kept secret. I looked around but didn't see the PM. I asked a suit, "Where'd he go?" The man answered by pointing toward the house. I looked around the side of the barn and saw him standing out front by the house, on the hill. I walked over to him.

"Is that your canoe down there?" he asked.

"Yes. Do you like it?" I inquired.

"It's a beauty. That's a cedar strip. You've got a nice setup here. This is the kind of place I'd like to have someday, when I retire," he said.

"Thanks. Not sure how much I can enjoy it now," I replied.

He turned to me and said, "Life isn't always fair. You and I have a lot in common. We stand out. See all those guards I have?" He looked back over his shoulder. I looked back and saw several suits standing there, watching us. "I can't go anywhere without them. Oh, chances are I could, but you just never know these days. I could meet a dozen guys who want to shake my hand and buy me a beer, then turn around and get stabbed in the heart by some extremist or psychopath looking for kicks, or just some guy who doesn't like my policies. A lot has changed. There was a time when you and I would have been honoured for our strength, but not today. We are targets. It's the same for actors, singers, and leaders. You're a leader. You know, you could work in the government. I'd get you a position anywhere you want; CSA, NRC, anywhere. But you will still be a target. You know that now, don't you?"

I had wondered if this was actually the PM. Who ever heard of a politician actually getting their hands dirty? Could this have been a look-alike? What would be the point of that? These were obviously Canadian authorities. Who else would have access to RCMP vehicles? But now, with this speech, I was sure it was the PM. We started to walk back toward the house and he said, "Is that all of it, in the crate?" I answered yes. "What are you going to do with that plane?" he asked.

"I will find a way to hide it," I answered.

"Perhaps you could let us take it, to Ottawa. We can keep it safe," he stated.

"No. I can safely hide it here. Look at all this bush," I turned and pointed out at the other side of the river.

"Alright. We won't be far away," he said.

I'm not sure what he meant by that. I don't know if he was looking out for me or for my technology. I had the uneasy feeling no one could be trusted. What if I went to town and came back to a hole in the ground.

TEN - The Departure

I had never felt like a target before, and now I was being hunted. I didn't know who the enemy was, when they would come or how they would execute their plan. I just knew my life was in danger. I did not want to lose all my research, nor did I want to be forced into submission. I had become very proud of my achievements and my independence. I had never been a fighter before, but my life had changed over the past year. I was no longer an introvert, hiding under the wing of a caretaker, whether that be my parents or the university. I was my own provider, my own boss, my own master. No one was going to push me around. I would not let anyone take me. If I couldn't stand and fight, I would hide, but I wouldn't give in.

If I was going to be threatened, I needed to protect myself. First order of business was to hide the plane. I stood outside and surveyed the property. Any open areas were unacceptable. I had to look to the trees. The hills had small pockets of space a plane could land, with a bit of clearing. I grabbed an axe and headed up the main hill on the west side of the property. I climbed through the trees, occasionally reaching small clearings where I could look down on the farm. I kept rising up until I was near the top. I found one small patch of young poplars and I measured an area just a bit bigger than the plane. I hacked at the bushes and trees to clear a spot. I had to whack the stems low to the ground so no spikes were jutting up that could hurt the plane. I pushed all the trees and bushes over to the side, opening up the site. I was sweating under the hot summer sun and I sat for a moment to look over the forest and river. It sure was beautiful.

I walked down the mountain toward the river, occasionally slashing the face of a spruce tree to mark the path. I continued down through the trees past the farm, right to the river. At this point I was familiar with the land. I went up to the barn, opened the wide doors and hauled the plane out on its plywood pad. I put my suit and the spare suit on the back seat of the plane. I collected some emergency supplies and packed them into a bag, stuffing them and the tarp behind the passenger seat. I inserted all the fully charged power pucks. I fitted the solar panels I made onto the bottoms of the wings and connected them to the power system. The rifter was disconnected. I had it in the lab where it was only partly ready. But it was not necessary for flight.

I sat inside without wearing the suit, sealed the lid and popped up in the air. I slowly flew higher, high enough up the mountain that I could easily spot the new clearing I made. I maneuvered over the clearing and gently lowered the plane, landing in the centre of the site. I climbed out of the plane, closed the lid and covered the plane with the tarp. Next I retrieved the bushes and trees I had cut down and laid them beside and on top of the plane to camouflage it. I did a good enough job that I could walk right by and barely notice the tarp. I hoped it looked equally hidden from above. Once again I had to walk down the hill. I retraced my steps back, checking for tree slashes as I went.

All I had left in the farm was my laptop and the rifter. I went to the lab and worked to maximize the capabilities of the rifter. I wanted to attain fifty thousand times speed of light. I was confident I would hit that number. I used a combination of rare earths and a combination of gases that I was sure would give significant amplitude. I could gauge up to fifty thousand, but amplification above that would require tests in space. I couldn't theorize it so fast. For the rest of the day I worked to assemble the rifter. By evening, I was tired and felt I had finished it. I brought it into the house and stood it up on the side table near the moon rock.

****

Next morning I planned a warning system. How could I do that? I could setup a signal at the road where the laneway starts. Anybody driving in would trigger the signal. I'd also need a way to block the road, to slow them down. It wouldn't stop anyone, but would give me time to react. I collected some fishing line, a switch, a battery and a roll of wire, and I walked down the lane a ways. It was easy enough to stretch the line across the lane and connect the battery to the switch.

From the switch, I connected the battery to the wire and ran it through the trees by the lane to the house, under the floor and up to a makeshift doorbell. If the line was depressed or stretched, it would trigger the switch and send a signal. But I doubted anyone would just drive in here, abduct me and drive out. That seemed unlikely. The only way I could slow someone down was place a few stubby logs and branches on the road that they would have to clear. I couldn't believe it took me most of the day to do this. It was probably the most low tech setup I had ever assembled.

Time for a well-deserved beer and dinner. Not sure I could relax and enjoy it though. I had tried to prepare for an invasion of some kind. Now I had to remain vigilant. I cracked open a cold one and sat back on the couch with my feet up on the coffee table. My cell phone rang.

"Hello," I answered.

"John, it's me, Peter."

"Peter, are you OK? I heard you were being held by the CIA," I said.

"How on Earth did you hear about that?" he asked.

"I had a visit from someone rather important. He told me what had happened to you," I said.

"I'm sorry, John. It was my fault. I contacted a friend in NASA and told him about our trip. I didn't know the CIA had tapped into our communications. I didn't divulge any of your secrets though. I couldn't tell them how your technology worked, even if I wanted to. But I shouldn't have told anyone about you. I'm so sorry," he apologized. "I suppose my friend was forced to invite me down to Washington. The CIA was waiting for me. They got your name from my cell phone. I told them you lived near the airport. That will only stall them a little while. They'll figure out where you really are. They're determined to find you. They just released me about twenty minutes ago. I had to call and warn you. This is imminent, John. They're coming. It's only a matter of time before they show up there. You can't let them get you, or your knowledge. Get out of there. Lay low for a while," he said.

"OK, Peter. I'll be careful." I hung up the phone.

It all made sense now. I showed Peter. Peter told a friend at NASA. The CIA tapped into it, tricked Peter into coming to Washington. Information was extracted and processed. An informant relayed the information back to Ottawa. The PM was informed and personally came to secure the technology. Maybe the RCMP were watching me now. Maybe I was under surveillance. Would they protect me against spies? Who knows?

I swigged my beer. It had a nice aroma of fruit and spice. This may have been the best beer I will ever get to brew. It was simple moments like this that made life great, and yet my mind was muddled with concern. I picked up my cell phone again. I had a bank account I hadn't used in a while, a joint account with my parents. It was handy while I was a student and young. I redirected all proceeds from the app to this account. So far I had made about $67,000. I transferred that over too. Then I sent an email to my parents:

Dad, Mom,

Hope you guys are doing well. The financial app I wrote with your help Dad is doing well. The profits are going into our joint account. Enjoy it.

Johnny.

I put my head back and rested my eyes. I felt drained. Though it seemed like only a few minutes had passed, it was hours. I woke to a thunderous noise which grew rapidly outside and then disappeared. A helicopter, high up; a big one. It had passed over. Was it gone? Was it looking for me? Something was going on. I had never heard a helicopter out here before. I'd heard and seen some in town, but small ones, certainly nothing like this.

I jumped up and grabbed the rifter. I ran to the front door and opened it to flee, but turned around to look back inside. There, before me was my home, the home I had come to love for the past year. It didn't seem right to be forced to run away from it. I hesitated for a moment. What would they do to it? Would they destroy it looking for my secrets? Would they soil it with their dirty, thieving hands? I couldn't fight them, I could only run away. I turned off all the lights and slipped out the front door. Again I was presented with a sight I didn't want to give up; the river. My river. I looked up, but there was nothing I could see in the dark sky.

I dashed down to the river, along the shore and into the trees. All I had was my cell phone to light a path. I climbed the bank looking for slashes on trees. It was hard to do, but once I found one slash I continued upward, tracking from one to another. It was slow moving and I stumbled over rocks and logs. I reached the clearing, pulled the branches and bushes off the plane, removed the tarp and cleaned the plane off of leaves and twigs.

I took out a few tools from inside the cockpit and started attaching the altered rifter. I kept fumbling. I was rushing and making mistakes in the dark. A screw slipped out of my hands and fell to the ground by my head. I grabbed my cell phone and shined the light around, madly searching for it. Leaves and twigs were scattered around, creating hiding places. I felt with my trembling hand. "Come on, come on. Where are you?" I cursed. I found it, flipped myself around and steadied my hand to insert the last screw. In it turned until it was tight.

As I lay under the nose, I heard the helicopter coming back. I could see above me lights from the helicopter. It was stationary for a moment. Then small lights emerged and began falling, slowly. What were these, I thought. Then it dawned on me; they were paratroopers. I finished with the rifter, slipped my suit on and climbed in. I pushed some controls and popped up ten feet off the ground very quickly. Then I began to rise slowly. I spotted a man cruising past me, shock on his face as he gazed into the plane at my helmet. His parachute snagged the edge of my wing, turning the plane sideways. I quickly compensated for it and, apart from a brief drop toward a spiky tree, righted the plane, pulling at the parachute till it ripped away. It must have seriously damaged his parachute. A moment later, I heard him hit the trees below me. I don't know who he was or if he was injured. That wasn't my concern. I saw many other tiny lights falling all around, maybe six, seven or eight.

I shot ahead over my home toward the river. The moon was out but not full. There was still a sliver of light along the horizon. Thankfully, I could just see the sinewy reflection of the river below. I followed along the river at a height of about five hundred feet searching below for lights. I wanted to find Ashenee's tribe. There was a chance I could miss her small camp. I'd never seen it before and, if it was hidden amongst the trees, it would be hard to find.

I moved along at about 90 Km/hour watching the south side, looking for the fork in the river. Out front, north of the river I saw a caravan of cars driving the highway toward my place. I counted eight or nine, some with flashing red lights. Who was that? Did the RCMP or the army identify the helicopter? Were they on their way to rescue me? I don't know. I didn't want to be in the middle of some international fire-fight. There it was, I saw it up ahead. I saw the glow of fire and the white teepees spread around in a clearing. I circled and then lowered the plane, slowing down, looking for a landing spot.

I shone my light down and landed on a grassy area. I could see several people coming toward me and others emerging from teepees to see what was going on. The spotlight was still on, facing down but illuminating the plane and surrounding area. I opened the cockpit lid and climbed out, removing my helmet.

"Johnny Crow, is that you?" came a voice from the crowd. It was not clear who asked, but I responded.

"Yes, it's me. Where is Ashenee?" The crowd of people stepped back, opening a pathway. I called out, "Ashenee! Ashenee!"

Ashenee walked forward through the crowd. "Johnny? What's happening? Why are you here? Is something wrong?"

"I think I'm in trouble," I spoke out of breath. "I think people are trying to take my plane. I think they also want to take me somewhere. I have to go away. I have to hide." I stepped forward and put my arms around her. "I have to say goodbye, just for now."

Ashenee whispered in my ear, "I want to come with you. I want to be with you."

"It's dangerous, Ashenee. I don't know where I'm going. I don't know when I'll be back. I don't even know if I will ever make it back." I tried to make her understand. I kissed her and told her I loved her.

The crowd had begun walking around the plane, touching and examining it. I looked around at the fire and teepees. I felt like I was at the point of two worlds colliding, right here next to a river on the edge of the forest by my plane; a collision of worlds within the world. Yet there was a bond that transcended all differences. A desire to be with another person. There was no chasm that existed between us, no ocean nor space.

Back in the plane, I sat for a moment. I tapped the controls and lifted off, staring out at all the gentle faces. I rose slowly about forty feet, flashed my spotlight twice to say goodbye, pointed the nose upward and then, with the touch of a button shot away like an arrow.

In no time I was leaving the atmosphere and heading into space. Once a reserved introvert, now a space cowboy. The planet lay below me. I was far out of the reach of any government. I entered coordinates that moved the nose of my plane, pointing me toward Alpha Centauri, a star system 4.2 light years away. I questioned my decision, just for a moment, and quietly muttered, "Are you really ready to do this?"

"I'm ready, Johnny Crow," came a voice from the back seat.

I smiled. "OK then, let's go!" I said. My thumb hit the activate button and everything went black.

Epilogue

I am out here. I am way out here. After learning about my journey, you're out here with me. All journeys are an experience. No one lives by spending their life hiding away. The challenges faced in discovery and exploration are worth all the troubles when, at last, a puzzle finally comes together. Whether you struggle to accomplish a mission or not is immaterial. The joy of discovery should never be limited to a lab, but to life. For me, the journey to a new town, finding a new home, making new friends and living new experiences was as rewarding as the great journey to the stars. After seeing space, I could never be confined to Earth again, even though it would always be my home. My horizons had forever been expanded. My life was now a new, shared journey. I was not alone anymore. I had become an adult, matured through life experiences. My journey is not over though; on the contrary, I'm just getting started. Whether it's a journey to discover a new world or the journey to discover yourself, it's a great trip. Always take the risk. I think I have narrated my growth and achievement well enough. Beyond that is another story. The universe is waiting to be explored.

About the Author

Matt Egner grew up in Nova Scotia and Eastern Ontario. From an early age he developed a love of science and exploration. He completed a Master's degree in Geology and worked for many years in mining and exploration camps. He then went on to work in software development. When he isn't writing or working, Matt enjoys acting, outdoor activities, beer and doughnuts. You may find Matt camped by a remote lake, gardening around the house, in a hot spring somewhere in Japan, or baking bread at home.